Iturned to face Dave and put al gwasannath. It may even have moment but didn't stop. He charg me over. I landed on my back, the _____ it felt like I'd been hit by a bus. The bus then landed on me, one meaty hand grabbing my chin, pushing my cheek into the gravel. I tried to twist my head to save my eye and bite his hand but could not make any movement against his strength.

As his thoughts, blazing with anger, flowed into mine I pushed the fear and pain I felt into him. I couldn't let everything go, that would damage him too much like that Otherkin soldier; it would become a police matter and I certainly didn't want that. Just push him enough to scare him off. I built the flow carefully, all the time conscious of the pain of my face pressed into the gravel, until he cracked and stopped. He gasped and rolled off me and then took off back the way he'd come, pelting across the yard as fast as his legs would carry him.

I lay on the gravel for a couple of minutes trying to get my breath and quell the nausea. I sat up, the anger that had surged through me from Dave still rumbling like a distant thunderstorm in my mind. I raised a hand to my cheek and found gravel; carefully I tried to pick it out. My phone rang.

DEEPER SHADOWS OF FAERIE

BY MARTIN OWTON

It took forever; I wrote a long statement for the uniformed sergeant then had three rounds of questioning, each with a different plain-clothes officer, none of them I knew. Understandable, I guess, with all that had happened, but it left me feeling completely hollowed out as they meticulously went through every line. I wanted to go home, have a bath and a long, long sleep, but I wanted to see Michelle more.

I thought someone might have said something like "well done for getting the prisoners back and stopping the raids,", but no one did. At least they gave me my mobile back and told me which ward Michelle was in at Southampton General.

I reckoned I would have an hour or so with Michelle before they threw me out. I hadn't figured out what I was going to say to her, it would depend a lot on how she was.

I phoned mother while I was waiting for the bus to take me to the General. To my relief she answered immediately.

"Charlie! How are you? Where are you?"

"Tired! I just finished with the police. I'm in town. I'm going to the General to see Michelle. How are you?"

"Frustrated. I've been dealing with the insurance company about the back door since I got home and it's driving me crazy. Charlie, you be careful when you see Michelle. She's a nice girl and I like her, but she's been through a lot recently. I get the feeling she's fragile."

So she didn't know.

"Last thing I want to do is upset her."

"Then tread very carefully. Look, why don't you bring her out to lunch when she's out of hospital?"

"I'd love to. I'll ask her this evening." If she's still talking to me.

We chatted a bit longer, then the bus rolled into view, and I let her go back to dealing with insurance company call centres. It was good to hear she was undamaged by what had happened; I wondered whether Jack had done something to give her distance from the memories of it. That would be a good skill to acquire if he had.

I sent Sharon a text to tell her where I was going, then, as the bus ground its way through the evening rush hour, I thought about what mother had said about Michelle. Much as I wanted to talk about what Jack had said to me maybe it would be better to leave it; Michelle had enough to deal with. The prospect of seeing her filled me with an excited glow despite my tiredness as we neared the hospital.

I got all the way up to the ward but didn't get to see her. Sat beside her bed, guarding her like a gross tattooed cat at a mouse hole, was Dave. His back was to me, but there was no mistaking the bulky body and thick neck. He didn't see me so I walked quietly away; that was a confrontation that could wait until another day. I went back to the bus stop deflated and even more tired. The headache I'd got from the Otherkin soldier's attack was still hovering in the background threatening to return.

Sharon was halfway down the stairs before I had the door of her flat open.

"Charlie. Are you OK? I got your text." She stopped short of hugging me, just.

"I'm fine, just tired and hungry." I pulled the door closed.

"Hungry I can fix." She reached for her phone. "Pizza OK?"

I collapsed on the sofa while she ordered and fetched a bottle of wine from the fridge.

"I know you've probably gone through it a dozen times, but I need to know what happened to Tim Wilson." She passed me a glass of wine.

"I didn't exactly see it. A bunch of Otherkin soldiers hit us as soon as we came out of the gate. There was a short fight. Everybody was fighting. I burned one guy and then got a smack on the head. The Queen stopped it, and when I stood up DC Wilson was dead. The King executed the leader of the soldiers right there."

She looked down at her glass and was silent for a while.

"He was a good copper and a mate," she said eventually. "We all know it happens and accept that risk. But still, it was a weird feeling at the station today."

"Did he have family?"

"He wasn't married, but there's a brother and parents, I guess. I hate funerals."

"You're back on duty?" I said after a pause.

"Yeah. My suspension disappeared shortly after the Chief Constable was briefed on the prisoners' statements. I even got an apology." She took a mouthful of wine. "There's nothing like being proved right."

"That's good. I'm glad I haven't ruined your career."

"Not yet at least. Could have done with you today actually."

"Why. What you got?"

"It's a nasty one." She pulled a face. "We busted a dodgy massage parlour and picked up a girl. Looks like she's been trafficked and then drugged to make her compliant. She's got no papers, we've no idea where she's from or how old she is. It would really help to know which language we should be trying to talk to her in."

I could not say no to this one. "I should be able to find that out for you. Tomorrow OK?"

"You sure? She's been through a really rough time."

"As rough as getting murdered?"

"Maybe not, more sustained trauma though."

"OK then. I'll give it a go." It felt good that she still trusted me enough to ask.

"I'll see if I can organise that for tomorrow then. I need to find somewhere to put her. She's at the General at the moment, but she can't stay there. What are you doing tomorrow?"

"Back to the lab, I suppose. I didn't get to see Michelle tonight, so I'll see her tomorrow. I need to catch up with Greg and Chloe." That sparked off a thought. "Have you seen anything of your pal DI Scott?"

"No. I think he listened to our advice and took some time off. You thinking of trying to break that compulsion he's carrying?"

"Yes, and dealing with Peter Murphy. No disrespect, but I'd like to be able to go back to my own place."

"I've got his number. I can text him."

"Give me a day or two to get my life back on track before we try to do it. I'll need my father to help and there's no telling when he'll be able to come." Except, of course, my life wasn't really going to go back on track; sorting out the situation with Michelle would help, but the trip to the Twilight Zone looked permanent.

"Sure. Let me know when you're ready."

The doorbell rang.

"Pizza," said Sharon and headed for the front door clutching her purse. I went to find plates and cutlery. She came back with two boxes. We ate the pizzas and finished the bottle of wine which finished me. I crawled off to bed and barely had the energy to undress before crashing out.

I really did intend to get to the lab by nine, but I didn't wake up until ten. Shower, a bite of breakfast and then a bus ride, and it was past eleven before I got there. I fended of the questions from my labmates and picked up my e-mail. Prof didn't seem to be around, so I read back through my lab book to try to remember what I had intended to do next. I settled for making another batch of an intermediate then called the General to see if I could talk to Michelle only to be told that they were sending her home. This was good news because, obviously, she was going to be physically alright, but now Dave would be around her all the time which would make seeing her without confronting him doubly difficult. I checked my phone; there was no text from her which probably meant that Dave was with her. I sent her an e-mail saying I was desperate to see her. I thought there was marginally less chance of Dave seeing that than a text to her phone.

Sharon called just after lunch to ask if I could see the trafficked girl.

"She's at the station at the moment, but I've got to take her to the women's refuge, and I can't take you there. Can you come down soon? I'd really appreciate it. I'll buy you dinner."

Put like that I couldn't refuse; I left my reaction gently refluxing and took the bus down into the centre of Southampton.

Sharon collected me from the front desk of the Civic Centre nick and took me through to the suite of interview rooms. She halted at the door of one.

"Be careful, Charlie. This girl's had a very rough time," she said then opened the door.

The girl was on the floor sitting in the corner with a blanket round her, long dark hair across her face. She looked up as I came in with too-wide dark eyes. I was slightly reminded of Michelle. I crouched down and reached out a hand to her, but she turned her head away.

I stayed crouched for a couple of minutes speaking softly to her, but she wouldn't look at me; not surprising really. I reached past the edge of the blanket and caught her hand; a minor violation compared to what she'd already endured, but I couldn't help her without contact. She tried to pull away, but I held on and her life flowed into my mind.

In some ways it was worse than Karen. That had been brief terror then agonising pain. This was brief moments of pain and endless relentless exhausting terror that I had to wade through to find her origins. I tried to get through to her that she was safe now and we would help her; I'm not sure it worked or if she was capable of understanding that we would not hurt her.

I found the information I was looking for then let go of her hand. She still didn't look at me.

"OK, Charlie?" asked Sharon from the doorway.

"Bad." I stood up and left the girl still huddled in the corner. Sharon closed the door but did not lock it, the girl wasn't going anywhere and had been locked up enough.

"You want a moment?" said Sharon.

"Yeah." I closed my eyes and concentrated on breathing trying to calm the anger that burned within me at what had been done to her. I knew people trafficking happened, but the sheer inhumanity of it threatened to overwhelm me.

Sharon passed me a plastic cup of water. I drank it staring at the blank wall until I felt I had control.

"Her name's Nicoleta and she's sixteen. She's from some town I've never heard of in Romania, Pitesti I think it is. It's a rundown industrial place, big oil refinery. Some guy she thought she was in love with told her he could get her a waitressing job here. He brought her over, then left her with some other guys and disappeared with her passport. It got nasty, very nasty. You're right. She's had a rough time." I shook my head in a vain effort to clear the awful experiences from my mind.

"Thanks, Charlie. You've helped her. I can do something now."

"If you need any help nailing the people who did this, let me know."

"I will. I promise."

She took me back to the front desk and I walked back to the bus stop, my head still filled with Nicoleta's terrible memories. I wondered if it would be possible for me to help someone recover from something like that. A good question to ask Jack next time I saw him.

I stopped off at the shops on the way back to the lab to buy the makings of dinner. I thought Sharon would appreciate a nice meal when she got home after today; I know she said she'd buy me dinner, but she didn't specify when.

I checked my e-mail when I got back to the flat; there was nothing from Michelle. She probably had Dave standing guard over her, watching her every move. The thought annoyed me, and I knew there was no way of avoiding a confrontation. I ran my hand over my face; it was still bruised from my last meeting with Dave. I had no reason to think his attitude to me would have changed.

I nearly called Michelle about four times while I was cooking dinner and waiting for Sharon to get home. Each time I stopped thinking I would probably make things worse.

By the time Sharon got home at half past eight the curry was thoroughly cooked, and I was starving.

"Sorry I'm so late, Charlie. I had to wait around for the Romanian interpreter to turn up before I could take the girl to the women's refuge."

"How is she?" A reminder that my problems were pretty tiny compared to Nicoleta's.

"Not saying much, but at least she's out of the station. I

needed to know that she understood what was going to happen to her, that she would be safe where she was going."

"And will she be safe?"

"Should be. The locations of these refuges are kept secret. That's why I couldn't take you there. Did you get wine? I could do with a drink."

"In the fridge."

The curry was pretty good, probably improved by the extra cooking time.

"I'll let you cook again," said Sharon. She reached into her pocket and took out a bag of mints.

We settled down to watch TV, but I couldn't settle and checked my e-mail about five times before I went to bed. There was still no message from Michelle.

I slept poorly, troubled with fear-filled dreams of being pursued by unknown men through a labyrinth of rooms, probably an echo of Nicoleta's memories. I checked my e-mail first thing and there was a message from Michelle, timed two thirty.

I clicked on it and waited, heart pounding, as it opened.

"I want to see you, too. Dave won't leave me alone. I had to wait until he was asleep to send this. He's got my phone and keeps me locked in. He heard from someone at the gym how we were together. I don't know what to do. Love you."

It was signed off with a line of kisses.

I read the message through a couple of times and sat staring at the screen feeling conflicted. I was angry about Dave and scared about what he might do to her now that he knew about us, glad beyond measure that she still wanted to see me. She'd said nothing about knowing our secret. Should I tell her or keep quiet about it? I didn't know what to do about any of it.

I thought of little else as I showered and made toast and coffee. I couldn't think of what to say in reply until I realised that it didn't really matter right now; she wouldn't be able to read it until the next time Dave left her alone.

By the time I got to the lab I'd decided that the way forward was to talk to Jack. I needed to talk to him to learn about compulsions anyway so that just made it more urgent. I could do with finding my own gateway to use, but until I did the easiest one to use would be the one near mother's cottage.

Sharon phoned just before eleven.

"Are you fit for a trip to the mortuary," she asked. "Got an interesting one that came in this morning."

"Sure." Bound to be more interesting than the lecture I was supposed to attend at eleven.

She picked me up in the blue Fiesta she had used on our first trip to the mortuary at Southampton General.

"Sorry to do this after yesterday, Charlie," she said. "But this one's a bit strange. Young guy went down to the Town Quay last evening and walked off the end. Pockets full of stones so he went straight down. The divers fished him out this morning. We've got a load on our database about him, and he's certainly not the suicidal type."

"You sure he walked, wasn't pushed?"

"Walked. A dozen people saw him."

Interesting. "OK. I'll see what I can find."

Sanjay, the technician, was on duty at the mortuary again. "Good morning, Sergeant," he said. "Very nice to see you. You're looking particularly lovely today."

"Thank you, Sanjay. Always good to see you," said Sharon. "Could we have a look at the drowning that came in this morning?"

Sanjay consulted his ledger then opened a door on the wall of refrigerated cabinets and slid the shelf out. He partially unwrapped the body then stood back.

I looked down at the sharp-featured waxen face and was surprised. "I know this guy. He's one of the people who kept Nicoleta. Whatever happened to him, he deserved it."

"OK," said Sharon. "But why did he try and walk across Southampton Water?"

"Let's see."

I laid my hand on his cold chest and let his memories flow into me.

"Charlie." Sharon's voice recalled me from the murky world of his memories.

"You OK? You were in there for a really long time."

"Was I?" It didn't feel that long, but there had been so much I wanted to know about.

"Did you get anything?"

"Oh yeah."

"Let's go in the office."

We left Sanjay to rewrap the body and went to his small office just along the corridor. Sharon sat in his chair and took out a spiral-bound notepad. I perched on the desk and took a moment to put the information in order.

"Let's hear it then."

"His name is Idriz, he's Albanian."

She nodded. "We knew that."

"He's into pretty much anything dodgy that makes money. Drugs, guns, trafficked girls, stolen motors going east."

"So what's he doing walking off the Town Quay?"

"Someone put a compulsion on him. It was just like it was with DI Scott."

"So has this guy had dealings with Peter Murphy?"

"Yes, he did. It's hard to explain, but it's like the memories are behind a distorted glass wall. I can the outlines, but I can't get into them in detail. But I can see images of Murphy in there."

"Not that we can touch him for it. A dozen witnesses saw our boy walk off the end of the quay with nobody near him." She laughed grimly. "It's the perfect murder."

"Except we know he did it."

"And he's probably done it to other people."

"All the more reason why we have to deal with him. There's loads more. Do you want the rest of it?"

"Sure."

I went through the details of Idriz's criminal enterprises, and she filled about five pages of her notebook.

"He's been one busy boy," she said when I'd finished.

"You going to be able to use this to go after the bastards who hurt Nicoleta?"

"Maybe. If she'll ID them and make a statement."

"And if she won't?"

"Then there's less I can do. I can put it all into the database, of course, flag it up for the Drugs Squad and the Human

Trafficking Initiative. Have they got any drugs stashed at the moment?"

"No. Moved those on last week."

"Pity. You said they had guns."

"Idriz had a couple. Kept them at a girlfriend's place."

"We'll go after those then. Did the others have any?"

"Don't think so. He was the armourer and enforcer. He handled them. If they needed them, they came to him."

"Let's hope they've been stupid enough to leave their prints on them otherwise we can't go after them immediately without Nicoleta's statement." She shook her head. "I'm sorry, Charlie, but it's going to be a question of gathering the evidence slowly and building the case."

"But then they can carry on and destroy more girls like Nicoleta."

"And if we go in too early, we could blow it, and give them the chance to get off. I know you don't like it, but that's the way it's going to be done."

Damn right I didn't like it, but Sanjay came in then putting a stop to the discussion.

We walked back to the car and Sharon drove me back to the University.

"What will happen to Nicoleta now?" I asked.

"That's a tricky one. Probably nothing for several weeks. She's a minor and a victim at risk and, potentially, a witness. Depends on whether she's willing to make a statement, or if she just wants to go home."

"Don't know if she's got much to go home to. She certainly doesn't come from a loving home and family who'll be missing her."

"Whatever happens I can't see any decision getting made quickly. Do you want to claim your dinner tonight?"

"Yeah, suppose so." I certainly didn't feel like cooking.

"Roberto's? Or do you want to try somewhere else?"

"Roberto's is good." Eating at Roberto's was still a novelty for me.

I worked through the afternoon and thought about what I was going to do. I'd spent a lot of time in Idriz's memories and knew exactly how evil a bunch of bastards his crew were. Sharon's slow collection of evidence might get them in the end, but they would damage a lot of people before they were brought down. I was in favour of something quicker, but for that I needed to learn a lot more and that required Jack. I sent mother a text telling her I was coming out tomorrow to go to the gateway then composed an e-mail to Michelle.

I told her to do nothing to annoy Dave, that I would find a way to deal with him, and that I loved her. A short message that said a lot. I was committed. I had contemplated not seeing her again and realised I couldn't do it. If she wanted to see me, I would always go.

I didn't get my dinner at Roberto's. Sharon texted me at six to say something had come up and she wasn't going to be able to get away. I spent the evening in the lab after getting a bite to eat in the union refectory. Cleaned up my batch of intermediate and thought a lot about Dave and the Albanians. Result: eight grams of clean material, no plan for dealing with evil bastards.

Sharon finally got in at eleven. The something turned out to be a parking dispute between neighbours in Millbrook that had got out of hand and resulted in two people stabbed and six arrests.

"Bloody nutters the lot of them," she said bitterly. "And the girlfriend's flat was clean when we went after Idriz's guns."

Mother had texted me to say she would be working until eight, so I went straight to the gateway when I got out to Langley. I wasn't at all sure whether Jack would appear; I could imagine how he could be very busy over there for weeks of our time. Nevertheless, I had to try. I sat down by the gateway and began his summoning song.

I shouldn't have worried because he turned up within a few minutes, smiling broadly as he appeared, seemingly out of nowhere.

"Charlie!" He looked around. "Is your mother not with you?"

"No. She's working. I'll see her later." I handed him the bar of chocolate I had brought. He sat down on a grassy bank and opened the wrapper. I sat beside him.

"How is she?"

"She seems fine. Did you do something to help her get over what happened?"

He paused to break off a piece of chocolate before answering. "Yes. I took some of the worst of her memories."

"Can you teach me how to do that?"

"In time, but there are other things you must first learn."

"Compulsions? I've been wanting to ask you about that."

"I can teach you a little, enough to control the gwasannath, but you would be better learning from someone else. They are complex and may unravel if you leave a flaw."

He broke off another piece of chocolate.

"So who could teach me? One of The Great?"

"You would want to learn from the best, wouldn't you?"

"Well yes. But I need to be able to do something now."

"There are those I could ask, but to weave a compulsion such as you need takes time to learn. How are you now at casting a glamour?"

"I don't know." Probably not good, I hadn't thought about it for a while.

"Show me."

I looked at his boots and tried to project the image of my feet covered by a matching pair.

"You need to practice that before you attempt a compulsion."

"But…"

"What is your haste?"

"Michelle is in trouble. I need to help her."

"What trouble?"

"There's a man who thinks he owns her. He was one of the prisoners. He got angry when he found we'd been together. Now he won't leave her, he keeps her in her house all the time. He has been violent to her before."

"And you thought to put a compulsion on him? To make him give her up?"

"Yes. He is too big for me to confront physically."

"Cannot your friend Sharon, the policewoman, help you?"

"Maybe. But I wanted to handle it myself."

"Foolishness. If she can help you, then ask her."

I nodded. He was right; it was just vanity to want to sort it out on my own. I felt I had to ask him about the other thing that had been gnawing at me since I last saw him.

"I keep expecting you to tell me that me and Michelle shouldn't be together."

"Why not?" Not the response I had feared.

"She is your daughter, my half-sister."

"Such things are not uncommon among our people. The Great do it to try and preserve the grym hud. You are one of us now. You need to learn to think our way."

Several tons of anxiety slipped from my shoulders like melting snow off a pitched roof. "I'm very glad to hear that."

"If she wants to be with you." He shrugged. "Why not?"

"How are things over there? What is Lord Faniel doing?" Plotting his revenge, I expect; he didn't strike me as the forgiving type.

"Lord Faniel is doing exactly as his father tells him." He smiled. "And most of his followers are trying to deny they ever did so. I think I will be spending more time around the court. The King is greatly interested in your world and seems to think I know about it. Perhaps you should come and answer his questions."

"I will come. I'll answer his questions and learn from The Great, but I want to get Michelle's situation sorted out first. There's another thing I need to get sorted, too. We have someone who is under a compulsion. Could you remove it and show me how?"

He thought about it for a moment. "Yes. That would be a good lesson, if it is a simple compulsion."

"I can bring him to a gateway." At least I hoped I could.

"I will come if I can, though I may be answering the King's questions." He cocked his head as if hearing someone call him. "I must go now." He stood up. "You need to practice your glamours."

I knew better than to try to follow him even though I knew where he was going. He vanished from sight before he'd taken five steps towards the gateway. I walked back towards mother's cottage feeling mightily relieved, but with a troll-sized problem still at the front of my mind.

Mother was still in her blue nylon care-assistant uniform so she must have just got in from work. I was slightly surprised she'd gone back to work so soon, but quickly realised that she needed the money. She hugged me long and hard.

"How are you?" she said with a real intensity.

"I'm OK. How are you?"

"I'm fine. It's strange. I remember everything that happened, but it's at a distance, like a dream, or a book I read."

"Maybe that's just the effect of the gateway. Stuff that happens over there doesn't seem so real."

"Could be. Did you get to talk to him then?"

"Yeah. He didn't stay long, but we talked."

"I need to get changed. Why don't you put the kettle on then you can tell me all about it."

I put the kettle and, while it came to the boil, looked at the new back door and around the kitchen trying to catalogue what else had got damaged by Lord Faniel's raiders.

"So what did he say?" she asked as she came in dressed in jeans and a Motorhead T-shirt.

"I want to learn about compulsions. He said he wasn't the best person to teach me."

"Really? Who did he suggest? Someone other there?"

"One of The Great."

She nodded. "You'd need to spend time over there."

"That's the problem. I need to be able to do something now."

"Why?"

I told her about Michelle and Dave.

"Was he the big guy in the barn that thumped you?"

"Yeah, that's him." My face ached at the memory.

"Are you completely sure she wants to get away from him?"

"Oh yes. That's why I need to be able to use a compulsion. To get him to leave her alone."

"But you don't need to be able to do a compulsion to get her away from him."

I thought about it for a while. "No, I suppose not. But I'll need it eventually."

"Let's focus on getting her away from him. She said he won't leave her alone, but there must be times when he has to."

"So far, the only time is when he's asleep, that's when she e-mails me. She said he keeps her locked in."

"So then we have to draw him out leaving the door unlocked. Any ideas?"

I thought about Dave and his activities. He had to work sometime, but presumably he locked Michelle in when he went out. He had to get to work in... his van.

"Maybe if we had a go at his van and set off the alarm that would bring him out."

"Do you know if it has an alarm?"

"I don't, but I'd think you'd need one round that part of Totton."

"So what are we going to do when he comes out to check on his van?"

"We?"

"Yes. We! I know and like Michelle, and I can see how much this matters to you. And I don't like men who treat women as possessions."

I was a bit surprised, but glad of the help.

"Once Dave's away from the flat, Michelle can make a dash for it. I can tell her to look for you, can you get her away?"

"Yes. I'll bring her back here. What will you do?"

"I'm still working on that. Run, I guess."

"When are we going to do it?"

"As soon as possible. I'll e-mail Michelle tonight, and we'll do it tomorrow if she's on for it."

"Sounds like a plan."

"Guess I'd better check that Dave's van is parked near the flat. I can do that on the way back tonight."

"Speaking of which, what time do you need to go?"

"If I catch the last bus just after ten, I can get off at Totton, check on the van and then get a train into town."

"I'd better get on and feed you then."

Dave's van was parked on the road a hundred yards up from the flat – ideal. I looked up at the blue television light spilling out of the sitting room window. She was up there with him, and I could imagine any numbers of ways he was abusing her. I desperately wanted to do something; go in there and make him give her up. I knew that would only make things worse and probably get both me and Michelle hurt. I walked away towards Totton station furiously plotting her escape, preferably with humiliation for Dave.

I got back to the flat pretty late, but Sharon was still up, watching late night television with a glass of wine and a bag of mints.

"You're late," she said. "I was wondering where you'd got to."

"I went to see my father."

"How'd that go?"

I told her about my meeting and how Jack had said he would remove Mike Scott's compulsion.

"That's great." She reached for her phone. "I'll text him to set it up. Be good to get that sorted, then we can go after Peter Murphy."

"Damn right. Can I get some advice? I've got a problem with Michelle."

"Sure. What's going on? I thought you were getting on well with her."

I hadn't talked to her about my relationship with Michelle, so I was a bit surprised at her comment, but then she is a copper and good at working things out.

"I am. Well, I was, until her boyfriend reappeared. You know the bloke I'm talking about. I should have left him over there."

"Ah, the jealous gorilla problem?" She took a sip of wine. "Tricky."

"Yeah, exactly that. He's taken her phone and keeps her locked in the flat, won't let her go out. I was wondering if there was anything you could do about it."

"Such as?"

"Send someone round to kick him out. It is her place after all."

She pulled a face. "It would be a damn sight easier if Michelle made a complaint. I could pass it over to the Domestic Abuse team. Without a direct complaint they're unlikely to do anything."

"She can't call, he's got her phone, and he won't let her out."

"Well, I can give you the number and you can report it, or I can get their e-mail address, but these guys are beyond busy. I doubt they'll do anything more than log it."

"OK." I decided against telling her what mother and I had planned; it did, after all, entail damaging Dave's van.

"And Charlie. Don't go diving in there and try to get her out. You'll just get hurt."

"No chance of that. I mean, you've seen the size of him."

I left her with that and went to write my e-mail to Michelle. I set down the plan I had agreed with mother as clearly as I could then sat, cursor poised over the "send" button, wondering if I'd overlooked anything. There was, of course, plenty of scope for making things worse, but I absolutely could not do nothing. I had to get her away from him. With a silent prayer I hit send.

I resisted the temptation to sit there hitting "refresh" and closed down the machine. It was very unlikely that she would be able to reply immediately, her previous replies had been in the small hours, so I went to bed.

Sleep proved elusive as horribly possible scenarios of everything going wrong played out in my mind. A dozen times over Dave caught up with me or Michelle, some bystander or a stray passing copper grabbed me as I ran from the van. Then, somewhere after two, a useful thought occurred to me; I needed a glamour to scare Dave off. I had a happy few minutes speculating about what would be most effective before settling on a gwasannath, then drifting off to sleep.

Michelle's e-mail was time-stamped 02.40: "Yes, I'll be ready, but for God's sake be careful – Dave is ready to kill you. I love you so much."

The last sentence filled me with a warm glow that lasted most of the morning. I sent mother a text to tell her that we were on for tonight and practised my glamour in the lab successfully enough that two of my labmates asked about my new boots.

I felt more confident, though whether I could pull off a full gwasannath was a greater challenge.

I worked until nearly eight, grabbed a bite to eat in the union, despite being too nervous to have an appetite, and then walked down to Swaythling to catch the train out to Totton. It was dark when I met up with mother, which suited my plans. If I was going to work a glamour, then I figured it would be better in reduced visibility.

Dave's van was still in the same place as last night. Mother was parked just around the corner, about fifty yards away. We sat in the car not saying much, waiting for the area to quieten down. By about ten nobody had walked past us for ten minutes so we decided it was quiet enough. I picked up the oak branch that mother had brought from her woodpile and walked towards the van. I heard her car engine start as I turned the corner. The street was deserted. I walked around to the far side of the van, struck the branch at the driver's side window. The branch bounced off the glass, the alarm shrieked, and the indicator lights flashed. I ran for the corner of the block, still clutching the branch. From there I watched curtains open in several flats, including Michelle's. A few seconds later Michelle's door opened, and Dave's bulky figure was framed in the doorway. He lumbered over to the van, and I kept my eyes on the doorway, hoping to see Michelle make her escape.

Michelle had not appeared when there was an angry yell.

"Hey you!"

Dave was standing by the van looking straight at me. He started to run. I considered relying on my ability to cast a glamour for a moment and then ran for it. I had no idea where I was going, just that I wanted to get him away from the flat and away from me. He moved pretty quickly for a big guy; much faster than I expected. He was closing on me as I took a left turn and then another, running flat out.

He chased me down a road lined with parked cars into a gravelled yard. Garages and workshops stood on either side with a brick wall closing off the far side, high enough that I didn't think I could reach the top and scramble over. There didn't look to be any way out.

I turned to face Dave and put all my being into projecting a gwasannath. It may even have worked; Dave slowed for a moment but didn't stop. He charged straight into me knocking me over. I landed on my back, the breath knocked out of me; it felt like I'd been hit by a bus. The bus then landed on me, one meaty hand grabbing my chin, pushing my cheek into the gravel. I tried to twist my head to save my eye and bite his hand but could not make any movement against his strength.

As his thoughts, blazing with anger, flowed into mine I pushed the fear and pain I felt into him. I couldn't let everything go, that would damage him too much like that Otherkin soldier; it would become a police matter and I certainly didn't want that. Just push him enough to scare him off. I built the flow carefully, all the time conscious of the pain of my face pressed into the gravel, until he cracked and stopped. He gasped and rolled off me and then took off back the way he'd come, pelting across the yard as fast as his legs would carry him.

I lay on the gravel for a couple of minutes trying to get my breath and quell the nausea. I sat up, the anger that had surged through me from Dave still rumbling like a distant thunderstorm in my mind. I raised a hand to my cheek and found gravel; carefully I tried to pick it out. My phone rang.

"Where are you?" Mother's voice.

"I don't know. Some kind of car park. Is Michelle with you?"

"Yes, she's here. Can you find your way back to the main road?"

Relief flooded through me. I got up and looked around, the yard was unlit, but there seemed to be streetlights beyond the row of buildings. I started to walk that way. "Maybe. I wasn't paying attention. Dave was chasing me."

"Are you OK?"

My ribs hurt and my hand came away sticky from my cheek. "Yeah. Couple of scratches that's all."

At the end of the row was an unmade road that joined an ordinary residential street. The sign on the corner said St John's Road.

"I've just joined St John's Road." I told mother.

I heard Michelle's voice in the background telling her where I was.

"Stay where you are. We're a couple of minutes away."

It was a bit longer than two minutes. I wrote a text to Sharon to tell I wouldn't be back tonight while I waited and was just starting to get worried that something had happened to them when mother's car appeared and pulled up beside me. Michelle was sitting in the back, so I got in beside her. She seemed, at least physically, unharmed. She threw her arms around me and kissed me passionately, and any doubts I may have had about her commitment to me vanished.

Mother pulled away briskly and headed for the Fawley road. I barely noticed where we were because Michelle was fully occupying my attention, and it seemed like no time before we arrived at the cottage.

It was past eleven; I was suddenly tired as the adrenaline flowed out of me, and ready for bed. Michelle kept hold of me as I fetched her small bag of things into the cottage.

"Take that upstairs," said mother. "Michelle can have your room. You're on the couch."

I looked at her in surprise.

"My house, my rules," she said. "On the couch."

I knew better than to argue.

She turned to Michelle. "Have you had anything to eat recently?"

"No, nothing much today," said Michelle.

"Good God, you'll fade away. Right, I've got some stew I'll warm up."

Mother bustled off to the kitchen. I took Michelle upstairs and showed her my room and the bathroom.

"What a lovely house," she said. "I always wanted to live somewhere like this."

I would have quite happily offered her to move in then and there, but, of course, it wasn't my decision.

We didn't talk much, but we were still upstairs when mother called up that the food was ready.

I was awake early in time to catch the bus into town. My ribs had stiffened up overnight on the couch, though they might well have done wherever I slept. It would take nearly two hours to get to the lab through the rush hour. I was really tempted to throw a sickie and spend the day with Michelle, but I'd left stuff running that needed to be worked on, and mother sent me on my way.

"Michelle's been through so much, she needs peace and space. I'm going to let her sleep for as long as she needs, then we're going to make some phone calls. She needs to get her flat and her car back and make sure that boyfriend of hers can't mistreat her anymore. None of this needs you. Give her a couple of days. Come back at the weekend."

I wasn't sure how they were going to ensure Dave couldn't give her any more grief without putting a compulsion on him, but it didn't seem smart to argue. I finished my cereal and walked to the bus stop just in time for the bus.

I had plenty of time to think as the bus filled up on its way into Southampton. Mostly I thought about Michelle; I was glad now that I'd had no chance to talk about us sharing a father. I didn't know if she knew, but I simply could not face the possibility that she might reject me if she didn't. If it meant deceiving her and stacking up greater trouble for the future, then so be it; that future might never arise. After all, the only other person who knew had no problem with it.

I changed buses in the centre of town and caught the Unilink. We were crawling up London Road when I recognised someone on the pavement. He walked past the bus talking on his mobile. He passed within six feet of me and there was no mistaking his face; he was the leader of the gang that had abused Nicoleta. Idriz's memories supplied his name, Besian.

Seeing him blew all thoughts about my situation with Michelle out of my mind. I was seized with an urge to get off and follow him. I stood up, but the bus lurched forward and dumped me back into my seat, and when I looked again, he was gone.

I burned with anger at the sight of Besian; the knowledge

of what he had done and was still doing. I sat rigid with my fists clenched, seeing again his abuse of Nicoleta, the memories I had taken from her suddenly fresh. By the time I reached the University that anger had cooled to a cold determination to do something. I was prepared to bet that Sharon's inquiries hadn't managed to get any further.

I got a text from Sharon mid-morning; Mike Scott was keen to get rid of the compulsion any time we could make it. I texted back "this evening" pleased that I was going to be able to get that ball rolling. She texted me back within five minutes "'6pm at my place." I just hoped Jack would show up.

I left it until after lunch to call Michelle, agreeing that she needed to sleep, but I evidently left it too late, and the call went straight to voice mail. I said I'd call her later and went back to work.

Mike Scott was at Sharon's flat when I got there a little after six. He was unshaven with sunken bloodshot eyes; he looked as if he hadn't slept since I last saw him.

"Do you really think you can get rid of this fucking thing out of my head?" he asked as soon as I came in, an edge of desperation in his voice.

"I'm sure my father can. I've seen him do it with lots of people."

"I hope to God he can," he said. "I can't live with the idea that something's controlling me."

"And when we get you fixed," said Sharon. "We can go after the bastard that did it."

"Can't wait," said Mike.

"I'm looking forward to that, too," I said. "He only tried to have me killed."

"Yeah. I know. Sorry." Mike said, his eyes on his feet.

"Let's hit the road," said Sharon. "Where we going, Charlie?"

"Netley Marsh," I said. I thought it would be a good idea to keep Sharon well away from my mother after the argument they had last time they met. I could really do with finding a few more gateways to use.

We hit the rush hour traffic heading out of Southampton. I sat in the back of Sharon's Mini since Mike was bigger than me.

I don't recommend it as a comfortable ride if you're over five feet tall, particularly if you have sore ribs. Mike fidgeted the whole time like a 40-a-day smoker on the second day of giving up.

It was well after seven before we pulled into the carpark in Netley Marsh, and I was able to stretch out my legs and restore the circulation.

"So what do we do now?" said Mike looking around the deserted car park. "I thought we were meeting your father here."

"We are," I said. "If he shows up. I'll go and call him."

He looked puzzled.

"Leave it," said Sharon. "It'll take too long to explain."

Mike seemed inclined to dispute it, so I left them their debate and walked up the track towards the gateway. I passed through tunnel of trees where Michelle had killed Lord Faniel's gwasannath only a few weeks ago and settled myself on a bank with the gateway glowing blue about forty yards away. I began the summoning song, hoping that Jack wasn't busy with the King or something. I didn't think Mike Scott would be too impressed if he didn't show up.

I sang the song through; nothing happened so I began it again, thinking as I sang about how difficult it would be to explain the failure to Mike. By the tenth time I was wondering about just taking them through to find Jack when he appeared right in front of me.

"I brought the man with the compulsion," I said. "He's back there with Sharon."

"Good. Let us see what may be done. Have you been practising your glamours?"

I started guiltily. "I tried. It didn't work too well."

"Then you must keep practising. Let me meet your friend with the compulsion."

We walked back towards the carpark where Sharon and Mike were sitting on the car bonnet smoking. They threw down their cigarettes and ground them out as we approached.

"This is my father," I said to Mike then turned to Jack. "This is Mike, who needs your help."

"Pleased to meet you," said Mike, offering his hand. "Do

you think you'll be able to do anything?"

"I would think so," said Jack, ignoring his hand. "Let us come away from the iron, it will disturb the flows."

Mike looked at Sharon, puzzlement across his face.

"Let's move away from the car, Mike," she said.

We walked back towards the gateway until the car was out of sight. Jack chose a grassy area between two trees and sat down.

"Sit here," he said to the still puzzled-looking Mike, pointing to a spot beside him. "Charlie, sit here."

I sat where he directed facing the two of them.

"Join hands."

Jack took my hand then reached for Mike's. I offered my hand to Mike. Mike hesitated a moment then with a visible effort he took both the offered hands. There was no rush of thoughts and emotions, just Jack's voice quietly asking what the compulsion was. I started to probe for Mike's memories of Pete Murphy and immediately ran into the barriers of smoke and glass. I pushed at them, but they simply absorbed the pressure, drawing the force away from the point of impact like a big squashy balloon. The more I pushed the further away they got.

"That's not how you do it," said Jack in my mind. "You draw it into yourself, if you are strong enough."

"How?"

"Suck it in and swallow it."

The barriers began to flow past me, at first slowly but with growing momentum.

"This is a weak compulsion," said Jack. "You try, you should be able to move it."

Not sure of quite what to do, I leaned forward to press my face into the barriers. When I felt resistance, I breathed in slowly and deeply. I reached out as if gathering in a large duvet and attempted to shovel great scoops of the barrier towards me. To my slight surprise the barrier stuff moved and began to flow. I smelled and tasted a strange musty flavour as I sucked in the material.

"That's it," said Jack. "You've got it. Keep drawing it in."

I sucked in several more lungfuls until the musty flavour

faded. Jack let go of my hand, and when I lifted my head Mike's memories of Peter Murphy were laid out clearly before me. I dived in absorbing as much as I could about this man who had ordered me killed before releasing Mike's hand.

"Did you get rid of it?" asked Mike, an edge of desperate anxiety in his voice.

"Yeah. You're clean," I said. "Can't you tell?"

I think he would have come apart completely if we'd said no. He buried his face in his hands and slumped forwards. Sharon came and knelt beside him and put her arms around him. Jack and I walked a few paces away to leave them space.

"Strange," said Jack "That was a crude and weak compulsion, but I think I recognise some parts of its construction."

"How would you recognise it?" I thought of the strange flavour; was that something distinctive?

"Everyone who works compulsions does them differently. In time you'll find your own way. When you've seen some of the different ways, you'll recognise them. There were parts of this one that only a few people use that I know of."

"Could someone learn it, develop their own technique without being taught?"

"If they did, I don't think they would end up doing it this way."

"So could the man who cast this compulsion have been taught by one of those people you know of?"

"It is possible, but then I'm surprised by how poorly it was done."

"Maybe they only had a few lessons," I said. "The man who cast it lives on this side."

"Then perhaps that is it. They were shown it a few times and then left to make their own way."

"Works pretty well in a world that doesn't know how to remove a compulsion."

"Indeed, crude but effective."

He turned and I followed his gaze to see Mike Scott and Sharon standing together looking at us.

"I owe you guys so much," said Mike. "I don't know how I can repay you."

"Start by putting Pete Murphy in prison," I said.

"Oh yes. That's the very least I can do," said Mike. "I owe him that for what he did to me, leave aside anything else."

"We've got to be smart though," said Sharon. "Got to make it stick."

I turned to Jack. "There's something else I need to be able to work a compulsion for."

"Practice your glamours," he said. "And I will find you a teacher."

"One that will come over here?"

He frowned at me.

"You said it would be a lot of work which I'm prepared for, but if I go over there to learn I'll lose weeks or months over here. There's no way I can do that."

He frowned again then abruptly turned away from me. "Practice your glamours. Now I must go. Farewell, Michael, I wish you the best of fortune in your quest to bring down Murphy."

He walked a few paces towards the gateway and then vanished.

"That's your father?" said Mike, surprise written across his unshaven face.

"That's him," I said.

"And can you do that? Just disappear like he did?"

"No. Not yet, but I'm going to learn." Along with lots of other stuff.

We walked back to the car, Mike with his arm around Sharon. I concentrated on imagining boots, building and projecting the glamour.

"Nice boots," said Sharon as I contorted myself to climb into the backseat of the Mini, my ribs giving me a sharp reminder. "Have I seen those before? Much better than your scruffy trainers."

"Yeah, nice, aren't they?" I said, glowing inside with satisfaction, then added. "Fifteen quid on E-Bay."

"Good deal," said Mike.

I found an almost tolerable position in the backseat, and we headed back towards Southampton.

"So any ideas about how we go after Pete Murphy?" I asked once we were on the main road. "Can you still get in contact with him?"

"Yeah, I still talk to him. I've told him I'm being investigated, and he hasn't pushed me," said Mike. "But we need to be careful. He's a very dangerous man."

"I know that," I said. "He tried to kill me. That's why I'm so keen to help bring him down."

"Like I said before," said Sharon over her shoulder. "We have to be smart. Build the case completely so that he can't wriggle out of it. That isn't going to happen quickly."

"Maybe I can get you the evidence you need if I can get close to him like I did with Tommy Rowe."

"This time's different though," said Sharon. "He knows about you."

"And I know about him. I just broke a compulsion he put on, I'm stronger than him."

"But you're younger than him," said Sharon. "And nowhere near as nasty as him."

"She's right," said Mike. "He's really evil bastard. You have no idea."

"All the more reason why we should bring him down as soon as possible. And I can help you with that."

Before they could answer my phone rang; my heart gave a little lurch as Michelle's number showed on the screen. I answered and a warm glow spread through me at the sound of her voice as she told me what she had done today. Mother had taken her to see a lawyer about her mother's estate, then to see the landlord about getting the flat put in her name and the locks changed to keep Dave the troll out. Then they shopped and cooked a meal together, which made me aware of how hungry I was and regret I'd missed it. I told her I looked forward to cooking for her, too;, she giggled and said "soon." Then she asked when she was going to see me. I didn't feel I could tell her that mother had ordered me to give her space, so I lied about having to do work stuff and said I'd see her Friday evening.

"I don't think I can wait that long," she said, which was great to hear, but damn frustrating.

By the end of the phone call we were driving through Shirley, nearly back at Sharon's place. We parked up, went into the flat and it was pretty evident that Sharon and Mike were more interested in each other than something to eat. I resorted to the takeaway pizza menu and left them to it, wishing I was out at mother's cottage with Michelle.

There was no sign of Sharon when I got up next morning and her door was shut so I assumed Mike Scott had stayed the night. I felt a little nibble of jealousy that they had enjoyed what I had been denied. Her door was still shut by the time I left for the lab.

I've never had a visitor in the lab before, so I was pretty surprised when I got a call from Prof's secretary around eleven telling me there was someone waiting to see me. I went down to Prof's office to find an average-looking guy in a plain suit sitting in the outer office – Nigel the spook. The guy who had stitched up Sharon and me only a few weeks ago.

"Mr. Somes." He stood up but didn't offer his hand; he knew about my talent.

"Nigel, I'm sorry I don't know your second name." I tried to stay polite in front of Prof's secretary.

"I was hoping we could have a little chat."

I would have liked nothing better than to tell him to shove where the sun doesn't shine, but I remembered the trouble he'd made for Sharon and thought of how much trouble he could make for me. Behind him stood the whole apparatus of government and it didn't seem smart to defy it openly.

"OK," I said warily, wondered what I was letting myself in for.

Prof's secretary showed us into a vacant seminar room.

I went and sat in the chair that Prof normally sat in beside the whiteboard. "So what can I do for you, Nigel?"

"You have a most unusual talent. I was hoping you might be persuaded to use it for the good of your country."

"Doing what?"

"I'm sure you're aware of the challenges we are facing with a variety of extremists looking to do us harm. One of the greatest difficulties is identifying those who are a genuine threat, sorting out the players from the dabblers. You could help us a lot with this and then getting to their controllers."

Well, yes, I could do that, and I saw the need for it; but it bothered me that he knew so much about my abilities. I remembered mother's warning against getting involved with the authorities; looked like it was too late.

The doubts must have shown on my face.

"You're what, second year of your PhD? So you'll be looking for a post-doctoral position in another year's time," said Nigel. "We can offer some support, grant money that you carry with you. A NATO fellowship."

That would make a huge difference to where I could go. With my own NATO money, pretty much any lab in the US, Canada or western Europe would welcome me.

"How big a time commitment are we talking about?"

"Only a few hours a month."

That wouldn't be too much of a nuisance, not for a NATO fellowship.

"And we'll pay you, of course. At our standard contractor's rate of seventy-five pounds an hour."

That was just too much money to ignore.

"OK."

"Good. I'm looking forward to working with you."

I wondered what his next move would have been if I'd said no.

"Are you available to start immediately?"

"If it's OK with my Professor. I just need a few minutes to get my reaction to a point where it's alright to leave it."

"You go and do what you need to. I will speak to your Professor."

I couldn't imagine even Prof would argue with MI5. I went back up to the lab wondering what I'd let myself in for.

I was still wondering twenty minutes later as Nigel drove me into the centre of town in his very ordinary Vauxhall Astra. He drove carefully, sticking to the speed limits and stopping at amber lights, and without small talk. To my no-great surprise our destination was the Civic Centre police station. We parked in the visitors' area, and I followed Nigel into the station. He showed a pass to the desk sergeant who let us both in without any questions or signing in, and then escorted us down to the custody suite. We stopped outside a cell, the name Tanvir Khan was chalked on the board beside the door.

"This lad's got some nasty friends and some bad stuff on his computer," said Nigel. "We'd like to know if he's a real headbanger or just a wannabe. Can you do that?"

"Should be able to," I said.

"If you could get his passwords to some of the jihadist websites he's been on, then that would be worth a bonus."

The sergeant unlocked the door and I stepped into the cell. A skinny Asian man with a straggly beard sat on the bed. He stood up as I came in; he looked pretty young, younger than me and looked almost pleased to see me. I reached out a hand, and then Tanvir recoiled as Nigel came in behind me. Tanvir's expression changed to fear and defiance. I heard the cell door close.

Nigel stepped around me, caught hold of him in an armlock and held up his hand for me.

"Don't take too long," Nigel said.

I reached forward and took Tanvir's hand, even as he tried to pull away. A great wave of his fear washed over me. I pushed through it, reached into the swirling thoughts behind. He knew what he was being investigated for, and his activities were at the front of his mind which made it easy for me.

"That didn't take long, said Nigel, when I'd finished. "Did you get anything?"

"Enough," I said.

"Let's go then." He let go of Tanvir and rapped on the cell door with the flat of his hand. The door opened, we left the cell and the sergeant locked it behind us. He led us down the corridor, showed us into a vacant interview room then left.

"Well?" said Nigel. He placed his phone on the table; in record mode I presumed.

"He's not a terrorist," I said. "He's just a scared kid who was trying to big himself up with his mates and is now shitting himself over what his mother will say."

"So no passwords to jihadist websites?"

"No. He's looked at a few, guest access only. He isn't a member of any."

"What about the videos on his computer?"

"He hasn't watched them. They were put there by someone he's only just met. Guy called Iftikhar Islam. He sounds like someone you ought to be looking at, though."

"Oh, we will." He retrieved his phone. "Would you be available to help us with him in the same way?"

"Yeah. Don't see why not."

"Well thank you, Mr. Somes. You've been very helpful. I reckon that to be about an hour's worth, so we owe you seventy-five pounds." He took a wallet from inside his jacket and counted out eighty pounds in ten-pound notes.

"Five pounds signing on bonus," he said as he handed me the money. I pocketed the notes, signed a receipt and followed him back to the visitor's car park. I thought about leaving Nigel to set Tanvir free and taking the Unilink back up to the campus, but decided the extra time spent in a cell would be therapeutic for Tanvir.

I didn't get back to the flat until mid-evening thanks to a misbehaving reaction that I couldn't leave. Sharon wasn't around so any prospect of claiming my dinner at Roberto's gently expired. I cooked and ate some pasta, then phoned Michelle to tell her about my excursion with Nigel.

I was still talking to her when Sharon rolled in just after ten. Her slightly flushed and bright-eyed look suggested she'd had a drink or three.

"I had a visit from our friend Nigel the spook today," I said when I'd ended the call and she had installed herself on the sofa.

"Yeah. I heard he was around. What did he want?"

"To know what was in someone's head. I didn't know he knew what I can do."

"I didn't tell him."

"Not saying you did," I paused. "But he knew."

"That's the spooks for you. It's their job to know stuff other people don't. So did you do it for him?"

"Yeah, I did. He bought me. The price was too good, plus I had an idea he could make life difficult for me if I didn't."

"Well, we know he's good at that," she said with feeling. "You be careful around him."

"I intend to be. Are you any closer to a plan for dealing with Peter Murphy?"

She shook her head. "Officially speaking, it's nothing to do with me. I should leave it to Mike and his crew."

"And unofficially speaking?"

"I'm totally up for doing something, but I'm still leaving it to Mike. He's got the connections, the resources and the motivation. Look Charlie, it will get sorted, just don't get impatient."

I had to be content with that; pushing it wouldn't help. She reached for the remote, turned the TV on and started channel hopping. That was the end for any serious discussions.

"I'll be going out to Mother's for the weekend. Spend some time with Michelle."

"You got her away from the gorilla then?"

"Yeah, she's staying with my mother for a bit. But I need a permanent solution to the gorilla problem."

"Staying with your mum? That sounds dangerous."

"Dangerous? Why?"

"What do you think they're going to talk about? You'll have no secrets left."

"Oh! I thought it was a good thing they were getting on OK."

It really had not occurred to me that anything but good could come from it.

"Then they'll be making plans for you and your life won't be your own. You might as well be married."

I didn't know what to say to that.

"Don't look so worried, Charlie. I'm winding you up. Well mostly." She grinned at me. "Are those the same boots you're wearing?"

"Yeah, why?"

"They look a different colour."

"No, same ones." I looked down at my trainers for a moment and tried to think of a reasonable explanation. "I just polished them."

"Oh right." She turned her attention to the TV and changed the channel.

I left the lab as soon as I could on Friday, just after Prof left at half five, and caught a bus down to the city centre then a second bus out to Langley. I texted mother and Michelle to let them know I was on my way and received an immediate reply promising dinner and many kisses from Michelle. That filled me with a warm glow that sustained me for the entire boring journey.

It was nearly half past seven and I was starving when I got there. Michelle must have been keeping a watch for the bus because she came running down the lane to greet me with an extravagant hug. Mother's greeting was a bit more restrained, but she was still pleased to see me.

Dinner was a really fragrant fish stew with mashed potato with a bottle of white wine.

"All Michelle's work," said Mother. "I just showed her how to work the hob."

"My mum's recipe," said Michelle.

"It's excellent," I said thinking the best way to show my appreciation was to ask for seconds. "Is there anymore?"

When we were finished Mother told us to leave the washing up. It was a mild evening with plenty of light still in the sky, so I walked Michelle down to the river and through the woods to the little beach that was Mother's meeting point.

"Your mum's been so good to me," said Michelle, snuggling against my shoulder. "I hardly know her, but it feels like I've always known her."

"Yeah, she's good like that. Took me a while to appreciate it."

"She's offered me to move in with her. Would you be alright with that?"

That was a surprise. It took me a moment to answer. "It's her cottage. I don't actually live there anymore so it's not really for me to object."

"But I'd be moving into your old room. Thing is, if I'm keeping the car, I can't really afford the flat on my own, and as long as I'm there Dave will always know where to find me."

"I'm hoping I'll have a permanent solution to Dave pretty soon, but until then it's good. At least I'll know you're somewhere safe."

"And she's going to help me get a job at the care home she works in. The money's better than Tesco, and it'll be something that'll help me get into nursing."

"Tough work, though." Mother sometimes talked about some of the people she looked after, and it made me grateful that I had better options open to me.

"So is nursing, but that's what I want to do. It would be good to start moving my stuff soon, and I need to pick up my car. Could you come with me tomorrow and get it? If we go in the evening, then Dave'll be working."

"You sure he'll be working? I really don't fancy running into him. I'm not ready to face him." That could be fatal.

"He usually works Saturday nights. Starts at eight, doesn't finish 'til three or four in the morning sometimes. If we get there at nine, we should be safe enough."

"Have you got a lot of stuff?" Mother's cottage wasn't exactly huge and uncluttered.

"I haven't got that much, but there's all mother's things to go through. I've been putting off doing it, but most of them can go to the charity shops."

It sounded like a thoroughly miserable job; I hugged Michelle in sympathy and said, "We'll make a start on it tomorrow."

She leaned into me, turned her head for the kiss, and we didn't talk for a while.

It was pretty well dark by the time we got back to the cottage. I looked around the sitting room, at all the furniture and pictures I'd grown up with and tried to imagine having to clear it; not something that would be easy to do.

"Hey, boots off," called mother from her armchair.

I grinned and let go of the glamour; I'd taken my trainers off at the door.

"Oh!" said mother.

"How did you do that?" said Michelle.

"It's a glamour," I said. "I've been practising."

"Cool!" said Michelle. "What else can you do?"

I concentrated for a moment and the boots reappeared, white rather than brown.

"Excellent!" said Michelle. "Keep going."

Another moment's thought and my jeans were black rather than blue. I was getting the hang of this and enjoying myself.

"Did Jack teach you that?" asked Mother.

"Yeah, it's something a lot of people over there can do," I said.

"How does it work?" asked Michelle.

"You have to imagine as strongly as you can the image that you want the glamour to show. It's hard to describe, but then you just kind of push it out."

Mother frowned at my description. "So it's some kind of telepathy?"

I thought about that for a while. "I suppose it must be. I'm projecting my image of something and imposing it on your mind. It only works on people who aren't as strong as you. Jack took me to his brother's house, and I could see past the glamour he'd put on it."

"So can you disappear the way he does when he goes back over there?" asked Mother.

"Maybe." I thought about it, trying to imagine the chair I was sat in empty. I pushed that image out to them and watched their faces.

"What are you doing Charlie?" asked Michelle.

"You can still see me, right?"

"Yes," said Michelle. "What are you doing?"

"That doesn't work then." I said, feeling a bit daft. "I was trying to disappear."

"No. Very solidly still here," said Mother. "Right, children. I am working early shifts this weekend so I'm heading to bed." She looked to me. "You know the rules."

I looked at Michelle, who smiled at me mischievously.

"I know the rules."

As soon as Mother had left the room Michelle came and snuggled up to me on the sofa.

"There's lots we can do that doesn't break the rules," she said.

We arrived in Totton just after nine on Saturday evening equipped with a roll of binbags. The Polo was parked where Michelle had left it, undisturbed despite Totton's reputation. Dave's van was nowhere to be seen for which I was deeply grateful; my ribs still hurt.

We climbed the stairs to the flat and once inside I looked at it with new eyes. Instead of a compact and tidy little home I saw shelves and cupboards full of stuff to be sorted through; this could take months.

"I'll start with my stuff," said Michelle. "Then we'll do some of Mother's."

I sat on the bed in her bedroom and held open binbags for her as she emptied drawers and cupboards. For someone who claimed to not have much she still had more than me, and we quickly filled four bags. We loaded them into the car and went back up into her mother's room.

Michelle opened a wardrobe and pulled out an armful of clothes. She laid them on the bed and then began to examine them one by one, folding them neatly and putting them in piles. She lasted about ten minutes before the tears came. She was holding up a dark blue dress which still had a protective plastic film over it.

"I remember buying this with her," she choked. "She never got to wear it."

I caught her in my arms and held her while she cried. After that we got a little distracted or I would have heard the footsteps coming up the stairs. As it was, I walked out of the bedroom with two bags of clothes in my arms and came face to face with Dave.

He looked almost pleased to see me.

"I was hoping you'd be here," he said with quiet menace. He took a brass knuckle out of his jacket pocket and slipped it onto his right hand.

"Get out of here!" Michelle yelled at him. "This is my flat and I don't want you here."

"Shut it," he said. "I'll deal with you later."

"You won't get away with it," she said. "You know we'll go to the police."

"You won't go to the police, not if you want to carry on living round here. I've got plenty of friends who can just make life shit for you."

I stared at him, paralysed by fear. I clutched the two bags to my body and wished I had a weapon, any weapon. A knife wouldn't be enough, he must have faced enough knives; a gun would be better. I poured my wish for a gun towards him, imagining the weight of it in my hand, the dark metal glinting under the strip light. I dropped the bags of clothes and clashed my hands together as if I gripped a pistol.

"Just fuck off," I said, lifting my hands to point at him.

He gaped at me and took a couple of steps back.

"Just fuck off." I repeated.

He turned and ran for the stairs. His footsteps crashed through the fabric of the building. He stumbled before he reached the bottom and I hoped he hurt something, but seconds later I heard an engine cough into life and then roar away. Then I had to sit down before my knees gave way.

"Where did you get that?" said Michelle so quietly it was almost a whisper.

"Get what?"

"That gun?"

"What gun?"

"The gun you..."

"No gun. Just an illusion, a glamour."

"But he believed it," she said. "Thank God, or we were in the shit. We should get out of here in case he comes back."

I was very happy to agree to that. I just needed a minute or two before I could be sure my legs would work.

Michelle drove us back to Langley, the back of the car filled with bags of clothes. I sat beside her thinking about how close I'd come to getting seriously hurt.

"We can't go on like this," said Michelle. "I have to be able to go back to the flat without him showing up every time."

"Yeah, but what can we do? Maybe we can get a court order until I can put a compulsion on him."

"You think he'd obey a court order? He's completely lost it over this. You should see the texts I've been getting."

"What texts?"

"From him, and some from his mates. I deleted them all."

"You didn't tell me."

"No. There wasn't anything you could do about them, and I thought it would just wind you up."

"Oh! Alright." Actually, it wasn't alright, but I didn't want to start an argument about it, we had bigger things to worry about. She was right that there wasn't anything I could do, but I thought she should have told me.

"So how soon can you learn to do a compulsion?"

"I've no idea how long it will take to learn. Let's see if we can contact Jack tomorrow and make a start."

"Good plan."

"Let's not tell my mum about tonight's run-in with Dave. I don't want to worry her."

"You sure?"

"Yeah. If we do, she'll just give us a harder time next time we want to do anything."

Mother had gone to bed by the time we got to the cottage. We quietly took the bags of Michelle's stuff up to my old room and put the other bags in the shed. We sat up watching rubbish TV for an hour or so before I made up my bed on the sofa and reluctantly said goodnight to Michelle.

I woke early, disturbed by the sound of mother going out to work. Rather than stay in my rather uncomfortable roost I decided to get up and make breakfast-in-bed for Michelle.

Her appreciation of my efforts delayed us, but by half past ten we were on our way to the little beach on the river.

"What did Jack actually say?" asked Michelle. "Is he going to bring someone over here to teach you?"

"That's the thing. He said he'd find a teacher. I explained I didn't want to lose a load of time by going over there, but he never actually said he'd bring someone over here. I'm getting nervous about it, now I think about it."

"You think you'll have to go over?"

"Maybe."

"I'll come with you."

I hugged her, but it didn't make me feel better.

We reached the little beach, and I apprehensively began my summoning song. Nothing happened as I kept repeating it, self-conscious as Michelle watched me.

"Keep going," said Michelle. "Maybe he has to go find your teacher to bring him over."

I carried on singing through the little melody for what felt like ages, then Jack was there. He just appeared right beside us with another man. Michelle leapt up and threw her arms around Jack while I looked at his companion. He was older than Jack, but I'd be hard put to say how old because his hair was still dark and his face unlined. Maybe it was something in his eyes as he looked me over.

Jack disentangled himself from Michelle.

"This is my mother's brother," said Jack. "He will teach you."

Jack's uncle smiled at me. I extended a hand, and he took it.

"I am happy to meet you, Charlie. I have heard a lot about you," he said, though I couldn't tell whether he actually spoke, or if I just heard it in my head. Probably the latter; as an illusion it was superbly done. Just the sort of person I would want teaching me. "You wish to learn the art of compulsions?"

"Yes. That's right."

"I was told you have much potential, and that is certainly true. Come and sit with me."

We sat on a grassy bank overlooking the river. I still held his hand and he spoke to me in calm authoritative tones, not unlike Prof lecturing.

"A compulsion is imposing your will on the mind of someone weaker or less skilled than you. The greater the disparity between the minds, the stronger the compulsion."

This much I already understood.

"The very easiest compulsion is to do something simple immediately. An example may be instructive."

With his free hand he beckoned to Michelle. She approached.

"Give me your hand." He must have spoken aloud as Michelle held out her hand.

I had never been able to read Michelle, but through him I was able to and followed him as he found her thoughts questioning what he wanted. He seized the thread and, with me following, wrapped his will around it, pushing fingers into its core.

"We shall have her sneeze when you say a certain word. Choose the word."

"Banana."

I felt him insert the instruction into her thought and then withdraw, sealing the thread as if in perspex.

He let go of her hand and the connection vanished.

"What did you do?" asked Michelle.

"Banana," I said.

She sneezed. Jack's uncle smiled at me.

"Was that example clear enough? Do you think you can do that yourself?"

"I think so."

"Then show me."

I looked at Michelle, who was still looking puzzled. "Give me your hand."

"What's going on?" she said.

"Trust me."

She reached out a hand. I took it and still holding Jack's uncle's hand, I rode his power into her mind. I seized on the main thought right at the front of her mind of "what's happening?" I pushed my will into it and inserted the instruction to sneeze when I said 'apple,' just as I'd seen Jack's uncle do. Then I sealed it, squeezing hard to fuse the new instruction into the thread. I pulled back and was pleased to find the thread felt pretty solid.

"That was well done." Jack's uncle spoke in my mind. I released Michelle's hand and the contact vanished.

"You did something again," asked Michelle. "What did you do?"

I didn't think it was fair to keep her in suspense. "Apple."

She sneezed again. "What did you do?"

"Just that. Made you sneeze when I said apple. It was a little compulsion."

"I didn't feel…"

"No. You're not meant to." Jack's uncle placed the words in my mind.

"Is that it?"

"Yes, to make you sneeze once. No more than that." I spoke his words.

"You need to practice this as often as you can before our next lesson," he continued for me only. "The lesson is over, now I think I would like to look around. It has been so long since I was last over here."

With what he had taught me I couldn't really refuse. I wondered when he was last here; given the way time moves differently over there to here, it could be centuries ago.

He kept hold of my hand as we walked back towards the cottage following the stream to where it joined the gravel track. The first thing he commented on was the road surface when we reached the point where the tarmac began. I explained how it was made and could almost see him thinking that it could be useful back home. Then he saw his first car; a Ford Fiesta, it was parked rather than moving, otherwise he might have just run. He walked cautiously around it twice as if it were some rare bird that might fly away at any moment. I hoped no one was watching us.

"This looks like some kind of wagon," he said after considering it a while. "But what moves it?"

"A self-propelled wagon," I said. "They're very common over here. Michelle has one. This is quite a small one."

"How does it work?"

I briefly explained the principles of the internal combustion engine then another car drove by at about thirty mph.

"They go so fast."

"They can go much faster than that."

He looked at me as if he thought I was lying. A plane droned overhead; he looked up and I followed his gaze to see the flight from Southampton to the Channel Islands go over. He watched it until it was out of sight behind the trees. I didn't need to be able to read his mind to sense his astonishment, it was written deep in his wide eyes and open mouth.

"Is that?" he asked.

"Yes," I said. "We have learned how to fly."

"There is much here I do not understand."

I thought I'd leave satellites, men on the moon, and the Mars Rover for another time.

We walked on up the lane to the cottage and went in the back door to the kitchen. Jack hung back at first, but his uncle came straight in and eventually Jack followed. Without thinking about it I filled the kettle at the sink and put it on. When I'd finished Jack and his uncle were both looking at me. It took me a moment to realise what had surprised them this time.

"Running water," I said. "That's something else most people have."

There was an exchange in that liquid tongue of theirs. I went to the fridge to get the milk out.

"Stores things that need to be kept cold," I said, conscious of their gaze. I passed Jack the milk so he could feel the temperature of it. They exchanged words again. Jack's uncle held the milk for a moment before passing it back.

"And this is all done using iron?" said Jack.

"Not all of it. I think you can do that without it." I pointed at the fridge. "And maybe the water."

I made tea for four and brought out a packet of chocolate digestives. Jack and his uncle looked at the tea doubtfully but drank it eventually and dug enthusiastically into the biscuits. We chatted a bit more, trying to work out when Jack's uncle had last been over here by the clothes the people he met had had worn. That the women wore long skirts was our only clue; could have been any time in the last three hundred years.

Once the biscuits were finished, they got up to leave. Jack's uncle took my hand.

"Practice and it will become easier. You have the talent," he said in my mind. "I will come again."

"How do I find you again?"

"You'll know when the time comes."

They walked out and disappeared. I knew better than to try to see where they had gone.

"What did you do?" asked Michelle as soon as they were gone. "You held my hand, and you did something."

"Made you sneeze."

"Is that it? You must have done more than that."

"No. Just a simple compulsion to make you sneeze when I said a trigger word."

"What was the word?"

"Apple. ...see you didn't sneeze again."

She looked bemused. "I never felt a thing."

"No. I don't think you're meant to. As far as I know you can't tell if you're under a compulsion until you run into it. DI Scott certainly wasn't aware of the one he was under until he started doing stuff, helping Pete Murphy and couldn't explain why."

"So you could have left a compulsion in my mind that I wouldn't know anything about until you triggered it?" she eyed me suspiciously. "So you could have planted this urge I have to kiss you?"

"Maybe," I said as she leaned towards me. "But I'm not telling."

I woke up on the couch on Monday morning with a stiff neck and just like the previous week had to hurry to catch the bus. This time the bus failed to arrive, so I had a half hour wait for the next one; consequently, it took forever to get into town, and I missed my connection with the Unilink and again had to wait for the next one.

The whole day seemed to be working like that; the key reagent I'd ordered hadn't turned up and my NMR spectra had to wait while the machine was rebooted. I was in the postgrad centre having a sandwich for lunch when my phone rang, caller Nigel the spook.

"Can you spare an hour or two?" he asked.

"Sure." If it meant getting paid I could.

"Could you come down to the Civic Centre station?"

"Now?"

"That would be good." I finished my coffee and, sandwich in hand, headed for the bus stop wondering who Nigel had got this time. Maybe the Iftikhar Islam who had given Tanvir Khan the jihadi videos.Twenty-five minutes later I was sitting in an interview room with Nigel, who looked as anonymous as ever.

"Before we can do anything else I need you to sign this," he said in his neutral regionless accent, a sheaf of paper in his hand.

"What is it?"

"The Official Secrets Act. It's purely routine. It just means you can't talk about any work you do here, but I can't pay you until you sign."

I liked getting paid, so I signed it where he indicated. He gathered up the papers and put them in a document case.

"What have you got for me this time?" I asked.

"Same as last time. Want to know if he's a headbanger or a wannabe. Passwords, usernames if he is a player."

"Sure."

I followed him out of the interview room and down to the custody suite where a uniformed sergeant took us down the row of cells. There was no name written on the board beside the door he opened. A stocky Asian guy with a bushy beard sat cross-legged on the bed and glared at us as we entered.

"What now?" he said. "I want a lawyer."

"Shut up and give me your hand." said Nigel.

"I want a lawyer," he repeated, shuffling backwards on the bed with his arms behind him.

Nigel stepped forward and grabbed him, wrestling him over onto his side. Stronger than he looked, Nigel.

"Any skin'll do, won't it?" he said to me. "Grab an ankle."

I moved forward and grabbed one hairy ankle, holding on as he tried to kick out. Then I was in his mind. I pushed through the initial blast of hatred into the thoughts behind, the things he was trying to hide. He kept on trying to kick out, but I held on and dug into his memories. Behind the hatred was his desire for righteous revenge which led me to the training he was planning. Beyond that were the e-mail exchanges and chatrooms where he shared these plans, passwords, and usernames.

"You got enough?" Nigel broke into my excavations after I don't know how long.

I let go of the ankle. "Yeah. I got plenty."

"This is assault. I want a lawyer," said the prisoner as Nigel released him. He was right; it almost certainly was assault, but he'd forfeited any sympathy from me.

We retreated out of the cell and the sergeant locked the door. We followed him back to the reception desk without talking, and Nigel took me straight back to the interview room. I sat down. He took out his phone, fiddled with it for a moment then laid it on the table.

"We're recording. Tell me what you got."

I took a moment to gather my thoughts. "His name is Iftikhar Islam and he's dangerous, a real hard-line believer. Despises what he sees around him. Sees himself as a holy warrior. He's set up to go to Syria for training. I've got passwords, usernames, e-mail addresses. He was talking to them about targets in Southampton." Some of them, pubs and clubs, were places I'd been to.

"Let's have them all then." He pulled out a pad and passed it to me. I wrote taking extra care to make it legible. After filling two pages I passed it back to him.

"There's a bunch of people he hangs out with and trusts." I recited the names, with brief descriptions. I then listed some other people he didn't trust.

"Excellent," said Nigel. He proceeded to ask me a lot of questions about the trusted people which made me think he already knew a fair bit about them. Then there were questions about his contacts in Syria and, finally, a bunch of names none of which our guy had any knowledge of.

When I looked at my watch it was half-past three; I'd been there over two hours.

"Okay. We'll hold it there," said Nigel. "But I might be back with more questions."

"Fine with me. If you need me to read him again." This guy was so obviously a threat that I'd happily scrape out every last memory if they wanted me to.

Nigel paid me and sent me on my way. I caught the bus back up to the campus one hundred and seventy pounds richer and with an altered view of Nigel. I still didn't actually trust him, but my exposure to what he was up against had given me a new respect for him, and the insight into the jihadist's thought processes was truly frightening. I've never been religiously inclined, but I just couldn't understand how someone could end up thinking like that.

I sent Sharon a text from the bus to ask whether I needed to buy something for dinner and got a reply back just as I reached the lab saying "there's nothing in so if you want to cook go ahead. Won't be back til 8 at least." That gave me plenty of time to think about what to cook.

I stopped in at the supermarket after sitting through a very dull visiting lecturer and picked up lamb chops and new potatoes for dinner. Sharon didn't appear until half past eight by which time I was damned hungry.

"You were down to see Nigel again," she said as the chops were grilling. "Did he want you to read that headbanger?"

"Yeah, but I'm not supposed to talk about it."

"Official Secrets Act? Don't worry about it. I heard the best bits. He spat at the custody sergeant and called him an infidel pig."

So much for Official Secrets.

"So how was your weekend? See Michelle?"

I decided I didn't want to mention scaring off Dave with a glamour of a gun.

"Yeah. Jack brought his uncle over and he gave me a lesson in compulsions. Here give me your hand."

"What for?"

"I want to try out what I learned. Don't you trust me?"

She looked at me sideways then slowly reached out a hand. I took it and dived into the dominant thought in her mind which was hunger. It took no time at all to insert a little trigger. I released her hand and she immediately reached for the biscuit tin.

"Hey, dinner in ten minutes," I said.

"I just fancied a biscuit," she said through a chocolate digestive. She looked at me suspiciously. "You made me do that."

"It was easy. You're hungry and you like chocolate biscuits."

She looked thoughtful for a minute. "Could you make me stop smoking like that? 'Cos I want to stop, but I've failed so far."

"Maybe. I need to think about how to do it. It should be possible. If I can't do it, I'm sure Jack's uncle could." And no doubt find it trivial and turn it into a lesson.

I carried on thinking about it as I dished up the dinner and then as we ate it.

"You'd normally have a cigarette now, wouldn't you?" I said as Sharon laid her knife and fork down.

"Yes. Why?"

"What do you want to replace it with?"

"What do you mean?"

"The best way for me to do something is to make you want something else when you start wanting a cigarette. So pick the something else."

She thought for about it for a while. "I've got some mints in my bag. Those'll do."

"OK. Just hold on to the thought of a cigarette and give me your hand."

She wiped her mouth with a napkin then held out a hand. I took it and went looking for her desire for a cigarette; it was not hard to find, right there at the front of her thoughts. I plunged in, gathering up the streams of thought, and began to impose my will on them. It seemed easy enough to divert her hunger so it would be sated by the mints. I caught the threads and wrapped my will around them as if I was joining electric wires under insulating tape. Satisfied with what I had had done I withdrew, resisting the temptation to examine her thoughts about Mike Scott.

"Done?" asked Sharon.

"I think so."

"You sure? I didn't feel anything," she said reaching for her bag and taking out the packet of mints.

I had thought it had taken a while, but that just goes to show how my time sense gets distorted while I'm doing it. She took out a couple of mints and put them in her mouth.

"So are you and Mike any nearer moving on Peter Murphy?"

"No. Mike's got to clear it with the Chief Constable and the National Crime Agency, and that means he's got to explain his existing relationship with Murphy."

"In a way that doesn't make him look bent."

"Correct."

"Not easy."

"Also correct."

"How about the Albanians?"

"No further forward," she sighed. "Waiting for the NCA and the Border Agency to get their shit together."

I hadn't really expected anything different, but I was still disappointed. "But I know where to find these guys. I can take them right to them."

"And when it reaches the top of their to-do list, you can."

She reached for the TV remote and began channel-hopping. I remembered the anger I'd felt when I'd seen Besian from the bus. Leaving it to the NCA and Border Agency wasn't going to get anything done, and more girls like Nicoleta were being brought in every week.

I sat with Sharon turning things over in my head as she flicked from one programme to another and ate her way through the packet of mints; she didn't go for a cigarette, though.

"See! You've gone all evening without a cigarette," I said at half past ten.

"Yeah," she said "And I really didn't notice. That's bloody brilliant. You could make serious money doing that."

"That's an interesting thought." I grinned at her. "I'm going to call Michelle, then go to bed. See you in the morning."

I decided I would start by taking a look at the café Besian owned down in Portswood. Idriz had liked to go there for the home-cooked Albanian meals and their hideously strong version of coffee, so there was every chance some of Besian's crew would be there, if not Besian himself. I could also do the week's shopping at the big Sainsbury's doubly justifying the trip.

I didn't have much of a plan when I left the lab just after six to walk down to Portswood; just have a look at the café, see the layout and who was around. I was thinking more about what to buy for dinner for the rest of the week.

The café was on a side road just off the main Portswood Road. There were a couple of reviews on the Union website I had read praising its cooking and authentic atmosphere, though I didn't know anyone who had been there. I had reached the corner of the road when I walked past a guy who was having an animated conversation on his mobile; the language was nothing I recognised but sounded east European. As he turned his head, I recognised him with a sudden chill in my stomach. It was Florin, Nicoleta's boyfriend; the man she had loved and trusted enough to follow to England. The man who had sold her to Besian's gang.

I had enough sense to keep walking, though I doubt he noticed me anyway; all his attention seemed to be on his conversation. He was one person I hadn't expected to find. So what was he doing here? Had a change of heart and come back for Nicoleta? Seemed unlikely. Gone back to Romania and brought another girl over to sell? A lot more likely. What to do? There was no question that what he done to Nicoleta was simply evil and he deserved to pay for it.

I made up my mind and walked back toward him. He was still talking, throwing his free hand around wildly as he walked in small circles; passers-by having to avoid him as he abruptly changed direction. It was the easier thing in the world to arrange for him to walk into me. He was mid to late twenties and solidly built, bigger in the shoulder and chest than me, but I caught him by surprise. Before he could react, I grabbed his phone hand and pushed into his mind.

It was instantly obvious that he'd brought another girl over from Romania. His phone call was about her; she had got away from where she was being held, and he was promising violent retribution if she wasn't recaptured. That made it easier. I wrapped my will around his thoughts and squeezed, embedding the compulsion in his mind. Satisfied with my work I withdrew and let go of his hand.

He looked at me and then ran still holding his phone, angling across the traffic crawling along Portswood Road and disappeared down St. Denys Road. I looked around; no one was paying any attention. I walked briskly towards Sainsbury's, just another evening shopper.

The next time I saw Florin he was laid out on a shelf in the mortuary at Southampton General. Sharon had called me about ten in the morning and taken me there to find out what his story was.

"Unknown male age twenty-five to thirty-five. A dozen witnesses saw him jump off Cobden Bridge into the Itchen just before seven last night. Nothing in his pockets. That's all know about him."

I looked at his corpse feeling nothing other than satisfaction. A thoroughly evil bastard had got what he richly deserved. It wouldn't help Nicoleta, but it would stop him doing the same to any more girls.

I put a hand on his chilled flesh and dived into his memories. I hadn't gone very deep yesterday, so I took the time to find out in detail what he had been doing. Several minutes must have passed before I broke the contact.

"Florin Lupescu, Romanian. Nicoleta's boyfriend; the guy who sold her to the Albanians. There's been others, too, and guns. Girls and guns come in, stolen cars go out, back to Romania. He's been doing it a few years. I can give you the names of the people back in Romania if they're of any use."

"So what's the connection to Murphy?"

I could have made something up, but I didn't need to. "I can't see that clearly. There's a compulsion obscuring his memories of Murphy, but he's definitely in there. Guns, I think."

"Nice lad then," said Sharon as she wrote in her notebook. "Got what he deserved."

"Pretty much."

She flipped the notebook closed. "Come on, I'll buy you lunch."

We went to The Cowherds for lunch. We sat outside and waited for our food; Sharon chewed mints and drank diet Coke;I had a pint of Doom Bar. It was cool with the threat of rain, and we were the only people at the tables.

"I don't see why Murphy would take this Florin out, unless he had direct dealings with him," said Sharon.

"We don't know how Besian responded to Idriz's death. Maybe he blamed Murphy and did something, and this is Murphy's retaliation. Or maybe he's taking the Albanians down one man at a time."

"Possible." She dipped into her bag for another mint. "We know he's capable of it."

"Shame we can't leave them to wipe each other out."

"Well yeah, but we can't. Mike's got a meeting with some bod from the NCA tomorrow so maybe he'll be able to do something after that."

"About time." After Florin I felt ready to take on Pete Murphy.

A waiter appeared with our food at that moment putting an end to the discussion. Sharon was halfway through her meal when her phone started playing Abba. She picked up and walked away from the table to begin her conversation. I had finished my ham, egg, and chips by the time she returned.

"I've got to go," she said, looking regretfully at the cold remains of her lunch. "I'll see you tonight and get the details on Florin's associates."

She hurried off to the car park while I went in the opposite direction heading for the bus stop.

I didn't get to give her the details on Florin's associates until after ten that evening. Not that it was going to matter. It was clear from Florin's memories that the people he did business with out there had their local police completely bought and controlled.

I spent the rest of the week thinking about how to put the rest of Besian's gang out of business. Sharon had happily accepted Florin's death as the work of Pete Murphy, but I thought it would be unwise to present her with further casualties too soon. I needed another plan and anything I could think of required a more sophisticated compulsion. I'd need a more sophisticated compulsion for Dave the troll, too. Having him take a flight off the Itchen Bridge would be too much of a giveaway. That meant I needed another lesson from Jack's uncle. I wondered how he would view what I had done to Florin. I had no regrets about my actions; Florin had ruined enough young girls' lives to thoroughly deserve his fate, but would Jack and his uncle agree? I remembered the soldier the King had executed for opposing our rescue mission and doubted they would object much. They seemed to have a more black and white view of wrongdoing. And if they didn't, well I'd face that, too.

Even though I'd talked to Michelle every evening through the week, I was desperate to see her by Friday, but I couldn't because both she and mother were working late shifts. I ate in the union on Friday evening as the undergrads were starting their weekend fun and then hung on in the lab until about ten to keep out of Sharon and Mike Scott's way. For someone who didn't want a serious relationship she was certainly seeing a lot of him. I was still waiting for him to say something about an operation against Peter Murphy.

I caught the bus out to Langley Saturday morning, determined that I would see Jack's uncle again over the weekend. I got to mother's cottage in time to enjoy a late breakfast.

"I really need to shift my stuff from the flat," said Michelle. "I've given notice, so everything has to be out by the end of the month. We need to do some this weekend."

"Do you think we did enough to scare Dave off last time?"

"He's stopped texting me."

"Does that mean he's given up?"

"I doubt it, but I can't wait. If I don't clear the flat, I'll have to pay another month's rent and I can't afford that, not with the car insurance due."

"I can scare him off again if he shows up." I mentally rehearsed the glamour of a gun. "But we need a more permanent solution."

We took Michelle's Polo and set out for Totton immediately. There seemed no point in waiting until the evening when Dave ought to be working, as he'd still shown up. I wondered what he would do this time.

There was no sign of Dave or his van when we got to the flat. We parked up about fifty yards from the flat and went inside and set about filling the boxes and bags we'd brought. I filled boxes with books and kitchen gear while Michelle tackled the remaining clothes until she declared we'd got a carload.

I was halfway between the front door and the car with carrying a big box of books when an amplified voice called out.

"Armed police. Put down the box and stand still. Keep your hands away from your body." I stopped and looked in the direction of the voice. A police car was parked across the forecourt in front of the kebab shop about thirty yards away. A police officer aimed a rifle at me over the bonnet. I slowly lowered the box to the ground.

"Take three steps back and lie down with your arms spread," the electronic voice ordered. I did as instructed, my mind filled with the image of the gun aimed at me. I really wished I could do Jack's trick of disappearing.

"What's going on?" Michelle's outraged voice called from somewhere behind me.

"Stand still. This is a police operation," said the electronic voice.

Boots scrunched on the concrete near me. I risked turning my head to see two policemen about six feet way. One pointed a gun at me as the other came and knelt over me. Heavy hands frisked me.

"Turn over. Keep your arms spread."

I rolled over still watching the gun and was frisked again.

"What's in the box?"

"Books."

"Nothing else?"

"Just books."

The unarmed policeman stepped over to the box and opened it while his mate kept me covered.

"Clear, Sarge."

"OK, let him up," said the electronic voice.

I cautiously got to my feet and dusted myself down, very conscious of my pounding heart and the gun still trained on me. The sergeant appeared from behind his car still carrying his loudhailer.

"What was all that about then?"

"We received a credible report of someone matching your description carrying a firearm in this area," said the sergeant. "We can't ignore reports like that."

Didn't sound like I was going to get an apology.

"And where did that report come from?" Michelle still sounded indignant.

"I can't discuss that," said the sergeant.

"No, well let me guess. I reckon it came from my scumbag ex. He'd do anything to stir up shit for us. You should do him for wasting police time. His name's Dave Nicholls, I can give you his address if you want him."

"That won't be necessary," said the sergeant. "Let's have your details then we can be on our way."

Reluctantly we gave him what he wanted and went back to packing the Polo. The marked police car left immediately, but two of the officers hung around in an unmarked car while we carried our cargo out of the flat. I didn't like the idea that they were watching us, but at least they would keep Dave away. When we came down with our last load they were gone.

"This shit has gone on long enough," said Michelle as we drove away. "I'm sick of it. We need to do something."

"Right," I said. "You mean a compulsion?"

"Can you do one that'll keep him away permanently?"

"Maybe. The trick is to make it permanent without damaging him. I could do with another lesson from Jack's uncle."

"Let's hope he turns up then."

We drove back by way of the charity shops in Hythe. Michelle stayed in the car while I dropped off the load. She said it was hard enough packing it all; she didn't want to see it given away.

We parked the Polo at the cottage and went straight out to the portal. As we walked down towards the river a tune I didn't recognise started circulating in my mind. By the time we reached the portal it had filled my mind, and when I tried to sing Jack's summoning song it wouldn't come, and I sang the strange tune instead. I tried again but still the strange song prevailed.

"Why are you singing that?" asked Michelle. "That's not the usual song for Jack."

I was about to explain when Jack's uncle appeared.

"I wasn't expecting to see you," I said.

"You were singing my song," he replied with a smile and took my hand.

Then I understood; he had left the song in my mind to activate the next time I went near a portal. Neat trick.

"And now you wish for another lesson? I will trade for another look around this world."

"Deal."

"You have been practising?"

"Yes."

"Good, and you used it, too, and now you fear my disapproval."

"He was an evil man." Nicoleta's face swam through my mind.

"He was, and you did no less than I would have done. It is not a gift to be used lightly, it is good that you consider before acting."

"I need to be able to work a more complex compulsion now. There is someone who we want to keep away from us, but without harming him."

"Tell me about it."

I took him through the story of our interaction with Dave. There was no point in being anything less than completely honest as he could lift the whole tale from my mind anyway and probably already had.

"And does Michelle agree with this?"

"She does." I turned to Michelle who was sitting watching us. "Give him your hand for a moment."

Michelle took his other hand, held it for about thirty seconds and then released it.

"Then let us think about how it may best be done," he said.

"Can't I just make him forget about her?"

"Not at all easily. They were together a long time, very many paths in his memory lead to her. You would have to divert every one to be sure of him not realising what you've done. If a single thread of your compulsion comes loose, then the whole thing may unravel."

"How should I do it then?"

"I would be much better to convince him that she was not the right girl for him, that he has chosen to move on from her. He is less likely to question it if he thinks it was his own decision."

Ingenious. I could certainly see the logic in that; I just

needed a reason for him to reject her. Maybe Michelle would have some ideas on that.

"So I put a compulsion on him so that he remembers dumping her for some reason, and that he has no regrets, then its job is done."

"Exactly so, but you need to practice creating the false memory. It has to be consistent, or the compulsion will not last. It would be best if I showed you how to do it. Can we use Michelle as our subject?"

I turned to Michelle again. "Can we try a small experiment?"

"What are you going to do?"

"Create a little false memory," I said.

"OK," she said dark eyes wide. "I trust you."

"So what do you wish to do?" asked Jack's uncle.

"Change what she remembers having for breakfast."

"Very well."

She reached out a hand and her mind opened to me. I searched for her memory of this morning and found coffee, cornflakes, and toast. I replaced the cornflakes with porridge and prepared to seal it.

"Add everything you can," said Jack's uncle. "How was it cooked, how hot was it, what did it taste of?"

I thought for a moment then added the memory of the porridge being poured from a saucepan, milk and brown sugar being added.

"That's better." He added the tip of her tongue feeling burned at the too-hot first spoonful to the memory. "Now seal it."

I wrapped my will around the memory covering the joins and squeezed, imagining it sealed in perspex and then pulled back.

"What did you do?" asked Michelle.

"What did you have for breakfast?" I asked.

"Porridge," she said without hesitation. "Why?"

"Sure?"

"Yeah. I remember burning my tongue on it. Why?"

"You had cornflakes. We changed the memory." She looked at me with furrowed brow, eyes full of questions. "That's what

I'm going to do to Dave, so he remembers dumping you."

A smile spread slowly across her lovely face. "I like that. That could work."

"Now I claim my reward," said Jack's uncle. "Show me something marvellous."

We walked back to mother's cottage. I let go of his hand and gave Michelle a short summary of what was needed to pay for my lesson.

"Take him inside, show him the TV and the PS3," she said. "That should do it."

We didn't actually do that. We got to the cottage and Jack's uncle was so taken with Michelle's Polo that he demanded we take him for a drive around. This surprised me as Jack had been very wary of anything iron, but his uncle seemed to have no such fears. Michelle drove; he sat in the front with me behind him holding his hand so I could answer his many questions.

We drove down the back lanes to Calshot and went to the beach. The towering chimney of Fawley Power Station impressed him, but what really got him was one of the big cruise liners. He sat in awe and watched as she made her way down Southampton Water and out past the Isle of Wight. There were a lot of people around windsurfing and the beach café was still open, so Michelle bought ice creams which impressed him still further.

"This is truly the food of the gods," he said with raspberry sauce running down his chin. "You have certainly paid for your lesson; indeed, I feel in your debt. I should like to travel on such a floating palace as that one day."

"That might be difficult to arrange. We could manage a trip on the Hythe ferry, though." That would actually be a pretty good jaunt sometime.

"The King should see this." He waved a hand at the diminishing liner. "And some of his nobles who claim to know so much about this world."

We drove back to the cottage and then walked with him to the portal.

"I've greatly enjoyed this. Call on me any time you need," he said before vanishing into the blue light.

"Did you really change my memory?" asked Michelle as we walked home hand-in-hand. "I totally can't tell."

"You're not supposed to be able to."

"Did you do it, or did he?"

"I did most of it, bit of guidance from him."

"So you can do it to Dave? You sure?"

"More practice would always be good but I'm fairly sure I can do it. What did you guys argue about?"

"Why?"

"I need to implant some reason in his mind for why you broke up. If I can use a real reason, then it's just going to be more convincing."

She thought for a moment. "He was always on at me to go to the gym and workout. But it's really boring, so I didn't go much."

"Aah right. That's not a lot to build on."

"There was other stuff, too," she said quietly. "He wanted me to do things with his mates."

"What sort of things?"

"Sucking their cocks and stuff like that while they all watched. Some of his mates' girlfriends did it. A couple of them seemed to enjoy it."

That surprised me. I had thought I knew about what people got up to, but clearly not.

"I only did it a couple of times to keep him happy. It was like an ownership thing, showing what I'd do for him."

That's something I really didn't want to know. I'd already made up my mind about what a bastard he was, but this just took it out into the stratosphere.

"That I can certainly work with." But then I won't ever be able to forget it.

We walked back to the cottage in silence. I couldn't think of anything else to say to her revelation, just hugged her close.

"We should do another trip to the flat tomorrow," she said once we were inside, and the kettle was on. "There's still so much stuff to shift and not much time."

"I can think of lots of things I'd rather do, but you're right we have to."

"Are you ready to face Dave if he shows up?"
"And put a compulsion on him? Yes. Time to get this sorted."

We had an undisturbed run to the flat on Sunday, so I didn't get to deploy my carefully constructed false memory of Michelle enjoying being a complete slut too much for Dave's comfort. I stored it away, sure that I would get to use it soon and tried not to think about the real events. I held my boots glamour as we sorted through the stuff, ready to change it to the gun at a moment's notice, but it wasn't needed. Dave didn't show. We filled up the Polo once more, and by the time we'd finished I could see an end in sight. We drove back to the cottage and mother's roast dinner feeling we'd done enough for one weekend.

My back had just about unknotted from sleeping on the couch when I got a call in the lab from Sharon late Monday morning.

"I've got another one in the General, jumped off the Isle of Wight ferry halfway across from Portsmouth. Coastguard picked up his body and brought him in to Southampton. Pick you up in fifteen minutes?"

"Is there lunch involved?" A fair question I thought since it was close to lunchtime.

"Cheeky! I'll buy you a sandwich."

The body in the mortuary was fat and middle-aged with a stubbly beard and thinning grey hair cut short. I laid a hand on his shoulder beside a tattoo mermaid and dived in. Much as I had expected his mind was filled with the fog and glass of compulsions. I tried to suck it in, but it wouldn't move. I tried again but then it occurred to me that as he was dead, the compulsions were probably locked; something I'd have to ask about. There was plenty more to investigate that wasn't obscured though so I followed that.

Sharon's hand on my arm pulled me back.

"Charlie? You still with us?"

"Yeah. Fine. Give me a moment." Sanjay was, as usual, watching from across the room. I followed Sharon out to

Sanjay's little office and stole his chair while she groped in her bag for a pen.

"Whatcha got then?" she asked, pen finally in hand.

"Peter Murphy again. Guy's name is Billy Porter. He's been dealing across the island for years. Murphy wanted in. Billy didn't feel like being a subcontractor. Thought he'd been in the game long enough and was hard enough to face Murphy down. Thought his reputation was overblown, so he went to see him with a couple of minders to sort it out."

"He was wrong about that then."

"As wrong as you can get."

"It's hard to mourn the death of a dealer like Porter, but this guy Murphy is an evil bastard." She put down her pen and reached into her bag for a mint. "Was there anything else?"

"I can tell you where he was buying his gear from and who his buyers were. Some of them were dealing on their own account from the amount they're buying."

"Go on then. I can pass the big players on to Mike and his team." She picked up her pen and wrote as I listed Billy's other suppliers and his regular buyers.

"Good stuff," she said. "There's a couple of names I recognise and maybe we can do something with them."

"So worth a sandwich then?"

"Yeah, worth a sandwich."

We headed back to her car and went in search of coffee and sandwiches.

"How did Mike's meeting with the NCA guy go last week?" I asked once we were underway.

"Good, I think he's got outline approval. But the ACC still has to sign off on the plan."

"So how long before we can do something?"

"Don't know. Could be a week, could be longer. Might not get approved. Can't do anything about it. Just gotta be patient."

We parked up by on Shirley Avenue and went into Santo Lounge which was getting busy with the lunchtime crowd to buy the promised coffee and sandwich. Promise kept; Sharon took me back up to the University.

There was a troll waiting for me when I left the lab that evening, lurking outside the main doors to the department. He didn't speak to me, just scowled malevolently at me, but his message was perfectly clear. *I can find you and I'm going to hurt you.* My first reaction was anger; that he was there projecting his toxic presence into my world. I was tempted to confront him then, but, in truth, I wasn't yet ready. Nor could I do what I needed to with people around. Fortunately, there were a couple of other post-grad chemists coming out at the same time and I was easily able to persuade them to come with me up to the Union building by offering to buy them a drink in the Stag's Head.

Dave shambled along behind us, keeping his distance until we went into the Union building. I didn't look to see whether he tried his luck with the security; I guessed not. He must have worked security here when they had bands on and would know the rules. Didn't really matter; he'd delivered his message.

It didn't take me long to figure out how he'd found me. Most of his mates had my University e-mail address; I'd given it out myself. My picture was on Prof's page of the department's website. Even a troll can use Google.

One of the good things about the Union building is that it sprawls across the campus and there are several ways out, all a long way apart. I don't know if Dave hung around at the door we came in by, but I chose to use another one on the other side of the building and caught my bus away from the campus. Tomorrow I would make a point of using a different exit from the department, beyond that I was going to have to deal with him sooner rather than later.

This all made me rather later than usual back to Sharon's.

"I was going to ask if you were available for a little adventure tonight," she said as I chopped onions for the curry I was cooking. "But it'll be too late by the time you're done."

"What did you have in mind?"

"A visit to one or two of the people on Billy Porter's list. There's been an upturn in burglaries, and the Super wants something done. I thought they might be able to assist us."

"Over in the Island?"

"No. Our Billy had friends all over the place, some of them in town."

"Tomorrow night do? I was going to make enough of this for two days so we can just eat it and go." Plus, I would be back earlier if I kept a look out for Dave and didn't have to divert via the bar.

"Tomorrow's good. These people aren't going away, unfortunately. We got any wine to go with that?"

Dave was lurking around the lab again the next evening much as I'd expected; this time I spotted him early and went out one of the side doors. As I sat on the bus, I wondered how long he stayed there and hoped he enjoyed the wait. If he persisted, I supposed I should get the University authorities on the case, but I rather liked the idea of him wasting his time hanging around the department.

Sharon came in just after me. We polished off the curry which tasted better than last night, and by half seven we were on our way to visit some of Billy's clients.

"James Marsh, known as Jay," said Sharon. "Originally from the island which explains his connection to Porter. Known user and got a couple of convictions for thieving. Still buying from our Billy, so probably still thieving."

We didn't have far to go, just down to the Polygon. We could really have walked. Might have been better if we had as there was nowhere to park, and we ended up some distance away from the house we were going to.

A lot of the houses round there are rented by students and are fairly scruffy so Jay Marsh's place didn't stand out. The front garden was a rubbish heap, and the paint was peeling from the door frame, but that was true of the house next door. The doorbell didn't work so Sharon thumped on the door. After several thumps it was answered by a nervous-looking brunette.

"Whaddya want?" she asked peering round the door. Her lined face and hollow cheeks made her look over fifty, and I could smell the stale tobacco from her.

"Is Jay in?"

"Nah. He's not here." Not a local accent, more estuary.

Sharon pulled out her warrant card. "Hampshire Police. You won't mind if we take a look."

The brunette hesitated a moment as if thinking about it then let us in. It didn't smell too good, a combination of damp, old takeaways and unwashed bodies.

Jay was a tall balding guy in, maybe, his forties. He lay stretched out on the sofa in the front room, but the brunette was partially correct – he wasn't there; he was flying somewhere out in interstellar space. I took hold of a hand and pushed into his mind, but there was nothing coherent there. Everything I tried to follow just dissolved as I tried to analyse it. I pulled out and shook my head at Sharon.

"Nothing. He's off his face and nothing makes any sense."

"Bollocks!" said Sharon with a grimace. "Okay, I'm going to take a look around then we'll move on."

The brunette stood watching me as Sharon moved around the rooms.

"What are you then?" she asked, her eyes hard.

"Special investigator," I said.

"Like a human search dog?"

"Yeah, that kind of thing." I wondered if I should make her forget my visit, but Sharon reappeared.

"We're done here, but we'll be back," she said to the brunette. "And when prince charming there wakes up tell him his mate Billy Porter is a goner."

We walked down the road away from the car.

"Don't know who the girlfriend is," said Sharon. "She's new."

"Where next?" I asked.

"Michael Vickers, lives on Morris Road," said Sharon. "User, thief, and small-time dealer. Supposed to have got clean, but he was buying regularly from the late Billy so he's worth a look. What I really want is where he's shifting the gear he's nicked to pay for it."

Michael Vickers was thin, sallow-complexioned with crude tattoos on his forearms; I wondered if he realised how much he looked like the stereotypical junkie. He tried to close the door when he realised who had been hammering on it, but Sharon was too quick for him.

"Evening, Michael," she said. "Just came by for a chat about a mutual friend. Not gonna make us stand outside, are you?"

"I got nothing to say to you," he protested as Sharon shoved her way in. I followed a couple of steps behind. It smelled worse than Jay's place.

"Now you know that's not true, Michael," said Sharon. "To start with there's Billy Porter to talk about."

"Who's that Mikey?" A female voice called from upstairs.

"Police," called Sharon.

"Stay up there, Tracy," called Mike.

Tracy immediately came downstairs. She was a very young-looking washed-out blonde with a pierced nose and the same crude tattoos as Michael, and clearly pregnant.

"Detective Sergeant Wickens, Hampshire Police." Sharon waved her warrant card at Tracy.

"He ain't done nothing," said Tracy.

"Then he's got nothing to worry about," said Sharon. "And I'm sure he can explain all about Billy Porter. Can't you, Michael?"

"I got nothing to say," said Michael. "You got a warrant?"

"I haven't," said Sharon. "But I can get one because we know all about the gear you've been buying from Billy. Do you want me to go away and get one then come back with the first team and take this place apart?" Her gaze switched to Tracey. "And have a word with Social Services about Tracey and her baby?"

Michael said nothing.

"Didn't think so," said Sharon. "Let's all sit down and talk about it, shall we?"

She pushed open the door to the sitting room and Michael reluctantly followed her in. He sat down in a grubby-looking armchair, Tracy sat on the arm beside him.

Sharon remained standing. "So tell me about the gear you've been buying from Billy Porter."

"I don't know no Billy Porter," said Michael.

"Come on, Michael, you can do better than that," said Sharon. "We've got Billy's records. We know who's been buying off him."

Michael stayed silent and looked at his feet, his hands

shaking a bit. Tracy beside him looked as if she might burst into tears at any moment. I felt sorry for her; she had made a really bad choice in Michael Vickers and now she was stuck.

"Got an answer for me, Michael?" said Sharon.

"Don't know nuthin about 'im."

"Really?" said Sharon. "Well, here's what's going to happen. Rather than listen to your lies my friend here is going to hold your hand and you're going to let him."

Michael looked up at me, incomprehension in his gaze. Rather than explain I just grabbed his hand and dived in. I didn't have to search to find his thoughts about Billy, they were right at the front of his mind. I absorbed all I needed then decided I would try a little experiment. I constructed a compulsion that any time Michael handled heroin he would see a vision of the grim reaper coming to claim him. That, I thought, should give him a serious incentive to get clean and give Tracy and her baby a better chance. I sealed the compulsion into place and withdrew.

"Alright, Charlie?" asked Sharon.

I nodded.

"Right, we're out of here," said Sharon. "By the way. Billy Porter's dead so you won't be getting any more gear from him."

She turned and walked out leaving Michael and Tracy staring. I followed her.

"Watcha got?" asked Sharon once we were back in the car.

"There an Asian guy down Bevois Valley that buys the phones and laptops. Told him the phones go out to Africa. Doesn't get much for them."

"Right," said Sharon, pencil poised. "Got an address?"

"I have. We should head down there now. Michael had a bag of nicked phones right there in the room. First thing he's going to do is offload them, he could hardly think of anything else."

"No wonder he looked so twitchy. You should've told me, but it'll work out better this way. Let's get going."

Less than ten minutes later we were parked up across the road from a takeaway chicken shop that I recognised from Michael's memories and undergraduate pub crawls.

"Our guy has the flat above the shop," I said. "Buys in nicked stuff and ships the phones up to London, sells the tablets and laptops on the net."

"Exactly the sort of scumbag I want to put out of business."

Michael Vickers turned up about ten minutes later, walking fast with a backpack over his skinny shoulder. He went straight to the door beside the chicken shop and rang the bell. The door was answered, and he went inside. Sharon took a series of pictures on her phone and caught him again when he came out five minutes later, the empty backpack flapping in his hand. He hurried off back the way he'd come; I wondered whether he was heading back to Tracy or to find another dealer.

"Bingo," Sharon said looking at the pictures she'd taken. "Need to write this up tonight to get a warrant first thing tomorrow. Just have to hope he doesn't move the stuff on overnight. Might well owe you dinner tomorrow night."

"We could wait it out, see if he moves."

"No. I'll chance it. We know where he is anyway."

She started the car and sped us back to her flat where she disappeared into her room, presumably to write up her report. I exchanged a few texts with Michelle then went to bed, content with my days' work.

Sharon was gone next morning before I got up. I didn't even hear her leave so it must have been before seven. The fridge was, as usual, almost empty. I wondered whether I should shop on the way home or whether I would get my dinner out; probably best to shop, I thought based on Sharon's previous. I used the last of the milk for my cereal then went to catch the bus up to the university campus.

I was expecting to get a text from Sharon sometime during the day to tell me whether the raid had found the phones. What I wasn't expecting was a call from Michelle just after lunch.

"He's found me," she said, her voice a tight whisper. "His van's outside the cottage."

I didn't need to ask who she was referring to.

"Where are you?" Fear gripped my stomach. I knew she'd been due to work an early shift this morning. "Did he see you?"

"No. I'm in my car. I spotted his van from down the lane, and I turned off."

"When's mother due home?"

"Not for hours, she's doing a long day."

"Stay where you are. I'll call you back."

I thought about the situation for a moment, my initial fear quickly turning into anger. It would take me an hour and a half minimum to get out there so that was not an option however much I wanted to. Who else was there? I pictured the lane and imagined where Dave had parked his van, then thought of Mrs. Godfrey. I'd bet he was parked outside her cottage. She had lived there all my life and more, so I knew her, not as well as mother who fed her cats when she went away to visit her sister, but well enough. The old phone directory in the lab yielded her number so I called her.

She answered after three rings. "Good afternoon, Mrs. Godfrey, its Charlie Somes. I was just wondering if there's a scruffy white transit van parked outside your house."

"Yes, there is. I was wondering whose it was. How did you know?"

"My new girlfriend told me. She's been staying with mother and she's afraid the driver is someone from her past she wants to stay away from."

"Oh dear."

"She'd like to keep away from him, so could you call the police and ask them to move him on. I think they'll pay more attention to you than to me."

"Well yes. If you think I should."

"I think you should. It would be a great help. Thank you, Mrs. Godfrey."

I called Michelle back, told her what I'd done and advised her to go to the Langley Tavern and have a leisurely coffee before venturing back. I went back to running my column nursing my anger. It was time to deal with Dave; we'd been lucky he hadn't caught Michelle; sooner or later that luck would run out. He had clearly lost all rationality, and I didn't want to think about what he might be capable of. The idea of a compulsion that made him remember rejecting Michelle as a complete slut was still the best

I'd got, so I have to go with that.

I was still thinking about how to deal with Dave when my phone bleeped with an incoming text. It read "Dinner at Roberto's tonight" followed by a smiley. An hour ago, I would have been delighted, but now it seemed rather insignificant. Still, I'd earned it, and it would be churlish to refuse so I texted back "Result! I expected nothing less."

My phone bleeped again a few minutes later. I was expecting it to be a reply from Sharon, but it was from Michelle. Dave had gone and she was in the cottage with the kettle on; the knot in my stomach untied itself.

My product took a lot longer to elute off the column than I had expected so I was late getting out of the lab; at least there had been no sign of Dave lurking. Sharon was already showered and dressed up when I got to the flat and was halfway down a large gin and tonic.

"Good result today, Charlie," she said, raising her glass. "No one had any idea that guy was there until we came along and cleaned him up. The boss is very happy, and the DCI came by specially to say well done."

That made me feel very good. I had a quick shower and changed into the best clothes I had with me.

"Thought we'd walk down and get a taxi back," said Sharon. "Then we can have a drink or two. I'm going in late tomorrow."

I suspected it would be more than two, not that I minded.

It was a good evening for walking with clear skies and a light breeze. Sharon filled me in as we walked on a lot of details about the day's arrest and what the search had found.

"Got some good leads on where he was shipping the phones to," she said. "But we'll have to pass those on to the Met, and they'll probably lose them."

Roberto's was packed with a queue at the door; just as well Sharon had booked. We started off with a cocktail each then hit the red wine along with the starters. I went with meat all the way, a plate of prosciutto followed by Florentine steak. Sharon had the deep-fried Calamari followed by wild mushroom risotto.

"So how's it working out with Michelle living with your

mum?" Sharon asked as we waited for our main courses.

"Seems fine. She gets on well with mother and likes working in the care home. We have still got a Dave problem, though."

"How so?"

"He started turning up at the Chemistry department and hanging around outside the main entrance. That's not really too much of a problem 'cos there's several other exits. But today he turned up at the cottage. Michelle spotted his van parked in the lane on her way back from work and managed to avoid him. I called a neighbour who got the local police to move him on, but next time we mightn't be so lucky."

"Wonder how he found it?"

I had wondered that, too. "Somes is not a common surname, and mother's in the phone book. I'm still on the electoral roll there, too. Even trolls can use the internet."

"What are you gonna do?"

"I need to get him on his own so I can put a compulsion on him. Can't do that with his mates around."

"Will that be strong enough?"

"I hope so. You're still off the fags, aren't you?"

"Yeah. But that's something I wanted to do."

"Peter Murphy was able to turn Mike Scott into a bent copper with little or no training against his will and keep him that way."

"Ok. So how are you going to get him on his own? Have Michelle tell him she wants to talk to him and set it up that way?"

"That's one way, but how do I stop him beating the shit out of me as soon as he sees me?"

"That's a problem you face whichever way you do it. Would it help if I came along?"

"Yes, it would." I'd been hoping she would say that. I'm all for solving my own problems, but not at the risk of sustaining the sort of damage an angry Dave could do me. The waiter arrived with the main courses at that point, and we discovered the bottle of red was already empty, so we ordered another.

That bottle, too, was dead, and we were contemplating liqueurs when Mike Scott turned up. I wasn't expecting him, but Sharon clearly wasn't surprised. More drinks were ordered, and I realised I would not be making an early start in the lab tomorrow. I did get from him that he was seeing the Assistant Chief Constable next week about the plan to take down Peter Murphy. I wished him the best of luck in getting the plan approved and assured him I was up for it. After that I played gooseberry as he and Sharon gossiped about colleagues, flirted, and generally behaved like I wasn't there. We ended up being the last customers in left in the restaurant, and I'm glad I wasn't picking up the bill.

I sat up front in the taxi and tried to avoid noticing what was going on behind me; good thing it was only a short trip. Mike and Sharon disappeared off to her room as soon as the taxi was paid for, so I drank a large glass of water and went to bed. The room was only spinning slightly.

The water did not save me from a hangover. Even though I was late up, there was no sign of Sharon or Mike. I made coffee but couldn't face eating anything beyond ibuprofen then dragged myself to the lab when I really felt like going back to bed. I struggled through the morning doing nothing very effective, skipped lunch, and dozed in the visiting speaker's seminar; just as well Prof was away in the US at a conference.

I was starting to feel better when Prof sent an e-mail round the group setting up a review meeting on Saturday midday as he'd missed the usual slot. This meant I wouldn't get out to see Michelle until nearly Saturday evening and pissed me off no end. There was no getting around it, though, so I texted her to let her know with a promise to call her later.

I left the lab as soon as I was decently able and went back to Sharon's. There was no sign of her and only eggs in the fridge so, finally hungry, I cooked myself an omelette, then talked to Michelle and went to bed. I was already asleep when I got a text from Chloe inviting me out for a drink.

Prof's Saturday meeting went on a long time but was really interesting as he talked about new chemistry that had been presented at the conference. Some of it was directly applicable to my project so, despite being desperate to get out, I had to pay attention and talk sensibly about how we could use it when it was my turn to discuss my work.

It was five o'clock before I got the bus to Langley. I sat at the back and sent texts to Michelle, mother, and then to Sharon to let them know I was on my way. I settled back in my seat and tried to put my thoughts in order; behind the buzz of excitement about seeing Michelle lay the anxiety that I had no real plan for dealing with Dave. I felt sure the compulsion would work if I could get hold of him; but how do that without him beating the living daylights out of me I didn't know. I didn't think Sharon being there would stop him. I hoped Michelle or mother had some idea.

Michelle met me at the bus stop, and I stopped thinking about Dave until much later, until after a very fine dinner of beef stroganoff actually.

"So how are we going to deal with Dave?" asked mother, a glass of red wine in her hand. "I certainly don't want him coming round here again, and Michelle needs him out of her life."

"I need him out of my life, too." To their surprise I had declined wine and held a glass of fizzy water. "I need to surprise him and get close enough to him to grab him before he wallops me, but it has got to be somewhere with no people around so that I've got time to put a compulsion on him."

"Some kind of an ambush then?" said mother.

"That makes sense," said Michelle. "'Cos the moment he sees you he's going to explode."

"So what are the options?" asked mother. "You know his routine."

Michelle thought for a moment. "He'll be working tonight and get back to his flat really late, like four or five in the morning. He'll sleep until midday, go down the pub for Sunday lunch then go to the gym. There's about a fifty-fifty chance he'll be working Sunday night."

"What about while he's asleep?" said mother. "Do you have a key to his flat?"

"I haven't got a key, and he shares the place with two mates."

"At the gym then."

I remembered how busy that was. "Have to be in the carpark

either when he arrives, or when he's leaving."

"Still gonna be people around," said Michelle.

"Unless you're inside his van," said mother.

"How would I get in? Do you have a key?" I asked Michelle, wondering if Sharon might know how to get into a van quickly and quietly. I had texted her to ask if she was around but had received no reply. I suspected Mike Scott was occupying all her time.

"No. But you might not need one," said Michelle. "If he hasn't got the lock fixed then the back doors will be open. It got broken into a few months back and he was too cheap to get a new lock."

"That's fortunate," said mother. "You don't think he'll have got it fixed?"

"No," said Michelle. "That van's shot anyway. Won't make it through another MOT, so he isn't going to spend money on it now."

"Let's go with that then," I said. "It's the least worst idea I've heard."

Mother looked worried. "Are you sure you can do this, Charlie? You could be in a lot of trouble if it doesn't work."

"I know. But I've worked on this a lot. I'm confident I can do it." I was lying.

The morning brought low cloud and solid soaking rain. We all slept in then had a leisurely breakfast that lasted until midday. Michelle made a guess about when Dave would get to the gym, and we headed off in mother's car with the aim of being there before him. We were wrong; his van was already sitting in the carpark when we got there. The rain was heavy enough that no one lingered outside so I picked a quiet moment and ran through the puddles with Michelle to test the van's back doors. Sure enough, they were open. I gave a thumbs-up to mother then climbed into the gloomy interior and Michelle closed the doors behind me. I settled down to wait for Dave; there were half a dozen unidentified boxes in the van, so I sat on one and listened to the rain on the roof.

I must have dozed because the driver's door opening startled me. Dave got in. I moved off the box, positioning myself to grab him, then froze as another man opened the passenger door and climbed in.

"I appreciate it, mate," said the other man. "I'll be fine if you can drop me at the petrol station on the corner."

"No worries," said Dave as he started the engine.

I sat immobile in the back as the van pulled away wondering what the hell I was going to do; all my plans had been based on Dave being alone. There was no way I could cope with two of them.

The van bounced across the carpark and pulled onto the road. I crouched down behind a couple of boxes that smelt of sweaty male gym clothes and tried to keep out of sight of the rear-view mirror; though, based on the way he thrashed the van, I'm not sure Dave ever looked behind him.

I figured my best chance would be when Dave dropped off the other guy. I hoped Michelle and mother were following, but I had my phone so I could call them anyway. I kept my head down but they didn't look back; instead, they talked about exercise regimes and mixed martial arts as Dave revved the van hard through the lower gears and accelerated through the corners. I had a struggle to keep from getting thrown around in the back.

After fifteen minutes or so the van pulled up. This was the moment. I gathered myself to grab Dave as his mate opened the passenger door. He paused for a moment to pull his jacket over his head and then ran for it as the rain sluiced down. The moment the door slammed shut I grabbed Dave, taking hold of his left ear. His foot slipped off the clutch and stalled the van as I pushed into his mind.

I concentrated on keeping him quiet as I climbed into the front seat then started digging for his memories of Michelle with his group of mates. They took only a moment to find, tinged with anger as was everything concerned with her. It was easy to rechannel that anger, to direct it at her for enjoying the experiences too much, and to twist the memory so that she had pushed him to let her do it. I inserted the false memory of him dumping her, complete with her tears and promises, and sealed it. It seemed expedient to also insert a good healthy fear of me before I withdrew so I did that, too, and then put him to sleep for five minutes to give me time to get away.

I closed the van door carefully so as not to wake him, then ran for cover from the still pouring rain. There was a bus shelter fifty yards away and I was soaked by the time I reached it. I looked around; I had no idea where I was. Dave's van started up and made a noisy U-turn in the middle of the road and sped off. I pulled out my phone which had been on silent mode in my pocket; four missed calls, all from Michelle. I hit reply and she picked up immediately.

"Are you alright?" she asked. "Where are you? We tried to follow you but couldn't keep up."

"I'm fine. Job done. But I don't know where I am." I looked around again. "I'm in a bus shelter. There's a BP petrol station just up the road, on the other side there's an off-licence, a kebab shop, and a hairdresser's."

There was a moment's silence.

"Okay," said Michelle. "I know where you are, just stay there. We'll be five minutes."

They weren't five minutes. I had my phone out poised to call them when mother's car appeared from the opposite direction I was expecting.

"Sorry. Got caught up in the one-way system," mother said as I got into the back seat with Michelle. "Are you okay? Did it go to plan? You looked soaked."

"I am soaked, but everything worked. We should be shot of him."

"Are you sure? I don't want him turning up again."

"He thinks he dumped Michelle. He remembers doing it and why. He should have no reason to question it."

"Good! Now which way do I go to get home, Michelle?"

I didn't see Sharon until Monday evening when she apologised for not replying to my text. She didn't say what she had been doing, but my intuition that she had been with Mike Scott was undiminished. I told her that we thought the Dave problem was sorted and that ended the conversation.

By Wednesday I was beginning to feel confident that we had indeed got shot of Dave. There had been no sign of him at the department or the cottage, and the abusive texts to Michelle had stopped. The chemistry Prof had brought back from the US seemed to be working, and I was about to start a column when my phone rang; it was Nigel the spook.

"Have you got a couple of hours?" he asked.

"At my usual rate?"

"Certainly."

"Then I'm available. Will I come down to the Civic Centre nick?"

"Not this time. I'll pick you up in half an hour."

"OK. I'll be in the foyer of the department."

He was fifteen minutes late when he pulled up in a silver Focus.

"Sorry. Spent ages crawling along the M27," he said, which had me wondering where he had come from.

I got in. He fiddled for a minute with his satnav before we set off down through Portswood to join the motorway link road. He didn't talk as we drove. We picked up the M27 on the edge of town heading east so I guessed we were going to Portsmouth. The traffic on the opposite carriageway was crawling along for no apparent reason; I hoped it cleared before Nigel brought me back.

I don't know my way around Portsmouth, so I assume Nigel took me to the main police station; it certainly seemed large enough.

"Same as last time," said Nigel as we pulled into the car park. "Usernames, passwords, phone numbers. Get whatever you can."

We went in the rear entrance and were taken straight to the custody area without any signing in. The sergeant walked us along the line of cells and stopped at the end one; the name chalked on the board was Ahmed. I followed Nigel into the cell expecting another bearded Asian guy and was surprised to see a girl. Dressed in normal western clothes she looked young, maybe seventeen, slim and pretty with long dark hair and big brown eyes. There was nothing but hostility in those eyes, though. I knew there would be no discussion with her, no consent to let me touch her skin, even though I was her way out if she was clean. My experience with Ifti the head-banger last time had washed away any sympathy.

She screamed as Nigel grabbed her and tried to scratch him with her nails. I caught one flailing hand and dived in. I had hoped to find she was only a wannabe like Tanvir, but no, she was in deep. All set up to go to Syria and offer herself as a bride to an ISIS fighter. Shame because she was predicted straight As for A level and had been going to do Chemistry.

Once I'd extracted the usernames, passwords, and phone numbers Nigel wanted, I decided I would do something to try and turn her aside from the road she had chosen. It was a much easier compulsion than the one I'd used on Dave, a fiery angel appearing in the cell half an hour after we left to denounce her as a heretic. I hoped that might be enough persuade her to change her course, not that I would ever find out.

I sealed the compulsion and released her hand and got a scratch for my trouble. Nigel let go of her; she lashed out and caught him solidly on the side of his left knee. He grunted with pain and stumbled to the door which opened when he banged on it. I hurried after him without looking back, and the door banged shut.

The sergeant took us back to the custody area and into an interview room; Nigel visibly limping. He sat down heavily and rubbed his knee before bringing out his phone and setting it up to record.

"What did you get?"

"Her name is Tareena Ahmed, and she's all ready to go and be a Jihadi bride. She's in contact with people out there and can't wait to go. Already picked out her holy warrior." I reeled off her Twitter handle, her usernames and passwords on jihadi websites, spelling them out letter by letter. "She's not in touch with anyone over here, and her family don't know about it. She thinks her parents are pretty stupid. It's all self-radicalisation on the net."

Nigel nodded heavily and rubbed his knee. "Is that all?"

"Yeah. What will happen to her?"

"Probably go into the deradicalisation programme for all the good it'll do."

He switched the phone off. "Let's get you back to Southampton."

Nigel said about as much on the way back as he had on the journey there. I wanted to ask him more about the deradicalisation programme and what had happened to Ifti the headbanger. Nothing that I really needed to know but still, my curiosity was engaged and wasn't going to be satisfied.

The westbound traffic had not improved, and we crawled along. Eventually I persuaded Nigel to override the satnav and come in through the eastern suburbs of Southampton. Even though I was getting paid for the time I spent in his car, I couldn't stand the boredom of his silence.

We finally pulled up outside the department; he looked at his watch. "I make that nearly two and a half hours. Shall we call that two hundred quid?"

"Works for me."

He took out his wallet and counted out the notes. I signed the invoice and took the money.

"Thank you for your help. That's good information you've given me," he said as I got out of the car. "It really is appreciated."

I walked back to the lab feeling pretty pleased with myself, though itching to know whether Tareena's vision had the intended effect. There was no way I was going to find out though, not from silent Nigel.

Sharon was late home and made straight for the wine in the fridge when she got in.

"Tough day?" I asked, unnecessarily as she sat down on the sofa.

"Tough enough; just frustrating. Nicoleta isn't going to testify. She's too afraid of reprisals against her family back in Romania."

"That sounds completely believable. We know Florin had the local police bought. What's going to happen to her?"

"She wants to go back to Romania."

"I can't imagine her family being very supportive. They're a pretty dysfunctional lot from what I got."

"Maybe so, but that's what she wants, says her grandmother will look after her, so I would imagine we'll send her back. There's nothing for her here." She took out a packet of mints out of her bag and put two in her mouth.

"So what's happening with the Albanians? Is the NCA on the case?"

"Haven't heard anything."

"Would you expect to?"

"Yeah. There would be a briefing just to make sure we keep out of their way."

"So there's nothing happening?"

"I didn't say that. There isn't an active investigation on the ground, but that doesn't mean nothing is being done."

"Is there anything we can do to give them a nudge?"

"You give me a reason to come down on these guys and I'll see it happens."

"Such as?"

"Guns are always good. You find me Idriz's guns that we missed then that'll be a good start."

"OK, I'll see what I can do." This wasn't going to be easy; I had got lucky with Florin, just running into him in the street. I'd need to find a way of getting close to one of the Albanians. Looks like I'd be doing my shopping down in Portswood for the next few days.

"You guys really should be bugging that café."

She looked at me sharply. "How do you know we aren't? Or the NCA aren't?"

That stopped me short; I didn't know. But then a thought came to me.

"You haven't known about it long enough for the approval paperwork to go through."

She threw a mint at me. "Smartarse! What's for dinner?"

"Thai Chicken curry."

I got down to Sainsbury's in Portswood a little before six in the evening and scooted round so that by six thirty I was standing opposite the Albanian café chatting to Michelle on my mobile. The café was pretty empty, and I briefly wondered what would happen if I went in and ordered something. I knew from Idriz that most of the gang ate there regularly so I figured if I waited then they would be along for their dinner. When I finished my call with Michelle, I kept my phone to my ear watching; just another student chatting on their phone.

Just after seven my waiting was rewarded; a black BMW M3 with blacked-out windows pulled up outside the café. Three dark-haired guys got out, all looking like archetypical gangsters with designer black leather jackets and shades despite the cloudy day. They left the car on the double yellow lines and went into the café.

I hung around for another ten minutes to see if anyone else would show up but they didn't. I needed to get back to Sharon's to start cooking so I made a note of the car's registration and headed back.

I went back the next evening, a little later and wearing a different jacket. The BMW was there, Besian turned up in a black Mercedes, and I could see about ten or a dozen men in the café. I came away confident that I could at least find them on a routine basis; now I just had to figure what I was going to do. It should be easy enough to find out from one of them where the guns were, but it was tempting to try to do more. Send them against Peter Murphy, for example.

That evening Sharon told me that Mike Scott had had his meeting with the Assistant Chief Constable and had permission to begin an operation against Peter Murphy.

"Not that it's going to happen straight away," she said. "He's got to document everything and get it reviewed, but he can start the planning. Thought you'd be pleased."

"I am. I'd feared they'd never let Mike near him again and I'd never get the chance to face him."

"We don't know if you'll get that chance. I doubt he mentioned that part in his proposal. This isn't about you. It's about putting Murphy behind bars with as few risks as possible. I know he tried to kill you, but that just underlines how dangerous he is. We know he has killed other people. He might just shoot you before you can get near him."

I left it there as there was nothing to be gained from further argument and got on with cooking the dinner.

I got up early and put in a few hours in the lab before catching the bus out to Langley. I got there in time for a late breakfast then we headed off to Totton to finish clearing the flat. I was pretty confident that Dave had been dealt with, but that didn't stop me being twitchy the whole time we were there. We got the last of the stuff bagged up, then cleaned the place thoroughly. I've lived in enough rented places to know how much cleaning you have to do to stand a chance of getting your deposit back. I think it was a shock to Michelle how much needed doing, despite them having looked after the place. It was gone eight when we finished and we were shattered, but the place was clean, and Dave hadn't put in an appearance.

Mother was working and I was too tired to cook when we got back to Langley, so we got a takeaway, watched a bit of rubbish TV, and crashed out early.

I woke next morning with Jack's uncle's song running through my head. I had planned to try and call him anyway so after breakfast we walked down to the portal. It took less than a single run through of the song before Jack's uncle appeared with a second older man. Both were dressed very plainly but in nothing than you would see today, smock-like tunics and baggy trousers; they looked like farmworkers from early Victorian photos.

Jack's uncle took my hand. "This is my good friend Toby," he said. "He has heard about the wonders of your world and wishes to see them. The Queen talks of little else it seems."

Toby smiled at us. He looked about fifty, greying but sharp-eyed and still trim and lithe; a glamour, of course, which I could not see through. He was probably one of The Great.

I relayed this to Michelle who came and took Jack's uncle's other hand.

"I'm sure we've plenty to show him," she said.

"And have you been practising?" Jack's uncle asked me as we walked back towards the cottage.

"I have, and I got rid of the problem man bothering Michelle."

"The compulsion worked?"

"It seems to so far. I don't want to go anywhere near him to find out, though."

"If you did as I taught you then I'm sure it worked. And now you are thinking about another one."

It took me a moment to realise he was talking about the Albanians. "I haven't yet decided what I'm going to do."

"Whatever you do, remember that the compulsion has to tell a complete story or it fails. I think it would be easier to just find out where the weapons are this time."

I was a bit disconcerting be given advice on something that he'd just plucked out of my mind, but he meant well and was probably right. "That's the conclusion I was coming to."

We reached the point where the tarmacked lane began, and Toby looked at it in puzzlement. He bent down and prodded it and spoke to Jack's uncle in their unintelligible tongue.

"He is impressed with the surface of the path," said Jack's uncle. "It would resist the rain?"

Their roads, I remembered, were essentially only tracks and paths, half of them probably impassable in bad weather.

"It does pretty well," I said. "Though frost can damage it."

This was passed on; Toby nodded sagely, and we resumed our walk to the cottage; I wondered how he would react to the car if he was impressed by the road.

He was predictably enough fascinated by it. He walked slowly round it a couple of times, examining it closely and was particularly interested in the tyres, bending down to feel them. Michelle unlocked the doors and we got in. Toby gave quite a jump as Michelle started the engine but settled as she pulled away. With four adults in the car, we couldn't go at much of a speed, but Toby sat there with a look on his face like a kid on a birthday treat as we drove through the back lanes to Calshot. Jack's uncle pointed out the power station chimney, so we stopped for Toby to look, and we explained briefly what it was for.

We moved on down to the beach, parking in the big car park

and went to the beach café. There was a fresh breeze blowing but not too cold for ice cream and a walk along the beach. The Solent was pretty busy; no giant liners this time, but loads of windsurfers and yachts, the largest vessel was the Isle of Wight car ferry going into Cowes. That wasn't what caught Toby's attention; he was looking at the sea. He said something to Jack's uncle who took up my hand again.

"He says this is the biggest lake he's ever seen and wants to know how large it is."

So he'd never seen the sea, and when I thought about it I realised I had no idea of the geography over there. Did they have seas?

"That's not a lake," I said. "That's the sea. Beyond the island that way it's about a hundred or so miles to France, but that way." I pointed west. "It's about three thousand miles to America." He looked at me wide-eyed and I could feel his confusion. "Don't taste the water, it's salty."

"We do not have this in our place," he said after a moment. "It is hard to believe, but I know you tell the truth."

He turned to Toby, and they spoke in their own language for a while until a helicopter flew up the Solent heading towards Portsmouth, and they watched in astonishment. Michelle arrived with the ice creams which proved as popular with Toby as they had with Jack's uncle. They were keen on seconds, but I thought it unwise to risk giving them indigestion; those cones probably contained more sugar than they'd had in their entire lives.

Michelle's phone rang then bringing another surprise for them, and I had to explain how she was talking to someone out of sight, who could possibly be anywhere in the world. I brought out my phone to show them how it works, but I think it was all a bit much for them.

We drove back to the cottage, showed Toby the fridge and then put on the TV. That really was too much for them. They watched open-mouthed as I explained what they were seeing and hearing.

"This is truly amazing," said Jack's uncle. "And all this requires iron?"

"Most of it. Iron is essential to making electricity."

"It would not be possible to have most of this in our place then."

"Most of it, no."

"I think His Majesty will be disappointed, but perhaps it is best. It would be a lot of change. Too much."

I thought about the places I had visited over there and tried to imagine them with tarmacked roads, electric pylons, phone masts, and TV and decided I didn't like the picture. "Places that change too quickly lose their identity."

"I think you are right."

"And we can come here if we want to see these things."

We watched a bit more TV, changing the channels to show them the variety, before walking back to the portal. Toby shook our hands vigorously and his thanks rang in my head.

"You must keep practising," said Jack's uncle. "You have done well so far, but still have a great deal to learn." Then they were gone.

"I wonder who he really is?" said Michelle as we walked back.

"Toby? Who knows," I said. "One of the The Great probably. He certainly held a very solid glamour."

"Strange them coming over here to see the sights now, after what happened before. Never thought we'd get tourists. Sounds like we might get the Queen soon."

"It is weird, but its good because it gives us influence over there if we need help. If Lord Faniel resurfaces for example."

"And we could make our fortunes selling them ice cream and chocolate."

"If we can find something over there worth bringing back."

After my usual uncomfortable night on the couch, I caught the bus into town and went straight to the lab. I exchanged a couple of texts with Sharon about dinner options on the way and then spent the rest of the day on a liquid ammonia reaction.

I got down to Portswood just after seven; it was still warm, so I dispensed with the jacket. The BMW was already parked outside the café, looking freshly valeted, and there were half a dozen men in the café. As I approached the black Mercedes pulled up, Besian and another guy got out and went into the café.

I'd thought of just bumping into them as they went into the café, but as I'd just missed them, I needed something else. Seeing the BMW looking so shiny gave me an idea. The owner was obviously proud of his wheels, so I went and casually leant against the front wing. I had cut a piece of polystyrene packing down to fit an old phonecase as I didn't want to risk my new phone in any confrontation. I pulled that out of my pocket and proceeded to fake a call keeping a watch on the café out of the corner of my eye.

It didn't take long; a stocky, dark-haired guy with a moustache came out of the café heading straight towards me. I didn't react as he approached.

"Hey! Get off the car," he said. I just looked at him and concentrated on my phone call.

"Hey! I'm talking to you!" He grabbed me by the arm which was just about the best thing he could have done as I was only wearing a T-shirt, and I dived into his mind.

It was easy; I didn't have to search at all, the guns were right there at the front of his mind. It took seconds; I pulled out and left him walking back to the café thinking he had given me a good scare. I walked in the other direction, seeking the cover of the supermarket shoppers.

I found a quiet aisle and called Sharon on my real phone. I prayed it wouldn't go straight to voicemail; this was something that couldn't wait. My prayers were answered when she picked up on the third ring.

"I've got your information," I said. "The guns are in a black BMW M3 that's parked outside the café right now. Most of the Albanian team are in the café. There're three 9mm pistols and one Uzi, all loaded. They're in the passenger footwell in a black sports bag." No wonder he'd been so keen to get me away from the car.

"Good man! I can make things happen now, but it'll take a bit of time. Can you keep an eye on them 'til I can get someone there?"

"Sure. I'll keep you updated by text."

It took ten minutes to buy ingredients for dinner then I went back up towards the café and found a spot where I could see the BMW but couldn't see into the café. I texted Sharon to tell her the car was still there and settled down to wait. It was rather dull, but the tension of when they would leave kept me interested.

After half an hour I updated Sharon that they were still in the café. A few minutes later she texted me back to say that someone was now in place watching them, and I should head home. I hadn't noticed anyone but that seemed a good thing.

I got back to Sharon's, cooked the curry I had planned and ate my share figuring she would be back pretty late. I didn't realise how right I was about that until I put Radio Solent on, and their news headline was that police had shot a man in an operation in Southampton. It seemed most unlikely that it wasn't one of the Albanians. Solent had no other details, so I sat down to wait for Sharon.

Sharon got in just after eleven.

"I heard the news," I said as I put her rice in the microwave.

"Yeah, it was all going so nicely until then," she said pouring herself a large gin. "We had three of them in the car, and one decided to play Bonnie and Clyde. You wouldn't believe the shit this causes. The IPCC are automatically called in, and they're crawling over everything."

"You going to be able to keep me out of it?" I was pretty sure I didn't want to be investigated by them.

She was slow to answer. "Should be able to," she said eventually. "But I can't have you anywhere near them now. There's just too many people watching."

"You got three, what about the rest of them?"

"We'll do everything we can to keep the pressure on them."

"But there's nothing to stop them just cashing in their gains and buggering off back to Albania."

"That's true. We can't stop them doing that at the moment." She took a swig of gin. "We've got three of them. I'd love to bag the lot, but sometimes you just have to settle for what you can get."

"They all deserve jail." I said as the microwave pinged.

"They do, but you don't always get what you deserve." She

took another swig of gin. "For what it's worth, I think they'll just put their heads down for a while then carry on. So you'll get another crack at them, but not until the IPCC have gone home."

She poured herself another drink as I served the curry and then tunnelled her way through it as if she hadn't eaten for a week. I left her to it and went to bed. I should have been pleased but I felt robbed.

When I got the phone call in the lab telling me I had a visitor, I was expecting it to be Nigel the spook, not DI Mike Scott. We went into a vacant seminar room to talk.

"Are you still up for taking on Pete Murphy?" he asked. "I didn't want to discuss it around Sharon."

"Because she doesn't approve?"

"Something like that."

"Yes, I am. I know Sharon thinks it's too dangerous, but I believe I can handle him."

"Good. I'm organising a meet with him, and I'll put your name into the conversation. I can't imagine it won't get a reaction. Give me your number. I'll call you when I've got more information."

I thought better of mentioning that he already had my number having taken it off the police records and given it to Murphy and gave it to him.

"Right, I'll be in touch," he said. "Probably best you don't mention it to Sharon just yet."

He left and, as I walked back up the stairs to the lab, I thought about what I was actually going to do. I could, of course, scoop out loads of details about Murphy's operations and pass them over to Mike, but it was tempting to do more. Like give Murphy a religious vision that compelled him to confess everything. Maybe a fiery angel with a burning sword; yeah, I liked that.

I saw Mike a couple of times during the week but always with Sharon around so neither of us mentioned Peter Murphy. It wasn't until Friday afternoon that I got a text from him saying 'Tomorrow, pick you up at 11am." I texted back "OK, pick me up from outside the Chem Dept." That worked pretty well for me as I wasn't due out to Langley until later in the day, but it would mean missing Prof's meeting. However, I reckoned Mike would be able to smooth over any objections being a DI.

Mike turned up twenty minutes late driving a black Astra, and we headed out of town to join the M27. I had expected that we would head into Portsmouth, but instead we left the motorway and took the A32 northward up the Meon Valley. Somewhere past Wickham we turned off into country lanes ending up driving down a tree-lined gravel road between green pastures, one containing sheep.

"This Murphy's country estate?" I asked.

"Something like that," said Mike.

"A couple of millions worth then."

"And then some."

My stomach tightened as the house came into view, and I remembered Sharon's warning "he might just shoot you before you can get close to him." This was the most dangerous thing I had done. I was risking my life on my guess that Murphy liked to deal with problems personally. He would try to put a compulsion on me rather than risk shooting me in front of Mike.

The red-brick house was large, solid, and seemed in good condition, though the outbuildings had an unused look about them. Mike drove around to the rear into what had been the farmyard and parked next to a very new-looking white Range Rover Sport.

"You sure you're OK with this?" asked Mike. "If you're not you'd better tell me now."

I hesitated and thought about it for a moment. "I'm fine. Let's go for it."

Mike switched off the engine and we got out. As we walked towards the house the back door opened and a man stepped out. Six foot plus with cropped hair and a hard-edged look to him, he stared at us with undisguised hostility but held the door open for us. It opened into a utility room with washing machine and American-style freezer. He closed the door and locked it, then grunted "come" in a way that suggested that he didn't speak much English. We followed him down a corridor into the interior of the house passing several closed doors until he stopped at one which he held open. Another grunt and flick of the head indicated that we should go in. We did so. He followed us in, closed the door and stood with his back against it.

The L-shaped room was wide and bright, furnished with a very expensive-looking white leather suite and matching carpet. The largest widescreen TV I'd ever seen hung on one wall. A heavily-stocked drinks cabinet stood against the wall beside the door. I thought they're not going to shoot me in this room, it would ruin the décor.

I recognised the man who appeared from the alcove even though I'd never met him. Pete Murphy was dark-haired, dark-eyed, maybe ten years older than me and about my height but with a deeper chest. A lot like I would look in my mid-thirties - if I lived that long. But then if he is half-otherkin it's not so unlikely; he's probably some kind of cousin.

"Glad you could make it, Mike," he nodded to DI Scott with a smile. "And this must be Charlie." He looked at me but did not extend a hand in greeting. "I've wanted to talk to you for some time. You've cost me money, and a good friend of mine is in a secure ward at Tatchbury Mount because of you." His voice remained even with no anger in it. "I was going to deal with you myself, but someone else has a bigger claim on you. Isn't that right, Faniel?"

My guts froze as if I'd dumped a cardice bath in my lap. A second person appeared from the alcove. He was tall, dark-haired, and walked with a bit of a limp. I didn't recognise him but that meant nothing; if it was Lord Faniel he would be wearing a glamour. I turned towards the door, but the monosyllabic minder took two steps forward and grabbed my arms. Then I felt a hand on my neck and Lord Faniel's voice in my head.

"It is so good to see you again, little meddler. You have cost me much blood and pain. Now it is time for you to pay." His voice boomed around my brain, drowning out my pleas for mercy.

My feet and lower legs exploded with pain. "This is what you did to me felt like."

I screamed until I passed out.

I woke up sprawled across the rear seat of Mike's car with

him leaning over me, my legs and feet still on fire.

"Are you OK, Charlie?" he asked, phone in hand. "Do you need an ambulance?"

"My legs! What's he done to my fucking legs?" I screamed. I pulled up my trouser leg to look at the damage which hurt even more. My shin was red raw with blisters most of the way to the knee. Just touching any part was agony.

"Looks fine to me," said Mike.

"What about the blisters?"

"What blisters? He didn't touch your legs. They look entirely normal. All he did was hold your neck."

How could he miss the angry white blisters? The pain was making it hard to think. He'd only touched my neck so why did my legs hurt? It had to be a compulsion. Because of what I'd done to him, I was feeling what he had felt. This insight did not diminish the pain.

"He's put a compulsion on me," I gasped. "No point in an ambulance. What I need is someone who can break it."

"Like what Murphy did to me? Who can shift it? Your dad?"

"No. He's not strong enough. But he should know someone who can." But who would that be? Who was stronger than Lord Faniel? Toby? The King?

"I need a gateway. Can you take me out to Netley Marsh? The place you went before." That was the nearest one I could think of.

"Right. You got a postcode for the satnav?"

"No. I just know how to get there."

"OK. You going to be alright until then?"

"Gonna have to be." There wasn't anything that was going to help short of general anaesthesia.

The journey passed in a blur of pain; that I knew it to be imaginary was of little help; I just had to endure it. After an hour or so I had to sit up and direct Mike for the last few miles. We reached the car park, and then he almost offered me his arm to support me as we walked to the gateway.

"So this Faniel guy who did this to you, who is he?" asked Mike as I tottered along.

"He's the heir to the throne over there, and he's the guy

behind all the shit we've had this year. The murders, abductions, and house burnings, all down to him. He's a really strong magician and a complete bastard."

"So what's his connection to Pete Murphy?"

"God knows! But it's not good news. I'm stronger than Murphy, but nowhere near Lord Faniel."

We reached the gateway, or at least we reached the point where it should have been clearly visible, but I couldn't see it. I walked slowly around the area, but no blue light peeped between the trees. The suspicion grew in my mind that Lord Faniel had removed my ability to see the gateways. No matter; it was still there and I didn't need to see it to summon Jack. I began his summoning song but came to a halt after a few words. I started again and again came to a halt. I couldn't remember how it went. Nor could I remember the song for Jack's uncle.

"Shit!" I sat down on a log and wondered what else he had done. I felt like crying.

"What's the problem?" asked Mike.

"He's blocked my ability to do anything with the gateway. I can't even see it." A dark thought occurred to me. "Give me your hand a moment."

After a moment's hesitation he reached out to me. I took his hand and...nothing.

"I can't do that either," I said. "He's blocked everything."

"No point in staying here then," said Mike. "Where do you want to go next?"

"Can you take me to my mother's place out at Langley?" If I couldn't call Jack, Michelle still could. She should have finished work by now; a powerful need to see her rose up in my mind. Mother would undoubtedly give me a hard time for getting into this mess by working with the police, but I could stand that.

"OK, but then I've got to get back to town."

"Fair enough." He's a Detective Inspector after all, not my personal chauffeur.

We walked back to the car with Mike supporting me most of the way.

"So how can this Faniel guy do this?" asked Mike.

"I don't know. I've only been learning this a few weeks. He's been doing it his whole life."

"Will your people be able to do something to fix it?"

"I just don't know. I hope so."

We reached the car and, exhausted, I slumped into the back seat. I gave Mike the address for the satnav and lay back trying to shut out the pain. This was shit and it was my own damn fault.

We arrived at the cottage, and Mike practically carried me to the door. Mother opened the door.

"What on earth have you done, Charlie?" she said as I tottered on the doorstep.

"My legs!" I gasped and collapsed onto her. She caught me and half-carried me into the sitting room and deposited me on the sofa.

"I'll speak to you in a day or so," said Mike over mother's shoulder.

Michelle hurried down the stairs and threw her arms around me. "Charlie! What's happened?"

"He says it's his legs," said mother. "Show me."

Together they carefully took my jeans off; I nearly fainted from the pain despite their efforts to be gentle.

"What's the problem?" said mother. "What am I meant to be seeing?"

"You won't see it," I gasped. "It's a compulsion. Lord Faniel made me feel his pain from when I burned him."

"Right. So what do you see?" asked Michelle. "'Cos I just see your legs untouched."

"Raw, weeping blisters up to my knees."

"There's no blood or anything on your jeans," said mother holding them up.

"Not as I see them." I could see the lower legs dark with blood.

"So if this is a compulsion then painkillers and stuff won't work 'cos it's all in your head," said Michelle.

"Think so."

"Worth trying anyway," said mother. She left the room heading for the kitchen cupboard that contained our collection of medicines and was back a moment later with a glass of water and a white box.

"This is the strongest we've got," she said, holding out the tablets. "Take two of these and we'll see what happens."

"What are they?" I asked taking them from her.

"Voltarol."

I swallowed them and drained the glass.

"If this is a compulsion then we need Jack," said mother.

"Jack's uncle," I said. "He might be strong enough to shift it, Jack isn't."

"I don't know his song," said mother.

"I did," I said. "But that's gone now, along with everything else I could do."

"Oh Charlie!" said Michelle and hugged me.

"I can call Jack, at least," said mother. "And he can bring whoever he thinks he needs. It'll take a bit longer, but it gets us there. I'll go straightaway. Is there anything else we can do?"

"Is there any ice?" asked Michelle. "Might help if we cool his legs."

"Barely enough for three gin and tonics," said mother. "But there's a tub in the garden shed. Bring that in, fill it with water, and he can sit with his legs in it."

"I'll try anything," I said, and meant it.

Mother left to go and call Jack. Michelle brought in the tub and filled it by bucket with cold water. I sat the sofa with my legs in the tub up to mid-shin in cold water and a blanket around my shoulders. I sat back and closed my eyes and tried to think of glaciers, snow drifts, the Solent off Lepe beach, anything cold. It helped a bit.

Michelle made tea for both of us then went back into the kitchen to start dinner. After a while she came and sat beside me.

"So how come you were anywhere near Lord Faniel?" she asked.

"Didn't know he was going to be there," I said. "Didn't know he was any part of it."

"So what were you doing?"

"Going after Pete Murphy. Mike Scott set it up. He's been approved to run an operation against Murphy, and he thought

I could wrap it up quickly. We went out to Murphy's place to meet him. I was betting that he would try to put a compulsion on me and when he did, I was going to read him. I was thinking of maybe putting a compulsion on him to confess, but I never got the chance. Lord Faniel was there and expecting us."

"So has he been behind Pete Murphy all the time, teaching him compulsions and stuff?"

"Possibly, or someone in his close circle."

She paused. "Could he be Murphy's father?"

"Who knows? It's a big problem whatever."

"I'm sure Jack will find a way of lifting this compulsion."

"I hope! I'm so screwed if he doesn't. But I was thinking beyond that to stopping Murphy and Lord Faniel."

"I thought the king had stopped him."

"We don't know exactly what the king stopped him doing. Raiding over here, obviously. But little bit of personal revenge, maybe not."

"Jack will know, and he'll pass on what he's done to you."

"Of course, but I don't know if it'll stop Faniel working with Murphy."

"We'll find a way. How are your legs feeling? Do they still look horrible to you?"

"Yeah, they do. The water helps. Don't think the painkillers have done anything."

She left the room for a moment to go upstairs and returned with a mirror which she held up in front of me.

"Look at your legs in the mirror. What do you see?"

I looked and saw the same blistered weeping flesh. "No different."

"Oh!" Her face fell. "I was hoping you'd see what we see. Didn't you say that a compulsion falls apart if you find a hole in it?"

"That's what I was told and it's a good thought. I guess they have mirrors over there, so he covered that. It's stupid really. I know it's a compulsion, but that doesn't stop it working."

She sat down next to me and put her arms around me. "Jack'll know what to do. I'm sure of it."

At that moment mother and Jack came in the back door. Jack

paused to take off his boots then came over to me.

"Am I glad to see you," I said.

"Your mother said Lord Faniel put a compulsion on you." He took my hand, concern written across his face.

It seemed a long time before he said anything more. "Yes, this is Lord Faniel's work; very tight and very strong. It is beyond anything I can do. We need my uncle or Toby, or maybe both."

As I had expected, yet I was disappointed he could do nothing to ease the pain.

"How is it that you came to be near him? I cannot reach the memory; he has hidden it."

"I had no idea he was going to be there." I thought the words rather than spoke them aloud not wanting mother to hear. "You remember the compulsion you removed from Sharon's friend? I was going after the man who did it, the man who tried to have me killed."

"Yes, I remember."

"Mother does not know this, and I am not ready to tell her yet." I remembered her reaction to finding I was working with Sharon and imagined similar when she found out what had happened.

"How far can you walk?"

I remembered my painful hobble with Mike to the gateway. I didn't think I could even manage that now. "Not far."

"Then I will bring my uncle and Toby here," he said releasing my hand.

"Do you have mirrors over there?" asked Michelle.

"Yes," said Jack. "Why do you ask?"

"I tried showing Charlie his legs in a mirror, but it didn't undo the compulsion."

"That would be an obvious thing to include, and Lord Faniel is too well-taught to miss it," said Jack. "It was a good thought, though, to seek such a flaw in the construction."

"Then let's try this." She held up her phone. "Show me your legs, Charlie."

I raised my legs as far as I could manage out of the tub; the flesh still red-raw and blistered to my eyes.

"Hold them there," she said fiddling with the phone. "Okay,

now look at this." She stepped over to me holding out the phone.

"What have you got?" I asked.

"Pictures I've just taken of your legs."

I took the phone and scrolled through the pictures. They were indeed of my legs, looking completely undamaged and normal. I brought up the live camera view and examined my legs on the screen; again, completely normal. There was a pop in my head as if something had snapped. The pain vanished as the compulsion unravelled.

"Brilliant!" I shouted, almost dropping the phone. "It's gone."

"What's gone?" asked mother.

"The pain, the compulsion."

"What?" said mother. "Just like that? How?"

"Yes. That's right," said Jack. "That's what happens if you find a flaw and confront it. I've only ever seen it happen like that amongst youngsters, though, when they first start learning. That was very clever thinking, Michelle."

I stepped out of the water tub and into Michelle's arms. It felt so good to be free of the pain that I cried on her shoulder.

After a couple of minutes, I dried my eyes then dried my feet. Mother made tea and we all had a slice of fruitcake to celebrate the return of normality.

"I will make sure the King hears of this," said Jack.

"What will he do about Lord Faniel then?" said mother.

"That is a good question. He is very aware of the debt he owes us, but Lord Faniel is his only son and heir. He may put further curbs on him, but ultimately there is little he can do if he flouts them."

Jack finished his cake and let himself out leaving me to face mother's displeasure.

"Tell me what happened," she said.

I told her the story much as I had told Michelle.

"This Mike Scott, he's police?" she asked.

"Detective Inspector."

"Well, I think you were extremely lucky. I warned you about getting involved with them," she said her lips thin. "Now they know about you they'll never let you go."

Just as well she didn't know about Nigel.

"I suppose you're going to carry on going after this Murphy."

"He tried to have me killed, and he's used his talent to kill several other people."

"That doesn't make me feel any better."

"He needs stopping."

"You could leave it to the police."

"I'm uniquely qualified to help them, and it's personal."

"I suppose you're big and old enough to decide for yourself. I wish you wouldn't, though. I don't think it'll end well."

She went into the kitchen to start dinner; the way she clattered the pans underlining her displeasure. My phone buzzed with an incoming text. It was from Sharon: "Are you OK? Mike's in bits over what happened." I texted her back to say it was all sorted. That would be another difficult conversation come Monday evening.

I guess it isn't surprising I dreamed of burning legs both Saturday and Sunday night and woke with leg cramps. It felt good to get back to the lab and immerse myself in the familiar world of chemistry that I'd come close to losing. I kept my head down as my labmates gossiped about their weekends and got on with setting up a new set of conditions for my ring-closing metathesis reaction.

I exchanged texts with Sharon about what shopping was needed, dreading actually going back to the flat and facing her. She wasn't back when I got there so I got on with the dinner. I was chopping onions for the curry when I heard her come in. I carried on chopping waiting for her to speak.

"Well, I'm glad to see you're alive," she said. "Do you want to tell me what happened? Mike wasn't really clear about some of it."

"Lord Faniel was there. Murphy handed me over and he put a compulsion on me. It wasn't anyone's fault, not Mike's, not mine."

"Except that you both underestimated Murphy. I told you how dangerous he is, and this just underlines the point. Stay out of it, Charlie. You were dead lucky this time. You're too nice to handle a bastard like Murphy. Leave it to the professionals."

"I don't imagine Mike will let me near Murphy again."

"I should hope not. There're plenty of other things you can help us with. God knows we're not short of scumbags that need locking up."

"You know I'm happy to help whenever."

"I know, but I can't use you too often without getting awkward questions. Is there any wine open?"

I went back to my cooking thinking that I would see what Mike had to say. I wasn't finished with Pete Murphy yet.

Mike Scott came by the lab next morning to see me. "Jesus, am I glad to see you okay, Charlie," he said. "I was shitting myself with what they did to you. Sharon told me your folks got you sorted and I'm so glad."

A small voice in my mind wondered whether that was out of concern for me or for the consequences on his career.

"So am I."

"Sharon gave me a very hard time for involving you and warned me having you involved again."

"That doesn't surprise me, but she's not my mother. I've had a lot of time to think about this. What happens when you bring him down?"

"He goes to prison for a long time."

"And given his abilities, he will be king of that prison within a week and your problem just got a whole lot worse. Even with a weak power of compulsion: prisoners, warders, even the governor will do what he says. They won't be able to resist. You of all people know how it works."

Mike was silent for a while as he digested the prospect. From the frown on his face, he didn't like it much.

"I can certainly see that," he said. "Do you have an alternative?"

"Yes." I wasn't going to mention my ideas on a short walk off the top of the Itchen Bridge; not to a copper no matter how well I knew him. "Lord Faniel's compulsion took away all my powers. I would do the same to Peter Murphy." No matter that I didn't know how to do that, I would learn by the time they brought him down or get help to do it.

"But can't Lord whatshisname just reverse that?"

"Yes. The second part of my plan is to cut off his access to Lord Faniel from the other side." Even if it was a plan in name only.

"You can do that?"

"Maybe. If I talk to the right people. The King certainly owes me a couple of favours."

"That would be very handy if you could manage it. I have no wish to meet Lord whatshisname again."

"I have…under the right circumstances." I had no idea of how to bring about those circumstances, but no matter; it was something else to work on. "What's happening with those Albanians?"

"Which ones? The three we nicked the other day? Remanded in custody. You were part of that, weren't you?"

"Yeah. What about the rest of the crew? Haven't pissed off back to Albania?"

"Still around as far as I known."

"Why haven't the whole lot been deported?"

"Have to ask the Borders Agency about that. We sent them the files. What's your interest in them?"

"They've had dealings with Pete Murphy. I thought there might be something there we could use."

He grimaced. "Not that I can see. But if you find something let me know."

Which meant he wasn't going to do anything about it, and that was fine by me.

"I certainly will. I still want to be part of bringing Murphy down."

"And I can still use your help, but I have to be careful. I'll let you know what develops."

I showed him out then went back to the lab. The thought of setting the Albanians on Murphy was looking more attractive by the minute. Convince Besian that Murphy was trying to put him out of business. It shouldn't be hard, after all Murphy had been responsible for Idriz's demise.

As I set up my column, I reviewed what I knew about Besian.

Everyone around him was either a relative or someone he had grown up with back in his hometown. I had seen him once in the street and once at the café he owned. I could spend a year trying to run into him again, so the café was the place to start. I knew he ate there sometimes, and he drove a black Mercedes. Messing with the BMW had worked well on his crew, so it was worth trying again on the Merc if it was there. I still had the fake phone with me, and it was forecast to be a fine evening, so why not?

The forecast was right, and I walked down to the cafe around 7. Portswood was busy so it was easy to wander around near the cafe without standing out. Some of the crew were already inside, and Besian rolled up about ten minutes later. I gave him a few minutes to get settled in the cafe then went and casually leaned on the wing of the Merc while faking a conversation on my phone.

I had my shoulder turned to the cafe, so I didn't immediately see the guy approaching me until he spoke.

"Off the car!" I turned; it wasn't Besian, but the stocky moustachioed guy from before and he was not happy. "Told you before!"

He stepped in and hit me with a short right hand under my ribs. It felt like he'd used a sledgehammer. I hit the pavement gasping for breath and found myself closely examining his boots.

"I see you again. I hurt you proper." He moved his foot so his boot touched my cheek.

He stood over me for a minute while I tried to breathe then hauled me to my feet by the waistband of my jeans. Fuck, he was strong.

"Fuck off now!" He gave me a shove to send me on my way and watched me as I staggered back to Portswood Road. I looked around to see if anyone had witnessed it, maybe filmed it, but no one paid me any attention. Feeling physically and mentally battered I started the walk back up to the lab. I needed a better plan; one which got Besian alone, and that was a problem I couldn't see a way around.

A possible solution did not occur to me until Thursday. I was surfing the Echo website and clicked on a story about a restaurant that had been prosecuted following an inspection by Environmental Health officers. That would be something that Besian would not ignore. If I posed as an Environmental Health officer and threatened to shut down his cafe, I would get to talk to him without his crew. I would need a glamour to make me look older and more authoritative, but that should be doable. A single touch and the cafe manager would lose any doubts and accept I was an inspector.

By the end of the day, I still liked the idea, but decided against mentioning it to Sharon. I did try out the "older Charlie" glamour on her and it worked well enough.

"You need a better haircut for that to look right," she said and was probably right. I'd let Chloe do my last haircut. I also asked her about the Albanians and the Border Agency and got the same answer as I had from Mike Scott. I didn't dig any further, didn't want her remembering my interest.

I practised my glamour and got my hair cut and on Saturday took the bus out to Langley after the lab meeting. I wore the "older Charlie" glamour on the journey, and the bus driver on the Unilink nearly didn't let me on because I didn't look like my ID. I call that a win.

I got to the cottage in time for a late lunch, then Michelle and I headed out for the gateway. We only had to go through the song once before Jack appeared with his uncle, and another man I did not recognise.

"Are you well?" asked Jack taking my hands. "No ill effects?"

"No, none. I'm fine."

"That is good to hear," said Jack, releasing my hands. "I have brought someone to see you."

I turned to look at the man who accompanied them. He was dressed in the same greens and browns as them, but his skin seemed to glow ever so slightly compared to theirs. It was really no surprise when Jack introduced him as the King. I did the deep bow and Michelle made the curtsey thing. He reached his hands to me, I took them, then his voice spoke inside my head.

"I have come to offer my apology for the acts of my son.

We are already deep in debt to you, and I hope you can find it in yourself to accept. He has given me his word that he will do nothing to harm you, nor encourage anyone else to do."

"And he will break all contact with the evil man on this side who helped him?"

"He will."

"And he will keep his word?"

A frown passed over his face. "To my shame I cannot be certain of this. He is no longer the son I knew. We are all worried by the weakening of the grym hud, but he has lost his reason and become a fanatic."

"And in blaming those who bring in new blood, he targets the very people who are the solution."

"How so?"

"How many people first settled your world?"

"The legends say there were ten families."

"So everyone is descended from one of ten men, that's really not very many. I learned about this in my genetics undergrad course. It is called Inbreeding Depression, and it causes populations to weaken over the generations. If you breed cattle, then you must know this."

"We used to steal cattle from this world, and men are not cattle."

"In this all animals are the same, men included. Are the people of mixed-blood weaker in the grym hud?"

"I don't know."

"It seems an obvious question to ask. Someone should find out." I was pretty sure I knew what the answer would be.

"I will ask it when I return. Thank you for your answers. Now, I have heard much of the wonders of this world but saw little when last I was here. Could you show me some of it?"

This I had been expecting "Of course. Is there anything you particularly want to see?"

"The water. They told me about an endless sheet of water. That I want to see."

"Certainly. We will go first to my mother's house. Follow me."

He released my hands and we headed back along the

riverbank towards the cottage.

Jack caught up with me.

"You should know how unusual this is. The king has never shown an interest in this side before," he said as Jack's uncle and the King chatted away in their strange language.

"We're in danger of becoming fashionable."

"You are indeed. The court is full of talk about this side. I have never been so much in demand as a dinner guest."

"What are they saying?"

"A lot of them ask about the chocolate and ice cream. Whether it's as good as they've heard."

"What do you tell them?"

"It's better," he said with a grin.

They reached the cottage with Michelle's Polo parked outside. The King looked at it and spoke to Jack.

"He says it's smaller than he remembers and wants to know how it works."

I went over and took his hand and, much as I had to Jack's uncle, took him through my basic tutorial on the internal combustion engine finishing with "But it's easier to show you."

We got into the car, the King in the front passenger seat and me sitting behind holding his hand to act as tour guide. Jack opted to stay with mother which saved us from being too crammed in.

The first things that caught the King's attention were the cattle in the fields were passed.

"They're so much larger than ours," he said after we had stopped so he could get a better look.

"How long is it since you stopped taking cattle from this side?" I asked.

He took a moment to answer. "Perhaps in my grandfather's time."

"That could easily cover a couple of hundred years over here. Time for a lot of selective breeding."

He nodded sagely then noticed the power station chimney which I explained for him exactly as I had for Toby. He stood in wonder staring at it for a couple of minutes before we moved on to Calshot.

The Solent was alive with windsurfers and sailing dinghies.

The King asked about the windsurfers, but just like Toby his attention was taken by the sea.

"I did not believe," he said. "But now that I see it."

We bought ice cream, which was as popular as on previous occasions. I then had to explain to the King how it was made.

"My wife and her ladies would adore this," he said, which again had me thinking about the possibilities of a chocolate and ice cream business over there.

Far above an airliner crawled across the sky leaving its contrail painted on the blue. The King followed my gaze with a puzzled look on his face.

"What is it?"

"Long distance air travel." I pictured a jumbo jet for him. "There could be five hundred people on board that."

"And where would they be going?"

"Spain maybe, or further down into Africa. Those planes can go thousands of miles."

He nodded silently and I wondered how much he knew of the world over there.

"I would like to see one close to," he said. "And perhaps travel in one."

"That's going to take a bit of organising." I thought briefly of how to arrange travel documents for him.

"Oh, not today. On another visit."

We finished the ice creams then walked to the Polo and headed back to the cottage to Jack and mother. We went in and I explained that this was a small house that two people lived in which surprised the King. He asked to see the "box that keeps things cold" so I showed him the fridge, then the electric cooker and the kettle, which I demonstrated by making a pot of tea.

When Michelle turned on the TV, he couldn't believe his senses, going right up to the screen and touching it, following the figures with his fingers. Inevitably he wanted to know how it worked. I tried to explain, but I'm really not sure how much he understood; he remained very impressed, though.

They finished the tea and the chocolate biscuits we had brought to accompany it, then made ready to leave, saying goodbye to Michelle and mother. The king took my hand again.

"Thank you for showing me a little of this world. It is full of more wonders that I could have imagined. I understand your fears about my son, and I will do everything I can to control him. I hope you will come again to my realm."

They left then, Jack leading them back to the portal.

"So that was the king?" said Michelle. "What did he say about Lord Faniel?"

"That he has given his word to doing nothing to harm me, but he can't guarantee that he'll keep it."

"Better than nothing, I suppose," said Michelle. "And honest of him to say so."

"He feels bad about it after all we've done for him. But it just reflects the reality of the situation. Faniel is his heir and there's not much he can do if he isn't going to disinherit him."

"Then we'd better watch our backs. He doesn't strike me as the forgiving sort."

The urge to do something about Besian and his crew kept nibbling at me, and the Environmental Health Officer idea still seemed the best scheme I had. It was easy enough to lift the Southampton City Council logo off their website, stick it on an official-looking ID and laminate it. I was gambling that the cafe staff wouldn't know what a real one looked like. There was an even chance that they couldn't read English.

I decided to go for it on Tuesday and arranged my work to leave the lab mid-afternoon. Post lunch seemed like a time when the cafe might not be busy. I could also come back if it was. I left my reaction refluxing and headed out. It was cool and damp enough for a raincoat, and I put on a tie on the way down to Portswood Road. I chose a moment with no one nearby to put the "old Charlie" glamour, hoping that I looked like a local government official clutching my black document folder.

There was only one customer in the cafe, an older guy reading an East European newspaper, so I went in.

"What you want?" asked the older woman behind the counter in heavily-accented English.

I held my breath and took out my fake ID. "Environmental

Health."

"Where the other guy?" she said, barely looking at the ID.

"One who come last month."

That was not the response I expected, and it took me a moment to answer. "He asked me to do a follow up inspection."

She shrugged. "We do everything he say."

"Then it'll be an easy inspection. I need to see the kitchen."

She opened the counter hatch to let me through. As I passed her, I caught her wrist and pushed into her mind. It took moments to set the compulsion and before I opened the fridge, she had her phone out to call Besian.

I carried on with the inspection while waiting for Besian. If they had done everything the previous inspector had told them to then I really didn't want to think about what he had seen. The kitchen was still dirty with no soap for handwashing, there were mouse droppings in the storeroom floor and black mould on the wall. Even though I was acting the part, I wanted to shut them down.

Besian turned up fifteen minutes later. He scowled at me and fired a series of questions at the manager in rapid Albanian. Then he turned to me, stepping close enough that I could smell the tobacco off him.

"Where the other guy, Ian?" he growled.

"He asked me to do a follow up inspection."

He scowled even more, and he chewed over my answer. "I give you the same deal as him," he said after about thirty seconds thought.

I didn't know what the deal with Ian was, so I said nothing, perhaps he took this as me holding out for a better deal. He reached into his jacket, pulled out a wedge of £50 notes and counted off ten.

"Five hundred, cash," he said, holding them out to me. *So Ian is on the take.*

"You fuck with me. I hurt you." He grabbed my wrist giving me the opening I wanted. It was easy. He was naturally suspicious, already angry about the guns bust and the death of Idriz so pulling those strings together and attaching Peter Murphy's name was only enhancing what was already there. I slipped him the location of Murphy's country house and gave him a little push to do something about it.

He released my wrist. I took his money; it would have been suspicious not to. "Just do something about the mice," I said. "They're a real problem."

I walked out sure that my heart was beating loud enough for them to hear it and struggling to maintain the "old Charlie" glamour. It would be a brave man who shut down Besian's cafe.

I made my way back to the Chemistry department losing the "Old Charlie" glamour at the first opportunity and taking off my tie. I was pretty pleased with my work; I'd satisfied my urge to do something and, hopefully, it would buy me a few peaceful weeks to get used to the new landscape of my life. If ever two people deserved each other it was Besian and Peter Murphy. One was as bad as the other, though Besian had cause as Murphy had done for Idriz. I thought of his threat: *You fuck with me. I hurt you.* He was now certain Murphy had fucked with him. It would be violent.

I saw rather less of Sharon for a while. Partly because the new chemistry Prof had brought back from the States was working giving me the chance to push ahead with my synthesis, and I spent my weekends out at Langley. She was also just around less; maybe due to the ongoing IPCC investigation, but she was also seeing more of Mike Scott. When she was around, I felt a coolness between us which I put down to me going against her advice with Peter Murphy, and I began thinking about moving back in with Greg and Chloe. That was until the missing schoolgirl.

My first awareness of her was a Monday afternoon news headline on The Echo website with picture of a fourteen-year-old girl who had not returned home on Sunday evening. Police were concerned for her safety as it was out of character for her to go missing. The picture caught my attention because she looked quite pretty, but I didn't recognise her surname and she wasn't from the Waterside, so I didn't think anything more of it. By the evening three different people on my feed had shared Facebook posts with more pictures appealing for help in finding her.

By the end of Tuesday, she was still missing. Her tearful mother and aunts were on the local TV news appealing for her to come home; her father made no appearance. It did not look good, and I thought the next thing I would hear was that the police had found a body.

Sharon called me at the lab on Wednesday afternoon.

"Have you got time for a trip to the mortuary?"

I didn't want to ask if it was the missing girl, but I had a bad feeling that it was.

"Yes, sure."

"I'll pick you up in twenty minutes."

She picked me up in the blue Fiesta.

"Is it the missing girl?" I asked.

"Yeah," she said. She looked tight-lipped and pale. I could easily have been convinced she had been crying.

"Shit." I'd been hoping it was another Albanian.

She didn't reply and I didn't feel like saying more so we travelled in silence. I wasn't looking forward to this and tried to separate myself from the emotion. The family and police needed the information. It was important that I supply it.

Sharon parked up in the staff car park and I followed her as she stalked off to the mortuary. Sanjay was on duty; when wasn't he? Did he live there? He knew what we'd come for and not to make small talk.

"I don't want to see the face," I said to him as he unwrapped the body. "Just a foot is enough."

"Okay." He moved his attention to the other end of the body and exposed her legs below the knee. I walked over to the body fiercely reminding myself of the reasons for doing it. I took hold of her cold right foot and dived in.

I had to go deep. She'd been dead since Sunday afternoon, but I found what I needed then pulled back. Sanjay knew by now to leave us alone and got on with rewrapping the body. We walked in silence to his office. Sharon took out a pad and waited for me.

"Jake Archer. One of her mother's on-off boyfriends. He was shagging her as well. She thought she was in love and told him she was pregnant." I choked up over the last sentence.

"Poor little girl," said Sharon huskily. She scribbled in her pad then snapped shut. "I need to get out of here before I lose it."

I followed her back to the car and gave her five minutes. I didn't feel much better myself. She was wiping her eyes when I opened the passenger door.

"You okay?"

"Yeah. It just got me. She's the same age as my niece." She looked at me with red-rimmed eyes. "Was it very bad?"

"Not as bad as Karen. At least I was prepared for it." I put on my seat belt.

"I don't know how you can do it. But I'm glad you do. I know I've been a bit sharp with you lately, and I'm sorry. It's just so stressful with the IPCC crawling all over us." She started the car. "I owe you another dinner for this."

Since she was in a mood to talk, I decided to bring up something that had been on my mind since the disastrous visit to Murphy's mansion. "I'm concerned about Mike."

"Why?"

"I don't know what happened at Murphy's place after Lord Faniel got his hands on me. He, or Murphy, could have reinstalled the compulsion on Mike. They'd know how it was removed, too."

She took a few moments to think about it. "Shit. It could be, couldn't it? How would we know? Would you be able to tell if you read him again?"

"Yes. I think so, but if it was Faniel I wouldn't be able to break it."

"Would Faniel do that for Murphy? Or would Murphy do it for himself because he thinks your ability has been cut off?"

"Impossible to know. I'll only find out when I read him."

"Then that needs to happen. I'll talk to him tonight. I don't think he'll be happy at the thought that he might have been done again."

"He may not have been, but we have to know."

As we drove back to the lab, I thought about what Mike could have learned from me since we were at Murphy's place. I was pretty sure that the only thing he could pass on to Murphy was that I had got my talent back; that would lose the element of surprise but wasn't a big problem for me. More of a problem could be anything Sharon may have said about Besian and his crew. All things considered it would be better if he was clean.

"I'll be late back," said Sharon as she dropped me off. "But I'll make sure Mike is around for you to read."

I went back to my reactions and fretted over how much Mike could give away until it was time to head to Sharon's to start dinner. She was late as predicted, though it didn't matter as I had made Irish stew and just kept it simmering. Mike arrived about twenty minutes later looking agitated.

"Do you really think he could have put that on me again?" he said as soon as he saw me. "I don't remember him touching me."

"You wouldn't," I said. "He can make you forget it happened. Let's find out. Give me your hand."

He reached out his left hand and I took it. It took moments to what I needed.

"You're clean," I said. "At least from anything done by Peter Murphy. I don't know if I would recognise a compulsion set by Lord Faniel."

He sighed and sat down heavily on the couch then, to my surprise, began to cry. Sharon came and put her arms around him. I went to the kitchen to give them space. When I returned, he was more composed.

"Thank you, Charlie," he said. "That's a huge relief. It scares the shit out of me to think that he might be able control me again. Last time nearly did for me."

"No need to thank me," I said. "We're in this together. It just shows why Murphy has to be brought down."

I woke on Friday morning with Jack's uncle's song running through my head. I couldn't do anything about it until later on Saturday, but I was curious to see who would appear with him this time.

The song was still there on Saturday morning; not strong but nagging at me throughout Prof's group meeting and the bus journey to Langley. I got to the cottage in time for lunch, then

Michelle and I headed out for the gateway as mother went off to work.

"My bet is the Queen," said Michelle. "After what the king said about the ice cream."

"Very possible. I hope she tones down the glamour from last time." I remembered her striking appearance with the ailing king out at Netley Marsh. "Or we're going to get a lot of attention."

Michelle was right. I had barely got halfway through the song before Jack's uncle appeared with two women. I recognised the Queen by her silver hair, though it was rather shorter than last time, and she didn't glow. She had dressed down from the flowing white gown to a plain green dress but still looked strikingly attractive. Even though I knew it was a glamour I was impressed. The second woman I did not know. She was more plainly dressed, and I think her face was her own; either that or I was strong enough to see past her glamour.

"Welcome back, your majesty," I said as she looked at me. She reached out a hand to me and I took it.

"My dear boy," she said in my mind. "I am so glad to see you unharmed. We are deeply ashamed of the deeds of Faniel."

The memory of the pain pulsed through my mind.

"I am deeply sorry that this happening to you," she said. "He assured us he would do nothing against you. We no longer recognise the son we raised. I fear for our people when he becomes king. He will bring division and bloodshed."

"Is there no way of stopping him coming over?" I said, thinking of the compulsion that had been put on Jack.

"Even if such a thing could be done, too many of the Great stand with him. They would remove it."

So much for that idea then, and I had nothing more to offer.

"Be sure that we will confine him if we can find a way," she said. "We came to see the wonders." That came as no surprise. "Era here is the mistress of the household. She wishes to see the box that keeps things cold."

That at least was something I could do easily. I expected they would want to try ice cream and chocolate, too.

"Yes. Those, too." She smiled at me and released my hand.

We walked back to mother's cottage with the three Otherkin chattering away in their strange liquid tongue. They clustered around Michelle's Polo with Jack's uncle pointing out parts, presumably explaining what it does, then nearly got wiped out as a car came around the bend. We chivvied them inside with the promise of a ride later.

We took them through to the kitchen, both ladies observing everything very closely. The queen took my hand again.

"Which is the box that keeps things cold?"

I took her over to the fridge and opened it. She and Era took a sharp step back as the light came on then looked at the contents cautiously. I reached in and took out a container of milk and held it out to Era. She took it and her face lit up, she said something to the Queen that I didn't understand.

The Queen turned to me. "This needs iron to make it work?"

"Yes, this one does."

She pursed her lips. "It would be so useful to us."

Era put the milk back, picked up a red pepper and examined it. She put that back and picked up a cherry tomato, giving it equal scrutiny.

"Tell her to try it," I said to the Queen.

The queen spoke to Era. Era brought it to her mouth, sniffed it and very cautiously bit into it. She gave a little squeak of delight and broke into a smile. She held out the tub of tomatoes to the Queen and said something to her. Probably "you should try one." The queen glanced at me as if seeking approval.

"Go ahead."

She carefully selected one and brought it to her lips. She glanced at me again then bit into it. Just like Era she smiled.

"That is...unlike anything I have ever tasted," she said. "But I like it. What is it?"

"We call them tomatoes," I replied. "They're easy to grow." That is to say mother could get them to grow, I couldn't.

"I would like to grow these."

"I can get seeds anytime, or small plants at the right time of year."

"That would be very much appreciated." She released my hand and turned her attention to a tub of hummus that Era was examining.

"Remind me to buy tomato seeds for the queen," I said to Michelle, who was watching with amusement.

"She likes them then?" Michelle grinned.

"Oh yes."

Era and the Queen spent another ten minutes investigating the contents of the fridge before turning their attention to the rest of the kitchen. After a few minutes the queen took my hand again and asked, "where is your cooking fire?"

I brought her over to the electric hob cooker, Era followed. I turned on a hotplate and they watched, fascinated, as it began to glow red. The Queen and Era had a short conversation, presumably about the cooker.

"This works by the same power as the box?" the Queen asked.

"Yes. There is an oven here heated the same way." I opened the oven door.

"So it needs iron?"

"Yes, it does."

"Then we cannot have these things, wondrous as they are." There was an edge of disappointment in her words. "Show us something we can have. What is that wondrous food I've been told about?"

That had to be either chocolate or ice cream, we had neither in the house so a trip to the beach was in order. We all crammed into the Polo with me in the back between Era and the Queen. They took a bit of a fright at the noise on starting, but quickly settled down to enjoy the ride over to Calshot.

I expected the beach to be busy as it was a nice sunny day, and I was right. We got lucky in the car park as we caught someone just leaving and grabbed their space and then made for the cafe. I had expected the Queen's attention to be caught by the wide expanse of the Solent, the kite surfers or the sailing yachts; I was wrong. What took her eye was the swimwear worn by the women on the beach. It was warm, and there were a lot of ladies in bikinis, though no one topless that I could see.

The Queen gripped my hand. "How can they show themselves like that?" I could feel her shock and was at a loss to reply.

"That's just what people wear," I said.

"They might as well be naked. I don't like this at all. I wouldn't dress like that."

There really was no safe answer to that so I decided to bail out. "I'll get the ice creams." I let go of her hand and went to join the queue leaving her to talk to Era and Jack's uncle. When I returned with the ice creams, she was deep in conversation with Era and from their expressions finding a lot of agreement. Jack's uncle received his cone with great enthusiasm. The ladies looked at theirs with suspicion until Jack's uncle spoke to them. I watched as they took a trial lick and their faces lit up with delight. I had bought large cones, so the next five minutes were occupied with their consumption.

"That was everything I was told it was and more," said the Queen. "But I expect the making of it involves iron somewhere."

"Same as the cold box, I'm afraid," I said. I know roughly how a fridge works; it needs something to drive the compressor and that usually means electric motors and magnetic materials, but maybe anything that turns a shaft could do it. Did they have watermills over there? Something to think about.

"If we could make it," said the Queen. "I would have it every day. But perhaps it would not taste so good to me then."

"It would not be good for your teeth," I replied.

When they had all finished and wiped their hands with tissues Michelle conjured from her bag, we walked along the beach a bit.

Jack's uncle was particularly taken with the kite surfers.

"That looks difficult," he said, taking my hand. "My sons, I think, would like that and I would like to try."

"I think the equipment does not need iron," I said. "It might be possible to bring it through the portal."

"But we have only a small lake, no open water like this."

"No coastline at all? How big is your land? I know very little about the world through the portal."

"A man might ride from one end to the other inside two days."

"What's at the edges?"

"Hills and more woods as far as you can see."

"What about the rivers that flow through the land, where do they go?"

"The same, more woods and hills. The occasional lake."

That just sounded weird to me, but then there was a lot I didn't understand about over there. In fact, there wasn't much I did understand. The Queen called Jack's uncle over then, so he released my hand ending the conversation, and shortly after we turned back to the car. Michelle and I walking behind them as I filled Michelle in on what had been said. Their discussion continued as Michelle drove us back to the cottage. They declined to come in and we walked with them, still chattering away, back to the portal.

The Queen took my hand when we reached the portal. "Thank you for showing us around. The ice cream alone makes it worthwhile. I would be very happy to see you again on our side."

"And you didn't get to try chocolate," I said. "I will bring some with me next time."

"You will be our honoured guest."

She released my hand and three of them passed through the portal.

"What did she say?" asked Michelle after they had vanished into the blue.

"She loves the ice cream, and we're very welcome to visit."

"That's nice, but I'd feel a lot better about going if they had Lord Faniel locked up."

"That won't happen. She said he still has too much support."

"Then I'm not going and nor should you."

That was fine by me; I had no intention of going anywhere near Lord Faniel until I had to.

I caught the early bus into town and got into the lab before Prof. I had left a cyclisation reaction running using the new conditions Prof had brought back from the conference, and I wanted to see what it had done. The first good sign was that it had not boiled dry and had changed colour. I took a small sample, set up a tlc and a LCMS run then went to get coffee.

When I returned there was a major new spot on the tlc and a decent size peak in the LCMS with the correct molecular weight. Fireworks started going off in my brain, but I knew better than to go and tell Prof. He would only tell me to isolate and characterise it, so I got on with that.

I columned it on silica with a long shallow gradient, that produced a lot of fractions to analyse and vac down. That took me until past six before I had thirty-seven milligrams of product clean enough to characterise. I made up the samples for the overnight NMR runs, then realised I needed to shop if I wanted to eat that evening as Sharon was most unlikely to have bought anything. As I was so late, I bought a couple of ready-meal Thai Chicken curries.

All this meant that I didn't get back to Sharon's until well after eight.

"I was wondering where you'd got to," she said. "I was just going to text you."

"Good day in the lab, so I needed to stay late. I've got dinner."

"Great," she smiled. "Did you bring wine 'cos I have news, too."

I had brought wine. I put the curries in the oven and set the timer then opened the bottle.

"So what's the news?" I asked and passed her a glass.

She took a sip before answering. "Someone hit Peter Murphy's place last night. Thought you might be interested."

I had been expecting something like this but couldn't let her know that. "What do you mean by hit? What happened?"

"Security camera showed four guys in two cars. Went in, shot it up with automatic weapons then torched it."

That certainly sounded like Besian's kind of operation. "What happened to Murphy?" Was it too much to hope they'd killed him?

"Missing. No one's seen him. The security camera goes blank just after the gunmen arrived. There are two bodies in the house, but they're not him."

Maybe Besian's crew grabbed him. "Who do they think did it?"

"Got to be the Albanians in pole position." She took a larger sip of wine.

I was happy she mentioned them first.

"We know they've got access to automatic weapons, and they've certainly got history with Murphy," she continued. "First place I'd look."

"Do you think they've taken Murphy?"

"No. I reckon he's gone to ground. Wouldn't you if they were after you?"

"Maybe he went through a portal to get away from them like I did to get away from his guys."

"You think he can do that?"

"Maybe. We don't know how much he can do. What happens next?"

"We have two bodies so it's a murder investigation, big one. Nothing to do with me, though. It'll be run out of Portsmouth. I expect Mike will have a part in it because of his investigation into Murphy. NCA might finally get into gear and take a slice of it."

"That should put the Albanians out of business permanently then." Which would be a pretty decent outcome. I still wanted something permanent for Murphy if he had survived.

"I wouldn't be so certain," said Sharon. "They've put a lot of effort into establishing their position here. You think they're going to endanger that by pulling this one stunt? I'll bet they contracted it out. Besian and his crew will all have solid alibis for last night, and the contractors are already out of the country. It'll make them keep their heads down, though." She held out her glass for a refill. "At least if the NCA get involved there'll be resources to mount a long-term operation against them."

That all seemed credible, if a bit disappointing. It wasn't the wipeout I had wanted, but it would certainly make life more difficult for them, and if Peter Murphy had survived, I couldn't believe he wouldn't retaliate. It still felt like a win.

The timer on the oven buzzed and turned our thoughts to dinner.

Next morning's meeting with Prof was one of the best I've had. He took a long time going over the proton and 13C NMR data I had gathered on the new product but was convinced I had made what I thought I had.

"This is an excellent piece of work, Charlie. It'll make a good communication in Organic Letters, and a short talk for you at a symposium" he said. "Now you need to see if it scales and try it with more substitution on the substrate."

This was the first time he'd mentioned a talk at a symposium, and I was pleased even though my stomach turned over at the thought of presenting in public. I agreed about the next steps, and I told him about the plans I had for making more substituted materials to put through the reaction. He agreed with them and made a couple of suggestions of how to make the molecules.

"If those work, and I see no reason why they should not," he said. "Then that is a paper fit for a good journal like Angewandte and a substantial portion of your thesis. I understand that you're doing important work elsewhere, Charlie, but I hope you will be able to find the time to complete this. You have a good future ahead of you."

I headed back to the lab with a renewed sense of purpose, then my phone rang. It was Nigel.

"Have you got a couple of hours?" he asked. "At your usual rate."

Despite wanting to get on with the project I said yes; after all, he was paying.

"I'll pick you up in forty minutes," he said.

"Fine. I'll be in the foyer of the department." I wondered what he had this time, probably another Jihadist. I took my spectra back to my desk then decided to head for the tearoom; there was time for coffee before he arrived.

He was five minutes late when he pulled up in the same silver Focus looking as nondescript as ever in the same plain suit.

"Just down to Civic Centre this time," he said as I fastened my seatbelt. No greeting, or "how are you?" and no conversation during the drive. I knew better than to ask him what today's job was.

He drove as calmly as usual down to the Civic Centre. We parked in the visitors' area and went into the station. Nigel showed a pass to the desk sergeant who let us both in as before without any questions or signing in, and then took us down to the custody suite. The sergeant stopped at a cell door, the name on the chalkboard was Mohamed Hussain, another Jihadist then. The sergeant unlocked the door. I followed Nigel into the cell and to my utter surprise I recognised the plump young Asian guy sitting on the bed. He was a second-year chemistry student I had taught in the undergraduate organic practical labs.

"Hello, Charlie," he said. "What are you doing here?"

Nigel turned to stare at me, for once his calm disturbed. "You know him?"

After a couple of seconds paralysis my brain engaged. "I've come to help you, Mo."

I reached out a hand to him, and after a moment he took it. I dived into his mind, and his confusion washed over me. I guess I was hoping to find this was a mistake since he had been a friendly and engaged student, but no mistake had been made. It was all there: closed Jihadi forums, prayer meetings with sermons from radical imams, contacts with Islamic State recruiters, and a splinter group of the university Islamic Society. Nigel had the right guy. I collected usernames, passwords, and contacts then added two compulsions; the first to forget he'd seen me, the second to see the same fiery angel that I had used with Tareena. Then I pulled out leaving him glassy-eyed.

Nigel banged on the cell door, it opened, and we left without speaking. The sergeant took us to an empty interview room and left us. Nigel took out his phone and laid it on the table. Speaking slowly and clearly, I went through all that I had found. Nigel listened silently; for all his expression changed I could have been reading out a shopping list. When I'd finished, he picked the phone and stopped the recording.

"Hussain recognised you. Is that going to be a problem?"

"No. He's not going to remember what happened."

"You're sure of that?"

"Yes."

He looked at me for a moment as if he was going to ask how I could be so sure, but then changed his mind. "Then we've finished here. I'll take you back to the University."

Nigel said nothing during the drive back. He paid me in cash for an hour and a half.

"Thank you, Charlie," he said as he handed over the money. "That was useful as always. I suspect I'll be seeing you again soon."

I got out of the car and watched him drive off feeling pleased with myself and a hundred and twenty quid better off. It wasn't until I got back to the lab that it occurred to me that I had shown him I could do more than just read people's minds.

I worked late again, working towards re-staging my successful cyclisation reaction with a more complex substrate and, after a brief trip to the supermarket, I didn't get back to Sharon's flat until gone eight. Mike Scott was there, and he caught me for a chat in the kitchen while Sharon was in the shower.

"I had a call from Peter Murphy today," he said, quietly even though we could hear the shower running. My first reaction was disappointment that they hadn't killed him.

"Where is he?" I asked. Brazil might be far enough away.

"He didn't say. Just said that he had gone to ground. Wanted to know who we thought was behind the hit."

"What did you tell him?"

"Told him we think it was the Albanians. He still thinks I'm under a compulsion remember. Then he asked where to find them, but I couldn't tell him 'cos, other than that cafe, we don't know."

I did. I knew where Besian had a swanky flat in Ocean Village with a girlfriend installed. I'd picked it out of out his mind when I put the compulsion on him. I thought he thoroughly deserved a visit from Murphy's crew, but there was no way for me to tell Mike without giving myself away.

"What'll he do if he finds them?"

"He didn't say but it won't be gentle. His girlfriend was killed in the hit."

Peter Murphy tried to have me killed so he can go to hell by the most direct route. His girlfriend cannot have been ignorant of what he was so my sympathy for her was limited, too, but Besian was just pure evil.

"Give me your hand," I said.

"What for?"

"Just trust me."

He held out his hand. I took it and slipped into his mind, planting the location of Besian's flat and leaving a little compulsion so that he would pass on the information and not remember this. It was done in seconds.

He looked at me slightly confused. "What were we talking about?"

He went to the fridge. "Do you want a drink while we're waiting, there's white wine here."

I did, to celebrate the progress with my chemistry if nothing else. Mike poured me a glass and one for himself.

"How would you feel about doing a favour for a colleague of mine?" he asked.

"What sort of favour?"

"Extracting a bit of information from someone who doesn't want to give it."

"Who is the someone?"

"A shop owner who is selling black market cigarettes and tobacco. Trading Standards busted a few, but they just paid the fine and carried on. Even the ones that had their liquor licences revoked changed their ownership details and reapplied. We want the people supplying them."

"So you want me to find out about the suppliers?" That sounded simple enough, and it's always good to have a copper who owes you a favour.

"Right. There's no risk to it. I'll show you the shop. You just go in, do what you do, and I'll be waiting outside."

"OK. When?"

"Some time when the place is quiet, want to go in when he's there, not his wife or nieces. Fairly early would be best."

Not so good; some of these shops opened really early, but I'd committed myself.

"Can't do tomorrow morning," Mike said. "Thursday's

good."

I couldn't think of a reason why not beyond laziness. "OK. Thursday."

"Six thirty?"

"Fine." It wasn't, but I'd dug my own grave.

Six thirty Thursday morning came too early. Mike was on time as he'd stayed over with Sharon. The morning traffic was still fairly light as we headed through town, across the Itchen and on to Sholing; another part of Southampton I knew nothing about. It was just before seven when we pulled up at a short row of businesses: an Indian takeaway, kebab shop, hair salon, and a tattoo parlour. Only the One-Stop Store at the end was open. We sat watching for five minutes; no one went in or out.

"Looks quiet enough," said Mike. "Put a hat on for the CCTV."

I hadn't brought one, so he gave me his. I got out of the car and walked purposefully to the shop. Despite its narrow frontage the interior went a long way back with packed shelves and chilled cabinets. I glanced at the middle-aged Asian guy behind the counter; he looked much like the picture Mike had shown me. I went to one of the chilled cabinets, selected a can of Coke and walked back with the can. I laid a fiver on the counter. As the shopkeeper went to pick it up, I caught his hand and slipped into his mind.

I had had enough practice to make it easy. I compelled him to write down the phone number he called to order the cigarettes, the name to use, and how much to pay. Then I made him wipe the CCTV memory and forget this had ever happened. I took my change and walked back to the car.

"Job done," I said to Mike passing him the paper. "This has all the major info. They call this number to order; the cigarettes are delivered by a guy in a van. The courier is paid in cash."

"Good man," said Mike looking at the paper. "I see this gets to the right hands. I owe you."

I opened the can of Coke; I felt like I'd earned it.

I took the bus out to Langley on Saturday after Prof's group meeting as had become my routine in a positive frame of mind. Prof was happy that my chemistry was moving forward, Peter Murphy had bigger things to concern himself with than me, being at war with the Albanians, and Dave the Troll was out of Michelle's life. That left only Lord Faniel and the awkward issue of Michelle being my half-sister. Lord Faniel was a long-term problem, but Michelle was very much on my mind. Things were going great with her, but I still didn't know if she knew. I knew it was something we should talk about, but I was totally committed, and the thought that she might be disgusted by it terrified me.

I was looking forward to a quiet weekend. No summoning songs were in my mind, so I had no need to be a tour guide. Michelle was intending on trying out a new dish on me which sounded exciting. She had really got into cooking since she had moved into the cottage, another example of what a good move it had been for her.

After her initial greeting Michelle showed me a letter that had arrived that morning.

"It's from the lawyer we went to about Mum's estate," she said, sounding anxious. "He says it will cost twelve hundred for him to do the probate."

"That's ridiculous. Her whole estate is hardly worth that, unless she had a Swiss bank account you haven't told me about."

"No. Just her current account, a building society account, and a few hundred in Premium Bonds."

I read through the letter. It was as she said. I had had no dealings with lawyers and knew they were generally regarded as expensive, but that sounded outrageous.

"There must be a cheaper option."

"If you can find one, I'll use it."

We opened up her laptop and started looking for information on estate duties. It rapidly became clear that we did not need to pay a lawyer to do this for us. The forms could be downloaded and there was a guide with online videos on how to fill them in.

"I think we can do this ourselves," I said. "She didn't have any property or shares or anything like that so most of the sections don't apply and can be left blank. It should be easy enough."

We printed off the forms and started to watch the videos, then Mother arrived back from her shift. Michelle disappeared off to the kitchen to start on her new dish for dinner, mother went for a shower, and I finished watching the videos. It still looked easy enough. If I can analyse scientific papers and patents, then surely I could do this.

Michelle's new dish was duck à l'orange which worked really well, and she was very pleased with. I would very happily eat it again and told her so. After dinner we chilled out and watched rubbish TV for the rest of the evening.

Neither Michelle nor mother were working the next day, which was forecast to be warm and sunny, so we went to the beach at Lepe, figuring it would be slightly less crowded than Calshot. It was certainly busy, and with the tide up the shallows were filled with bathers. We passed a pleasant day there, splashed around in the shallows, ate the picnic we had brought, and just relaxed. The Langley Tavern tempted us in for a drink on the way home, so it was mid-evening when we got back. Michelle opened up her laptop to look at the news.

"There's something going on in Southampton," she said after a moment. "It says police are dealing with a major incident in Portswood."

I looked at the report. There were just a couple of lines of the bare details.

"It could be anything," I said, but my immediate thought was to wonder if Peter Murphy had caught up with Besian and his boys. If he had, then I would be hearing about it soon.

Soon was Monday afternoon when I got a call from Sharon. "Can you do a trip to the mortuary? I think you'll be interested in this one."

"You know I'm not going to say no."

"I pick you up in twenty."

I was itching with curiosity by the time she arrived, but she refused to tell me what was going on.

"I want you to have no preformed ideas with this one," she

said. "I need a clean unbiased response from you."

That just made me more curious, but she wasn't going to say any more, so I shut up and let her drive. She sped us through the afternoon traffic to the General. We parked up and went to the mortuary to be greeted by the ever-present Sanjay. He nodded at me as we walked in.

"Good morning, Sergeant. I've been expecting you. Which one are you looking at?"

That caught my attention. *So there's more than one.*

"All seven," said Sharon. "He doesn't need to see the faces."

Seven! What on Earth has been going on?

Sanjay walked over to the bank of fridges, opened a door and pulled out a body. He unwrapped a leg and stood back.

"Tell me what happened, Charlie," Sharon said.

I stepped forward, laid my hand on a cold hairy shin and dived in. The first feeling I picked up was complete surprise and confusion. The dead man had had no idea of what was going on. I went deeper to find out more, until I felt Sharon's hand on my arm.

"Time for the next one," she said. Sanjay rewrapped the body while I put my thoughts in order. We took a few steps away so I could tell Sharon my findings out of his hearing.

"Albanian," I said quietly. "Besian's first cousin. Besian shot him, and he didn't know why. He'd known him all his life."

Sharon pursed her lips and nodded slowly. "Good work. Try the next one."

Sanjay had the next one ready for me, so I took hold of another cold leg. This man was much the same, surprised and confused by his execution. As I dug deeper into his memories, I felt no sympathy for him, though. I pulled out and stepped away from the waiting Sanjay to speak to Sharon.

"Same as number one," I said. "Besian accused him of betrayal and shot him."

"Better have a look at Besian then," said Sharon and consulted Sanjay's list. "That's number five please, Sanjay."

Sanjay finished rewrapping the last body, slid it back into the fridge then opened another door. *This will be fascinating* I thought as I approached the body.

It wasn't fascinating, it was deeply confusing and frustrating. Nothing to do with recent events was accessible. Every time I tried to approach the area it all went dark, and nothing I could do illuminated it. Reluctantly I pulled out and stepped away from the body.

"Watcha got?" asked Sharon once we were in the corridor.

"Nothing. It's all hidden from me."

"How come?"

"Compulsion, I think."

"Murphy's work?"

"No. I would recognise one he laid. This was done by someone far more powerful. My guess is Lord Faniel."

"Shit. That just makes things more difficult."

It was hard to disagree with that, and it made me wonder about the relationship between Lord Faniel and Peter Murphy. What was the connection between them? Why would he come over and put compulsions on people for Murphy?

"We're finished here then," said Sharon. "Thank you, Sanjay," she called through the doorway.

I followed her back to the car. We got in but she didn't immediately start the engine, reaching instead into her bag.

"See, I'm still being good," she said pulling out a packet of mints. "This would have been a cigarette a month ago." She took one and sucked on it for a few seconds. "So this is what I've got. Murphy found a way to get to Besian. He takes Lord Faniel with him. Faniel puts a compulsion on Besian to summon his team to the cafe one by one and kill them, then kill himself. Faniel goes back to the other side, Murphy has clean hands, and his opposition are gone. Have I got it all?"

"I think so. I'm not going to cry over Besian and his boys. They were evil bastards and we're well rid of them, but Murphy with Lord Faniel backing him is a problem that's only going to get bigger."

"So can we expect any help from your friends on the other side?"

I remembered the Queen's words: *too many of the Great stand with him*. "They have tried and failed to restrain him."

"Going to be down to us then," Sharon said and started the

engine. "Just like it always is."

Sharon dropped me at the lab, and I went back to work with plenty to think about; top of the list, how to stop Lord Faniel helping Peter Murphy. The King and Queen had clearly failed to stop him from that side so there wasn't anything to be done there. Lord Faniel had already demonstrated that he was much stronger than me, so any direct confrontation was out unless I got help. Or he was weakened; I don't know where that thought sneaked in from but after initially discarding it, I picked it out of the bin and turned it over a few times. I remembered how weak the King had become at the end of his trip to hospital over here. Jack had also said something about the iron in this world weakening him over time, too. Was that something I could use with Lord Faniel? Worth exploring, though there was the sizeable difficulty of capturing him to consider, and then keeping him close to a large lump of iron for several days before he was down to my level. Would anything I did then endure when he regained his strength? I needed help on this, and lots of it.

I told Michelle about it that evening, leaving out my contribution to Murphy finding Besian. She agreed with me that we were well rid of Besian and his gang, even if the actual way Murphy did it was horrific, and that we had to try to find a way of stopping Lord Faniel coming over and dealing with Murphy. I outlined my idea of trying to trap Lord Faniel on this side until he was weak enough for me to put a compulsion on him, but she was doubtful.

"I don't see why he wouldn't be able to throw it off once his strength returned, not unless you can do it so subtly that he doesn't notice it."

"I'm not at all sure I can be that subtle."

"Then get someone else to do it. Toby maybe? Jack will know."

"We need a long talk with Jack this weekend then."

I got an update from Sharon on Thursday evening.

"We got the post-mortem reports, and we were right. They all died of gunshot wounds, and one has all the characteristics of being self-inflicted. The bullets have gone off for ballistics and we all expect that they will be from the same gun. The verdict is murder-suicide, case closed."

"And no link to Murphy?"

"Nothing that would stand up in court, so it's not going anywhere."

"But you, me and Mike all know there is."

"We do, and Mike certainly isn't going to let it go. Don't worry, there's plenty more going on with Murphy. He's on the radar of the NCA now. We'll catch up with him eventually."

I had heard this before and didn't feel any more positive about it now. "He can do a lot of harm before then, especially with Lord Faniel helping him."

"He can, and we'll do what we can to stop him, but it has to be within the law. I know you find that frustrating but stay out of it. You were very lucky last time you went near him. He could have killed you. You know I'll bring you in if there's something you can do, but it's tricky with the NCA involved. There's so much more scrutiny."

What made it more annoying was she was right. Murphy was dangerous, and I'd got too close to the edge with him last time. I should leave them to get on with it and concentrate on Lord Faniel.

"Okay. But don't let him touch anyone, even for a moment," I said. "And bring them to me if he does."

"We'll make sure everybody knows. Mike's not likely to forget. You're not the only one with a personal reason for bringing down Murphy."

M ichelle agreed with Sharon.

"Leave it to the police," she said. Mother was at work, and we were in the sitting room of her cottage. "Have you forgotten how much it hurt last time?"

"No! I haven't." It makes me sick just thinking about it.

"Then stay away from him. We've enough to think about

with Lord Faniel. I'm sure Jack will say the same. I don't ever want to see you in that state again." She sniffed and her eyes started to moisten. I reached out and put my arms around her ending our discussion. I would leave it to the police.

After a pleasant diversion we walked down to our usual spot by the river to try for Jack. It took several passes through his summoning song, with a break for a pair of passing mountain bikers, before he appeared. He greeted Michelle with a hug and me with a firm handshake before Michelle brought out the chocolate.

I recounted all I knew of Lord Faniel's involvement with Peter Murphy and the Albanians while Michelle fed him squares of Fruit and Nut. He nodded sagely as I told the tale, savouring the chocolate.

"Are you sure the compulsion you found was Faniel's work?" he asked when I had finished.

"No! But it wasn't Peter Murphy's. I know his work, and this was far too strong and tight."

He looked thoughtful and took another piece of chocolate, sucked on it for a while then spoke. "Lord Faniel had a visitor from this side recently."

"Murphy?" said Michelle.

"I don't know. All I know is that a man came through a gateway who was confused about where he was, didn't speak our tongue but asked for Faniel."

"That could well be around the time the Albanians hit his house," I said. "We know he said he went to ground. Question is, how did he find a gateway and know how to use it?"

I glanced at Jack; he looked solemn but said nothing.

"It has to be Lord Faniel," I continued. "But why? What's the connection between them? Could Murphy be Faniel's son?"

"I thought he was opposed to men from over there having children with women here," asked Michelle.

"No," said Jack. "He is just opposed to them bringing those children over. That would not stop him finding a lover over here, but I have never heard that he did."

"Perhaps he just hid it well," said Michelle. "You can understand why he would. It wouldn't go down well with his supporters."

"Yes. That is very possible," said Jack. "And would explain the connection which otherwise I cannot."

"Whether that is the connection or not, we need to find a way of stopping him coming over," I said. "Murphy's a major criminal who kills people, and Faniel is deeply involved."

"That's not going to be easy," said Jack. "He has broken his pledge to this father."

"Who is the heir after him?" I asked.

"He has no brothers, nor does the King, so it will be a cousin, but he's not been raised for the position," said Jack. "Why?"

"Maybe we should talk to him. If the police catch Lord Faniel this side it will go very hard with him," I said. "He will not be back for a long time. If he thought this cousin is being lined up to take over from him, it might stop him coming over."

"I doubt Lord Faniel would consider that a serious obstacle," said Jack. "And I doubt he has given your police a second thought."

"He will when they put him in a cell for a few days," I said. "How long would it take for all the power to drain out of him?"

"That's hard to guess at," said Jack. "I certainly notice if I spend a long time here, but I've never been here for many days. He's stronger than me so it would take longer, but after three or four days, I think he would be essentially powerless. Remember how the King was when we brought him back?"

"Would it be sooner if he was close to a lot of iron?" I asked.

"Yes, that'll have a big effect. I notice it with just a short trip in the car."

"So if we catch Lord Faniel on this side and chain him to a big lump of iron then would he get weak enough for you or Charlie to put a compulsion on him," said Michelle.

Jack didn't reply immediately and took another piece of chocolate. He sucked on it before replying. "Yes, I think so."

"What happens when he goes back through the gateway and recovers his strength?" I asked, suddenly nervous; this was the key answer.

Jack again took his time to answer. "I don't know. I have

never heard of this situation."

"Who would know?" asked Michelle.

"I don't think anyone would know for sure," said Jack. "I will ask some of them, but I doubt I'll get a firm answer. Is that your plan then?"

"I wouldn't call it a plan yet, just an idea," I said, embarrassed that I didn't have more substance to offer. "I just wanted to know if the basic idea was flawed."

"You should keep thinking," said Jack. "This sounds very risky."

"Everything's risky with him," said Michelle. "And the biggest risk of all is doing nothing. If he's broken his word to his father about coming over here, then what other promises has he broken?"

"I haven't heard anything to suggest that he's doing anything else," said Jack.

"Perhaps he has learned how to keep his plans quiet," I said. "Would it be so great a surprise for him to be plotting a takeover? How many would truly stand against him? He had a lot of support last time."

"There would be plenty to oppose him."

"Would they be enough?" I asked. "And would they actually do anything?"

"That's hard to know. I think they would. But this is all guesswork."

"It is," I admitted. "But it's based on what I've learned about Lord Faniel, both directly and from you. He's a desperately ambitious bastard who'll stop at nothing to get what he wants and will hurt anyone who gets in his way."

"That is all true," said Jack.

"And we got in his way," said Michelle.

"Yes, we did," said Jack. "And he will not forget that."

"Damn right he won't," I said. "You might think its guesswork, but it will go hard with us if he takes over. He's not a patient man. I expect him to make a move." I don't really know where that intuition came from, but it felt right as soon as I said it.

Jack nodded slowly looking thoughtful. "It could be. I cannot say he will not. I will urge greater vigilance when I return. Now show me your latest glamour."

Recognising the end of the conversation I showed him "old Charlie," embarrassed that I hadn't practised as much as I should.

"You need to practice more," Jack said. He turned to Michelle. "Make him practice. Twice a day."

"Do you really think Lord Faniel will try to take over?" said Michelle as we walked back to the cottage.

"The more I think about it, the more likely it seems," I said. "He was humiliated by what happened, and I reckon he wants revenge big-time. Anyone who stood against him is going to be made to suffer for it."

"And Jack is top of the list. He seems very relaxed about it."

"He does, and that worries me."

Just then her phone pinged with an incoming message. She pulled it out and looked at it.

"Dave's got a new girlfriend," she said. "Looks like I've got rid of the bastard then."

"Who says?"

"Becky. She's Liam's girlfriend. She's not really a friend. I think she wanted to get a reaction out of me." She quickly typed out a reply as we walked.

"What did you say?"

"She has my sympathies." She grinned at me.

I gave the Lord Faniel problem a lot of thought during the next two days but came up with nothing. I wondered how long we had before he moved; that he would move seemed a near certainty. In the meantime, I was preparing the components to test my cyclisation with more substituted substrates. This should give more information about the reaction mechanism, make it more generally useful and a stronger publication. It could also make the reaction go in reduced yield or stop it dead; it is amazing how much difference a methyl group can make in the right (or wrong) place.

I was vaccing down the product from such a reaction when

Nigel called just after lunch on Tuesday.

"Do you have time to talk today?" he asked.

I thought about it a moment. I wanted to get on with the chemistry, but this sounded important; Nigel was too busy to do social calls. "I can make time."

"I can be there in half an hour; would that suit you?"

He must want something fairly urgently. "That's alright with me. I'll meet you in the foyer."

I had just enough time to finish vaccing down the product, make up a sample of it, and add it to the queue on the NMR machine. Nigel arrived in the foyer moments after me wearing the same plain suit. At least his shirt was different this time; a daring shade of pale blue rather than white.

"Is there anywhere quiet we can talk?" he asked.

At this time of day, the seminar rooms were usually empty, so I bagged one of those.

"Thank you, Charlie," he said once I'd closed the door and sat down. "I want to talk to you about the last two people you saw for us."

It took a moment to remember; I'd had a lot going on. "Mo and Tareena?"

"Yes. Those two." I noted that he didn't take his phone out to record the conversation. "Their engagement with the deradicalisation programme has been remarkable. The best responses we've had, which seemed too much of a coincidence until I recalled that Mohammed Husain recognised you. You said it would not be a problem, which leads me to believe that you did something more to him than just extract information. Is that so, Charlie? Is there more you can do?"

He had me bang to rights, but his tone was interested not accusative, so I decided to come clean. "Yes. I can do more. I gave them both a vision of an angel denouncing them as heretics, and I made Mo Husain forget he'd seen me."

Nigel nodded slowly. "And is that the extent of it, or can you do more? If you have further abilities, they could be very useful to us. Obviously, we would pay an enhanced rate for this."

I liked the sound of an enhanced rate. "What sort of things

would you want?"

"We been able to do a lot with the information you've given us, but there's no substitute for someone on the ground. Could you help us with that? You would be working with people who've committed to going on Jihad."

"Have the angel tell them to work for you?"

"Essentially yes. If you can do that."

"Isn't that putting them in danger?"

"These are people who have already decided they will die for a cause," said Nigel. "You've seen something of what we are facing, and we've been able to frustrate a lot of plans, but we only have to fail once, and people will die. You would be saving lives, possibly many lives."

I thought about Ifti the headbanger's plans to bomb pubs I go to. He would have killed dozens of people on a Friday or Saturday night and glorified in his cause. The people who set him up for it would rejoice and create more like him. I remembered how he felt about the people around him and decided I didn't owe him, or others like him, anything.

"I think I can do that." In fact, it should be easy. A straightforward obey compulsion like Peter Murphy used on Mike Scott would do it, but I was sure that with a bit of thought I could come up with something more elegant.

"I'm glad to hear that. Would you be available tomorrow? It will need several several hours of your time."

Tomorrow? He must have been confident I would agree and several hours sounded like a lot of money. "If it's OK with my professor."

"I'll talk to him directly. I'm sure he'll appreciate the importance of it."

Which meant there was no way Prof would object. "What time tomorrow?"

"Can you be here for eight? We have a fair distance to go."

Earlier than usual, but not a problem. "Sure. Do I need to bring anything?"

"I don't think so. The facility is well-equipped, and there's a reasonable canteen for lunch." Nigel stood up. "I'll see you tomorrow."

As usual he did not shake hands. I saw him out then went to see if my NMR had run.

I had the rest of the day to think about what I was going to do. It was good to know that the fiery angel had been effective on Mo and Tareena, so I didn't intend to change much; just refine it a bit. It would still denounce them as a heretic, then add that they were far down the road to hell and unless they worked to destroy the enemies of God they had so foolishly joined with, then they would never know God's favour. This assumed that they were believers, but every jihadist I had encountered so far had been, though it was a small sample.

I didn't tell Sharon about it; she was late in anyway and bitching about the IPCC. I poured her a glass of wine, fed her, and listened without comment to her complaints. She did mention that the ballistic results had confirmed what they thought, which meant the official line was that the case was closed.

"We all know Murphy's involved, but we don't have anything we can use," she said. "Yet."

I left that there. I knew Peter Murphy was in the system now and they would bring him down eventually. I had other priorities right now, like Lord Faniel.

I got to the department well before eight, but Nigel was there ahead of me. He was wearing the same shirt; that made me think he had stayed locally and underlined how important I had become to them. He greeted me with a business-like "good morning," but said nothing more as we walked to his Focus in the visitors' car park. We got in and he drove off heading towards the M3.

It was peak rush hour so I could understand Nigel needing to concentrate on his driving. The traffic eased off once we were past the A34 junction, but he still didn't talk.

I asked him where we were going and got a terse "South-East London" and nothing more. I gave up; South-East London was at least an hour and a half away, so I sat back and tried to doze.

It was ten thirty by the dashboard clock when I woke up. The Queen Elizabeth II Bridge was visible behind Nigel's shoulder as we turned off the approach road onto the A206 heading for Thamesmead. I had no idea where we were going until we turned into an entrance road with a sign for HMP Belmarsh and Courts. I figured we weren't going to the court. We parked up in the Visitors' Car Park and walked to the main entrance.

After a brief consultation, Nigel's ID got us an escort straight past security, down a corridor, and into a small waiting room with a coffee machine. We both had a coffee while our subject was made ready for us.

"Is today's subject as religiously motivated as the others were?" I asked Nigel.

He took his time over answering, no doubt considering his words carefully. "He has spent months arguing with the imams in the deradicalisation programme and has not moved his position a millimetre. For every verse they quote he has an answering verse. It is reported that he reads Islamic scriptures all the time in his cell."

So deeply religious; the fiery angel for him then.

"Excellent," I said. "That'll assist my approach."

"Good. My colleagues will be very interested to see how this plays out. He is very influential among the jihadi prisoners here."

"It will be interesting to see how the other prisoners react," I said. "Do you want him to talk to them about it?"

"No, they have channels that can pass on information about any changes. He would be blown before we even started."

"That would be inconvenient." *Just as well he mentioned it. I'll need to include an instruction for him to keep his revelation to himself then.* "I'll make sure he doesn't talk about it."

A prison officer appeared at the door to tell us the prisoner was ready for us. We followed him through a security door, up a set of stairs, and through another security door. Finally, we were brought into a small plain room that smelled slightly of bleach, the officer who had brought us standing with his back to the door. The prisoner was standing against the far wall flanked by two further officers, both big guys. Dressed in grey sweatshirt and pants, he was about my height and glared at us from behind a heavy beard.

"I will remember you," he snarled. "My brothers will take your heads."

He didn't move, though, and I realised he was handcuffed to the officers.

"Are you ready?" Nigel said to me.

"Yes." I stepped forward. The prisoner spat at me, and the officers yanked violently on his arms to keep him off balance as he tried to kick. The only bare skin accessible was his face so I grabbed for his right ear. He twisted his head and tried to bite me. I caught his ear then pushed into his mind through the surface of anger and hate. There had been plenty of time last night to formulate my compulsion and it was easy enough to add an injunction to secrecy. I wrapped it up tight and sealed it, then withdrew making sure he would not remember even being in this room. I did not bother to learn his name.

I let go of his ear and stepped back with all three officers looking at me with varying degrees of incomprehension.

"Done?" asked Nigel.

"Yes," I said, feeling pretty pleased with my work.

"Let's go then." Nigel nodded to the officer who had brought us in. The officer stepped away from the door to let us leave then tracked us to the security doors and punched in the code to get us through. He brought us back to the security check at the main entrance, we were waved through and left without a word.

"Did you achieve what you wanted to?" asked Nigel as we walked to the car park.

"Yes," I said. "He will become keen to cooperate within a couple of days. He won't tell his jihadi mates, and he won't remember being in that room."

"Good!" He sounded genuinely pleased. "We'll pay you when he does. If you give me your bank details, I'll have in transferred."

I'd been so caught up in getting the compulsion right that I'd forgotten they were paying me. I glanced at my watch, already midday.

"I look forward to it," I said. "What are we doing for lunch?"

Lunch was burger and chips bought from the motorway services and eaten in the car on the M25 as Nigel wanted to get me back to the lab and him on his way before the rush hour traffic. He was successful in that. I was back in the lab before four and he was on his way to wherever. I didn't have time to put on the next reaction in the sequence, but at least I could set up one to make more starting materials - you always need more starting materials. I did that then went shopping for dinner.

Mike Scott came around after dinner and grabbed a word with me while Sharon was in the bathroom.

"You remember that little job you did with the shopkeeper over the dodgy cigarettes?"

"Yes."

"Thought you'd want to know what you got was very helpful. We're raiding the suppliers and could do with you along. Have you the time?"

That sounded interesting. "When?"

"Saturday."

"What time?" I said, thinking of Prof's group meeting.

"Want to be at the site before midday. They're expecting a truck in the afternoon. We could be in for a wait; you might want to bring a book."

Still more interesting than Prof's group meeting, and I didn't have anything new to present anyway. "I'm in, if you explain to my Professor."

"No problem. I'll text you a pickup time."

The sound of the toilet flush ended the conversation. Clearly, he didn't want Sharon to know about this; I didn't know why.

I had expected that Mike would pick me up from Sharon's place, or even stay over on Friday night, but his text gave me a pickup point a couple of streets away. Saturday morning was grey and damp so walking to meet him in the rain was not the best start to the day. He was late as well.

"We're keeping this secret from Sharon then?" I said as we

headed off up Hill Lane in a plain grey Mondeo.

"She doesn't want too many people to know about you," he said.

"I can see the logic in that." Even though a number of senior police officers must know about me, along with a bunch of spooks.

"Yeah. But sometimes if you want favours from people you have to offer them back."

"So what favour am I doing today?"

"Finding who the top man is. There's serious money moving around in this, and we want the guys at the top. They probably won't be there today, but they'll have a man on the ground. That's who you're looking for."

"OK. Should be able to handle that."

From Hill Lane we took Winchester Road then Basset Avenue heading towards the M3. Not going anywhere in Southampton then. At Winchester Mike turned off the motorway onto the A31. We went past Alresford then took a minor road off a roundabout heading into the country.

"Where are we going?" I asked.

"They've got a shed on a little industrial estate just up here. We'll go past the turnoff then park up. It's pretty quiet on a weekend so we can't go in until the truck turns up."

Mike slowed as we went past a wide gravel track with a half a dozen business signs on a wooden post pointing up it.

"That's it up there," he said.

I could see a collection of industrial buildings a couple of hundred yards along it. We drove past then pulled into a wide gateway a few hundred yards on. There was one other car there already, a silver-grey BMW with three men in it. Mike got out and went to talk to the guys in the BMW. They appeared to know each other so I assumed they were police. I pulled out the book I'd brought with me, "The Girl with All the Gifts" and tried to remember where I'd got to.

After a few pages Mike came back.

"All set," he said. "We've got a couple of spotters watching the yard. The reception crew are up there. There's only one way in. We've got a vanload of uniform just up the road, a couple of

HMRC lads and a couple of dog units in case anyone tries to go cross-country. All we need now is the truck."

Mike wandered back to the BMW, and I went back to the book.

The truck showed up after about sixty pages. There was a flurry of activity by the BMW; police baseball caps were donned, and I could see across the fields a plain white canvas-sided truck making its way up the gravel track.

The BMW started up, and Mike hurried back to our Mondeo. A marked Police minibus packed with coppers came down the road at speed followed by an unmarked Astra. The BMW pulled out behind them. My stomach tightened in anticipation as Mike started up and followed at a more sedate pace.

The truck was parked next to an ugly industrial shed with its rear doors open; up close I could see it had Slovak plates. Two plain-clothes guys were in the body looking at the cargo; HMRC I presumed. The police had half a dozen guys lying face-down in the yard. Two of the BMW guys were armed and had their guns drawn, the third one was searching them one by one for weapons. Four of the uniformed officers were legging it across an adjacent field after another guy. As I watched, a police dog unit appeared at the far end of the field. The dog was released, and the fugitive collared in less than a minute.

"Looks like we got the lot," said Mike.

One of the armed men turned and waved us over.

"Let's see who's the boss," said Mike as he opened the car door. "Make it look like you're just talking to them."

With them face-down there were no clues as to who looked the boss, so I went to the nearest guy. He wore a dark fleece and tracksuit bottoms and his hair had flecks of grey. He turned his head to look at me as I put my feet down next to him.

"Keep still," growled the armed copper standing a couple of yards back.

I knelt down and put my hand on his neck below the ear. This close he smelled of old cigarettes. I entered his mind; it was immediately clear that he was not the man we wanted. I pulled away and stood up.

"Slovak truck driver," I said quietly to Mike. "Doesn't know what the cargo was. Totally confused by what's going on."

"Not interested in this guy," said Mike to the armed copper.

I moved on to the next man as the truck driver got to his feet and was hustled away by a uniformed copper.

The next man didn't know much more, but at least he knew who was in charge.

"Brian," I said quietly to Mike. "We're looking for Brian, he's the boss."

With them face down it was initially tricky to spot Brian. I had a picture of him wearing a blue beanie, but none of them were. I walked up the line and found him holding his beanie in one hand leaving his bald patch exposed. I knelt down and placed my hand on the back of his thick neck. He flinched to my touch.

"Hold still," I said and pushed into his mind.

I got a surprise. I had expected to be able to find all the details of who was running the show and where the money went but I couldn't. It was all wrapped up out of reach behind a compulsion. I knew who had laid that compulsion, too.

I pulled out and walked away from the prisoners.

Mike followed. "What have you got?"

"Peter Murphy. Everything Brian knows about this show is wrapped up in a compulsion, and I recognise Lord Faniel's style."

//I can't figure it," said Mike as we headed back toward the M3. "Why would Murphy be involved in this? He's got his operation and he doesn't need a sideshow."

I had been thinking about that, too. "Maybe he saw a profitable little operation on his doorstep and just took it over. Kept the original people running it but took a chunk of the profits."

"So it may originally have been Brian's operation?"

"Could be, or it could be someone else. Whatever, he is important enough that Murphy needed to control him and used Faniel to do it."

"Why didn't he do it himself?"

"Who knows? But it gives you another angle to get to him.

You won't get anything from Brian, though. He's wrapped up tight."

"Old-fashioned police work," said Mike. "His phone and his bank accounts will give us enough and tie him to Murphy now we know to look for the connection."

"Just warn anyone going to arrest Murphy about touching him."

"Yeah. Not sure how I'm going to phrase it, but I need to say something."

I thought they probably wouldn't get to that point for a couple of months, and by then I had a feeling that things would have evolved with Murphy and Lord Faniel.

Mike dropped me back in the centre of town and I caught the bus out to Langley. I wasn't really any later than a normal Saturday. Mother was still at work, so Michelle and I had a few hours to ourselves. It wasn't until we were cooking dinner that I told Michelle about the morning's events.

"So is he growing his empire now he can get Lord Faniel to do the compulsions to control them?" Michelle said after I'd told her about Brian.

"Could be," I said. "But we don't know how long he has been controlling Brian. He might just have had Lord Faniel do an improved compulsion."

"Why is Faniel doing it for Murphy? What's the connection?"

"No idea."

"Could Murphy be sending drugs over there?"

That was a possibility I hadn't considered. "Could be. If they love ice cream, then how much more would they love cocaine? It would certainly explain why Lord Faniel is doing stuff for him."

"And Lord Faniel is exactly the sort of person who would use it."

"Yes, he is." I imagined a troop of his cavalry all coked up and charging through the countryside. Not a good thought.

"Something we can ask Jack about tomorrow," said Michelle. "Now pass me the oregano and thyme."

I was asleep on the sofa when a noise woke me. It was still dark, and it took me a few moments to identify what I was hearing. The noise came again; a solid banging from the kitchen. I reached out and groped for the switch to put the table light on and checked my watch; a quarter to two. I made my way slowly to the kitchen. It sounded like someone banging on the back door and I wondered who it could be. Police or any other official would be at the front door and I didn't think Lord Faniel's people would knock. I put on the light and couldn't see anyone through the kitchen window. I took a carving knife from the drawer before unlocking the door. I opened the door a crack to see out. Jack stood in the doorway, behind him Toby and the Queen. This had to be something bad.

I put the knife down and pulled the door wide. The three of them came into the light. Their glamours could not conceal the anxiety on their faces.

"What's happened?" I asked closing the door.

"Lord Faniel has seized the palace," said Jack an edge of anger in his voice. "The King is his prisoner."

I sat them round the kitchen table and put on the kettle. I wasn't sure what to make them, but they looked like they need something warm.

"What's going on?" Mother swathed in a blue dressing-gown and furry slippers came into the kitchen, followed a moment later by Michelle.

"Lord Faniel has taken over," I said.

"How?" said Michelle.

"Just marched into the palace and took over," said Jack. "At least some of the household guards are with them. Toby was out riding with the Queen. One of the grooms rode out to warn them. They came to me. I brought them here. It seemed safer than anywhere over there."

"How much support do they have?" I asked.

"I don't know. I came straight here."

The kettle boiled and mother went to make mugs of hot chocolate. "We'll need more milk tomorrow, Charlie," she said quietly to me.

"I'll shop tomorrow morning," I said as quietly, feeling flush with the Nigel's payment in my bank account.

"We're going to have to rearrange if they're staying."

That would certainly be a problem. I expected the Queen would want her own room. So that was me sleeping in the shed with Jack most likely. I knew Greg had a 4-man tent he used for LARP campaigns, maybe I could borrow that.

I passed around the mugs of chocolate then sat down with mine next to Michelle. Jack and his uncle conversed quietly in their own language, their faces grave. The Queen was quiet and looked dazed.

"You were right," said Michelle quietly, snuggling against me.

"Yeah, wish I wasn't, 'cos I don't know what to do next."

"You don't have to," she replied, looking at Jack and Toby. "I bet that's what they're talking about now."

"You're right, but I'm still worried."

"They'll come up with something." She gave me a squeeze.

"I hope so." Beyond the consequences for over there, it would make Peter Murphy's position stronger if Lord Faniel was King.

When the hot chocolate had been drunk sleeping arrangements were made. The Queen took mother's room, mother went in with Michelle, and I went back to the couch. Jack and Toby gave every sign of staying up all night in the kitchen.

Jack was gone when I woke up. Toby was still around, sitting in the kitchen.

"He has gone to find out what is happening," Toby took my hand and told me. "I remain to look after the Queen."

"They'll be looking for him, won't they? This is dangerous."

"I'm sure they are looking for him, me and the Queen, and it is dangerous. But if we are going to oppose them then we need to know the strength of their support, and ours. Don't worry about Jack. They will find him very difficult to catch."

I remembered how he had got us away from the squad trying to arrest us near his brother's house the first time I went over. I had made the opening, but he had certainly taken his chance smartly enough.

"He is a very resourceful fellow, you have seen this."

I wondered momentarily about the young soldier who had been in command of that patrol. I thought I had hurt him badly.

"Indeed you did. But he put himself in that position."

"Do you have a plan?"

"There can be no plan until we have a lot more information. Now how do we make more of that drink we had last night? The Queen liked it very much."

He released my hand, and I went to fill the kettle from the cold tap, making a mental note to buy more hot chocolate.

He took my hand again. "Where does the water come from?"

As the kettle boiled, I explained about the tank in the attic, fed by the mains supply. I had got halfway through explaining the water supply and sewage system when the kettle boiled. I made mugs of chocolate for the Queen, Toby, and Michelle. I knew mother would prefer tea and I made coffee for myself. Toby took the Queen's mug into her, and I went into mother and Michelle with a tray. I could hear the radio, so I figured they were both awake.

"Who's up?" asked mother.

"Me and Toby. Jack's gone back over to find out what's happening."

"Of course, he has," said mother. "After I asked him not to."

I said nothing; Jack can fight his own battles.

"Are you going shopping this morning?" asked mother. "Because I haven't got enough for breakfast let alone lunch. What do you feed a Queen?"

"Ice cream," said Michelle and giggled.

"And hot chocolate," I said.

"I haven't enough of either," said mother.

"I'll come with you," said Michelle.

We went in her car, so she drove and headed for Waitrose in Hythe rather than the Co-op in Holbury.

"Don't worry so," Michelle said turning cautiously onto Lepe Road. "He'll make it back."

"I hope you're right. Lord Faniel is a bad enemy and he'll be a bad king."

"Jack knows that, and you can trust him to be careful. I've known him a lot longer that you have. He's really smart."

I was about to reply when my brain caught up with what she had said. I turned it over a couple of times to make sure I'd heard what I thought I'd heard.

"How have you known him longer than me?"

She looked at me as if I was simple. "'Cos he's my dad."

"So you know..." I struggled to articulate the question. It had been an ominous shadow looming over me, and I'd put off addressing it;, now it was suddenly right in front of me. I felt a moment of utter panic before reason asserted prevailed. *If she's known for ages, then she must be OK with it. She wouldn't be here otherwise.*

"I've always known."

The panic vanished as quickly as it had appeared.

"And you're OK with it?"

"With all that's gone on this year, I don't know what I'd have done without you. You're the best thing that has ever happened to me. All the important people are cool with it, and no one else needs to know."

"Does mother know?"

"Of course. How could she not? We talked about it. Jack had already talked to her, so she'd had time to think it through."

I nearly cried with relief. "That is so good to hear. I've been so scared of talking to you about it, in case you didn't know."

"You thought I might dump you?"

"It seemed quite possible. I mean, it is a big taboo."

"Well yeah, I guess it is a little weird, but it's not like we grew up together."

She slowed down to stop for the Rollestone crossroads traffic lights then leaned over to kiss me before the lights changed.

"You're mine and I'm not going to let anyone take you away from me," she said, then released the handbrake and pulled away from the lights. I felt as if I'd swallowed a sunrise.

We did a big shop at Waitrose as we both felt it very likely that mother would have guests for a long time. We stacked the trolley with stuff for the freezer and a week's worth of basic foodstuffs which I paid for.

"There's every chance Jack might come back with more people," said Michelle as we loaded up.

"I don't mind so long as he makes it back," I said. "But we'll run out of bedspace very quickly if he does."

"He'll be back."

We loaded up and drove back to the cottage where I had to lie to mother when she saw all we'd bought and asked me how I'd managed to pay for it. I told her that I was no longer paying rent for my room in town and Sharon wasn't charging me. I didn't feel great about it, but I knew that we would argue if I told the truth and we had too much else going on.

"So long as you're sure can afford to do it," she said after I'd told her. "I won't pretend it's not welcome."

The Queen and Toby were sitting in the kitchen drinking hot chocolate when we brought in the shopping. *Just as well I bought plenty of hot chocolate and milk.* The Queen looked less dazed, and her glamour was immaculate. *I wonder how long that will last?* She beckoned to me and reached out her hand which I took.

"Your family have been so kind to us," she said. "I hope very much that we can find a way to repay you."

"I hope so, too."

"I fear it will not be very soon. I still cannot believe that he has gone so far. We closed our eyes to the signs too many times."

"It will be a long hard road back," I said. "But we will help you where we can."

To my surprise she began to weep. I didn't know what to do. There didn't seem to be anything I could say. I stood there holding her hand before Toby came to my rescue, taking her hand and speaking to her softly in that liquid tongue of theirs. I had no idea what he said, but it sounded soothing, and her tears dried up in a couple of minutes. I stepped away and let them talk.

Michelle looked at me, questions in her eyes.

"I told her we would help her where we can," I said. "I didn't know what else to say."

I left the cottage on Sunday evening to free up sleeping space for those staying.

"You're back early," said Sharon, when I arrived at her flat. "Argued with your mum?"

"Not quite." I explained and what had happened.

"Any evidence of Peter Murphy being involved?" she asked when I'd finished.

"Not so far, but there's a lot we don't know yet. You think he might be involved?"

"We know Faniel has helped Murphy extensively, and nothing is for nothing."

"It sounds possible. We'll know more when Jack gets back." I decided to keep the theory about the cocaine traffic to myself. While it seemed plausible, we had no evidence for it.

Jack was gone nearly a week. This had me really worried until Michelle reminded me of the weird relationship between time spent over there and here. He probably spent less than a day over there and was at mother's when I got there on Saturday. He had brought two more people with him.

"They're in danger," he said. "Lord Faniel has his groups of the Great going around putting compulsions on everyone who might oppose him. I had to bring them over before they were caught."

"We'll need some tents then," I said, wondering if our old one was still in the loft. "Will there be more coming?"

"Possibly yes, but we cannot stay here."

"Well yes, we'll run short of space."

"That is not what I'm talking about. Lord Faniel already suspects the Queen is here. We have to move her before he sends his men here."

I glanced at the very solid new back door that replaced the more fragile one smashed when they last called. They knew their way here and that gave us a problem of where to shift our guests to. Not just the guests either; mother and Michelle, too.

"I can't immediately think of anywhere to take them."

"There are woodlands all around us."

"Those are all owned by someone. Everywhere round here is. We can't just set up camp without permission."

"We are in danger if we stay here."

"How long have we got before they arrive?"

"Who knows?" He shrugged. "Things are very confused over there, and Lord Faniel is not someone who makes logical decisions."

"What about Mrs. Barrett?" said Michelle from the doorway. I didn't realise she had been listening. "She said if you ever needed anything you should ask her."

It was true she had said that. She also had a large house with grounds, there was a portal nearby, and I wouldn't need to explain "over there" to her. It was still a call I hesitated to make; it felt like her offer was one of those you never expect to get called in.

"Go on, call her then," said Michelle. "There's no reason not to, and she could really help us."

At her insistence I dug her number out of my phone's calls archive and called. It rang three times before it was answered by a woman with an east European accent; Anna who had brought in the tea tray perhaps?

"Could I speak to Mrs. Barrett, please? This is Charlie Somes."

"Please hold while I see if she's available." I waited, expecting to be told she was not available. I was surprised when her cut-glass voice came on the line.

"It's good to hear from you, Mr. Somes. You're well, I hope."

"I am, but I wondered if you can help me."

"If I can. What do you need?"

I explained the situation to her.

"I think we can do that. There's space enough, and we've got a marquee we can put up in the garden. If you bring your people over, we can all put it up."

"That's wonderful. Thank you. I'll get them organised and bring them over," I said and ended the call.

"Result!" I said with a grin.

Jack looked at me quizzically. "She will help us?"

"She will. Get your people ready to go and we'll take the

first group over." I paused. "And then you get to explain to mother why she needs to go with them."

A pained expression crossed Jack's face for a moment. "The queen should go first. I'll go and tell them." He disappeared indoors.

"She won't want to go," said Michelle after Jack had left.

"I know."

I didn't recognise the Queen when Jack brought her out. She had no glow around her, a shapeless brown tunic instead of the flowing white dress and the long silver hair was now thin and grey. Her lined face and hands those of a woman who had lived fifty or so hard years, which is, I guess, what she had done. She smiled at me but otherwise looked pale and tired. Toby looked older, too, with a bald patch and liver-spotted hands. Life this side was clearly not suiting them, but it gave me hope that if we could trap Lord Faniel and hold him on this side long enough, then we could deal with him.

Michelle drove us over to Beaulieu in the Polo with the Queen and Toby sitting in the back, Toby holding the Queen's hand.

"This is nice," said Michelle as Mrs. Barrett's house came into view at the end of the gravel road. "I won't mind staying here."

"Tell mother," I said.

Michelle parked up next to a battered Land Rover with a trailer and we got out. I could see around the side of the house three men laying out a big white tent on the lawn. Mrs. Barrett certainly hadn't wasted any time.

The front door opened, and Mrs. Barrett came out to greet us. She looked much better than the last time I saw her; the dark shadows under her eyes had gone and she had lost the gaunt look.

"Mr. Somes. It's good to see you again," she said. "And before you start, I'm very happy to be able to do something to thank you for what you did for James. Now who are my guests?"

I introduced the Queen, Michelle, and Toby and warned her that more were on their way.

"We'll find room for all of them," she said leaving me in no doubt that she would.

I briefly told her about how to talk with them, then Michelle and I headed back to Langley.

"How many bedrooms do you think she has?" asked Michelle as we drove across the heath away from Hilltop. "There's a second level of windows above the ground floor."

"I don't know. I've only been inside on the ground floor. Could easily be eight. There might not be beds in them all, though."

"That's OK. I've slept on the floor before."

I didn't take long to get back to the cottage. Jack was standing outside with a scowl on his face. I guessed the discussion with mother had not gone well.

"Did you deliver the Queen?" he asked. "Is she happy there?"

"She'll be fine," I said. "And very well looked after."

"It's a really nice house," said Michelle.

"You'll all be very comfortable there," I said. "Mrs. Barrett is lovely."

"We're not going," said Jack. "We're staying here to defend the house."

Now I understood the scowl.

"That didn't go so well last time," I said.

"No! It didn't, but this time we know they're coming," said Jack. "Can you make some more of those firebombs?"

"Yes." I knew the starting materials were available in the labs.

"How soon?"

"It's an hour's work. But I have to go into the university."

"Can you do that today? They might come at any time."

"I can take you in," said Michelle. "I'd like to see your lab."

"Okay then," I said. The lab should be pretty quiet at this time. "We'll take the other two folk to Beaulieu then go into town. We should go to the fireworks shop, too. They were very effective last time."

"Do you really think they'll come?" asked Michelle as we drove across the heath towards Dibden Purlieu having dropped our passengers in Beaulieu.

"Yes," I said. "The Queen may be his mother, but as long as she's out of his hands she's a danger to his rule."

"He'd really harm his own mother?"

"He'd most likely prefer to hold her like his father, but if it came to it, he would. I think it's entirely consistent with his character."

"Can we stop him?"

"In the short term, yes," I said. "The firebombs I'm going to make should drive them off, though I'd prefer a couple of guns. Longer term, I don't know. It's not sustainable to keep the Queen and the others over here. You saw what she looked like."

"I did. At least that shows your idea about weakening Lord Faniel could work."

She paused as she slowed right down for a pony and foal ambling across the road.

"Mrs. Barrett's been lovely, but she'll want her house back soon," she said once the animals were safely across.

"That, too. We need a plan. I'll try to talk to Jack while we're guarding the house."

"You're staying with them then?"

"Yes. For a couple of nights at least." I really didn't feel I could leave it to them. It was still my home.

"I'm going to Mrs. Barrett's. I had enough of Lord Faniel and his followers last time."

"I think that's your best option." That was a relief. I really didn't want her around if the Lord Faniel's riders turned up and was glad we wouldn't argue about it.

The conversation paused as she negotiated the Heath roundabout and the unexpectedly busy A326 and didn't pick up again until we were on the Marchwood bypass.

"Do you think Lord Faniel has a summoning song?" Michelle asked.

"If Murphy wants to call him then I guess he must have."

"Is it possible to find out someone's summoning song if they haven't taught it to you?"

"No idea. I hadn't thought about it 'til now. Would be useful if we could."

"Probably means it's really difficult then."

"Something else to ask Jack about."

I spent nearly a hundred and fifty quid of Nigel's money on airbombs at the fireworks shop, then we moved on up to the University campus. There was only one other person in the lab, a Chinese post-doc who just smiled at me and carried on with what he was doing. His English was not great, so I just smiled back. I put on my lab coat and found a pair of safety glasses for Michelle then went to open my fume hood. The bottle of pinene should be in the cupboard under my hood if no one had borrowed it; to my relief it was.

"How many people are there in here usually?" she asked, looking around the lab.

"Eight. Everyone has their own hood and there are four service hoods. The desks are through there." I pointed to the office area at the far end. "Here, put these on." I passed her the glasses.

I extracted a bottle of dry toluene from the solvents cupboard and gloved up, then dissolved the pinene in just short of half a litre of toluene. Michelle watched as I syringed eighty mil portions into half a dozen hundred mil conical flasks then went to the fridge to get the 800ml bottle of trimethyl aluminium solution.

"This is tricky stuff to handle." I said closing the fridge door carefully.

"I'll keep out of the way," she said stepping back.

I turned on the nitrogen supply, stuck a needle in the cap of the trimethyl aluminium solution, flushed out each flask with nitrogen, then sealed them with rubber septa. Using a smaller syringe, I added 10 mil of the trimethyl aluminium solution to each flask through the septa, then carefully washed the syringe and needle with IPA. The final task was to stretch parafilm over each septum as an extra seal.

"Done," I said stepping back and stripping off my gloves.

"Cool," she said. "It's fascinating to watch you work. Is that what you do all the time?"

"Only some of it. I spend much more time purifying the

results of reactions than running them." I tossed the gloves in the bin and opened the cupboard behind it to get some bubble wrap. I wrapped each flask in a couple of layers and stood them up in a good stout box.

"Right, we're done here." I pulled down the front of the hood then took off my lab coat and hung it up. I carefully picked up the box and we left the lab.

When Michelle and I arrived back at mother's, there was an electrician installing motion sensitive security lights front and back. I wondered how much extra he had charged to come out over the weekend. Still, it would be worth it to give us extra warning if they came at night.

We quietly unloaded our cargo and Michelle headed off to Beaulieu. I left a couple of firebombs on the sills of each of the upstairs windows above the doors, then one bomb beside each door. The airbombs were designed to be seated in the ground, so I filled plant pots with soil and left a couple by each window with matches and airbombs.

"I heard about these," said Jack. "They worked well, but will they work again now Faniel's men have seen them?"

"Their horses haven't seen them before." I'd seen forest ponies spooked by fireworks, and I didn't think their horses would be any different.

"That's true, if they came on horseback."

"They'll also rouse the neighbours who'll help us. We can win this."

"Yes. I think we can."

"Then what? Do you have a plan for what we do next?"

"I don't. I just know that we have to keep the Queen out of his hands. If he takes her then there is no more to be done."

I had hoped for more.

"I still think if we can find a way to get him over here and trap him then we will be weakened enough that we can stop him," I said. "We've both seen what being over here has done to the queen."

"Yes, if we could catch him over here. But how do we do that?"

"How hard would it be to find out what his summoning song is?"

He looked at me as if I'd asked him to fly. "Very difficult. Unless you can take from the mind of someone who knows it. I don't know what anyone else's song is, it's not something you tell anyone."

So much for that idea then. "How do you choose a summoning song?"

"We have lots of songs. You choose a song you know well. Not everyone can sing, so pick one that's easy."

"So you could end up with the same song as someone else?"

"I suppose, but I've never heard of it happening. Only a few would use them."

"How many do you use?"

He looked at me like a kid caught with his hand in the biscuit tin.

"Come on. I've heard Michelle's version of your song and it's completely different to mine and mother's."

"I use several," he said after a moment. "They're not the best-known songs, but I've never been called by one and found someone I didn't know."

At that moment mother called up the stairs putting an end to the conversation.

"Charlie, can you take my car and get fish and chips? I've nothing for dinner otherwise."

"Okay." I looked at my watch. It was nearly eight and I realised I was hungry.

Over fish and chips, we agreed a rota that would have one of us awake at any time. Then I went to bed with it still light as I would be woken at four in the morning. I must have slept because I wasn't aware of mother coming into the room to wake me until she shook me by the shoulder.

I got up and made myself coffee, then went back upstairs to keep watch. Last time they had come in by the backdoor, so I figured that was where they would try again. I settled myself to keep watch from the window above it. It was just getting light, and the dawn chorus was at full volume. I opened the window and watched the garden and the trees beyond where the forest began, wondering again if Lord Faniel's team would come today and what the hell we were going to do to stop him.

Time passed; a couple of squirrels came out and got busy digging in the little area of grass we called a lawn. I was thinking of getting another cup of coffee when the birds stopped singing. The squirrels stopped digging and sat up looking towards the bottom of the garden then fled for the nearest tree. I looked there. Ten or so figures emerged from the trees walking towards the garden fence. The helmets and swords some bore showed they were not locals.

I ran the seven steps to the door of mother's room and went straight in; this was no time for politeness. Mother and Jack were cuddled together, both asleep. Jack was nearest so I shook him firmly by the shoulder.

"They're here."

Jack sat up sharply. "Are you sure?"

"Ten men armed with swords, coming into the back from the forest."

I hurried back to my post, closing their door behind me. I stood back from the window hoping they wouldn't see me and took out my phone to film them crossing the fence. Viewed through the phone's camera they were all shorter than they appeared to my eyes as they advanced towards the house.

I lost sight of them under the windowsill and heard the thump as they attacked the new back door. I put down my phone and moved to the window picking up one of the firebombs. I leaned out and took aim at the group of raiders clustered round the door; they were tightly packed so I could hardly miss. I didn't want to risk damage to the new door so didn't target the man closest to it.

The flask hit a helmet and shattered, spilling liquid fire across the shoulders and down the back of a raider. His comrades leapt back from him as he screamed in pain and terror. Three of them stood, unarmed, a few yards back. They looked older and more richly dressed; the Great who had come to subdue the prisoners. I reached for the second firebomb as they looked up at me. Before I could throw there was a shattering bang that made me nearly drop it. Jack or mother must have set off an airbomb; that would wake the whole neighbourhood. The raiders looked at each in confusion as the burned man slapped at his back and shoulders, screaming all the while. As they dithered, I threw the second firebomb. It smashed on the paving slabs spreading liquid fire up the legs of two of the Great. A second airbomb detonated overhead. The raiders fled for the trees, two of them supporting the first man I'd burned.

I watched them go, conscious of my heart pounding like a death metal bassline. Mother and Jack came into the room, Mother's face an angry scowl.

"Great work, Charlie. That's sorted them," she said. "Did you get any of them?"

"Three, I think. One soldier across his back and shoulders and two of the Great with hot feet."

"Good! I hope they're in fucking agony. Maybe it'll teach 'em to leave us alone."

The police turned up about half an hour later; not really surprising with all the noise we'd made. A uniformed constable knocked on the front door. I answered the door as mother was cooking an early breakfast.

"We're looking into reports of explosions and group of suspicious men in this area this morning," he said. "Have you seen or heard anything?"

"Yes. They were here and attacked us. The explosions were us driving them off."

He looked surprised and groped for his notebook. "Can you give me your name first."

"Charlie Somes," I spelled it for him. "And this is my mother's house."

He located a blank page and began to write.

"You said they attacked this house. What time was that?"

I glanced at my watch. "Just before six."

"Can you describe them for me?"

"I can do better than that. I've got video of them." I pulled out my phone, brought up the movie and passed it over to him. He watched it through a couple of times.

"It looks like they were carrying swords. Is that what you saw?"

"Swords, and some wore helmets," I said. "This is connected to those farm raids a few weeks back. It's the same bunch of people. DI Brown and DS Wickens at Southampton Central are the people to tell you more."

"Ah right." He looked relieved at the prospect of being able to hand it over to someone else. "And the explosions?"

"We set off some fireworks to drive them off."

"Did that work?"

"Yes. They scarpered back into the forest." Obviously, I didn't want to mention the homemade firebombs. He wrote for a minute or two.

"You should have called us, Mr. Somes."

I looked at him, he seemed about my age. "Really? Ten of them with swords. Where's your nearest armed response unit at six am on a Sunday?"

He closed his notebook and looked embarrassed. "I'll pass this report to DI Brown. No doubt he'll want to talk to you. Don't delete that video, whatever you do."

I watched him down the path to the gate then closed the door and went back to the kitchen.

"Police?" asked mother.

"Yes. Told him what happened, and he said we should have called them."

"Fat lot of good they would have been."

"That's rather what I told him."

We had breakfast, then Jack said he needed to tell the Queen and the others about the attack, so we got into mother's car and drove over to Beaulieu. I had expected everyone to still be in bed, but they were all up. Jack immediately went to talk to Toby and the Queen, mother and I found Michelle.

"You're up early," she said. "Something going on?"

"We had a visit from Lord Faniel's raiders," I said.

"What happened? Are you OK?"

"We're fine. About ten of them came out of the forest and tried to get in the back door. I hit them with a couple of firebombs, and they pissed off."

"Did you get any of them?"

"Yeah. One guy's neck and back on fire and a couple of the Great got hot feet."

"Good! They won't do that again."

"No. But Jack thinks they'll be back."

"Makes sense if Faniel needs the Queen as much as he thinks."

My phone rang just then with a call from Sharon. I put it on speaker so Michelle could hear.

"Morning, Charlie," she said. "I've just had a report come in with your name in it."

"Didn't realise you were working today."

"My turn in the barrel. I just wanted to get the facts straight about this before I kick it upstairs. I'm presuming Lord Faniel's men."

"Yeah. Ten of them, armed with swords. A couple of the Great. Trying to get into the cottage just before six. Drove them off with firebombs and fireworks."

"After the Queen?"

"Yes, but she's not there and we were expecting them. I've got them on video."

"Good. Just in case anyone has any doubts about it."

"Can't see why anyone would after what happened."

"Nor me. But you never know. Are you back tonight?"

I thought about it for a moment. "I will be. I think we have some time now before their next move."

"I'll talk to you more about this then. See you tonight."

"What do you think the police will do?" said Michelle.

"I don't know, I'll be grateful for any help at all at this point."

I took the bus into town around six after a nap induced by mother's roast dinner and the early morning watch. Sitting on the bus I thought about what police help might mean and what we could do to solve the problem of Lord Faniel. I was pretty sure they didn't have the resources to offer us twenty-four-hour protection. A patrol car passing by a couple of times a day would do nothing to deter Lord Faniel's raiders; it would most likely put the officers in danger if they arrived at the wrong moment.

We needed some much more serious people; Steve, Jimmy, and Geordie and a few more like them would do it. Maybe I needed to speak to Nigel; if Lord Faniel remained King, then he would want revenge for our part in his humiliation and, very likely, resume raiding over here. That seemed like something Nigel should be concerned about. That would not solve the longer-term problem, though; the only solution to that seemed to be removing Lord Faniel from the throne and ensuring he never took it again. That meant removing him permanently, probably by killing him. The idea was chilling, but it was the inescapable and logical conclusion.

"Talk me through it then, Charlie," said Sharon passing me a glass of red wine. "The report I got doesn't have much detail."

"We were expecting them, so we were keeping watch."

"We?"

"Jack, mother, and me."

"Where is the Queen and the other folks?"

"We moved them to Mrs. Barrett's house in Beaulieu. Michelle's there, too."

"Good thinking. So you were on watch. What time was this?"

"Just before six. I was watching the back because that's where they got in last time. First thing I noticed was the birds all stopped singing. Then I saw them coming out of the forest. I went to wake mother and Jack, came back and then filmed them crossing the fence into the garden."

"Show me that."

I took out my phone, pulled up the video and passed it to her. She watched it through three times.

"Scrawny little bastards when you see them without the glamour, aren't they?" she said handing me back the phone. "Can you send me this?"

I took the phone and sent her the file. "Their swords are real enough, though."

"So then what happened?"

"We were prepared. I'd bought some airbombs and made a

batch of that homemade napalm. They tried to break in the back door, and I dropped flask of napalm on them from the upstairs window. Mother set off an airbomb, then I hit a couple of the Great with another flask, and then they fucked off the way they came."

"Did you cause any casualties?"

"Two of the Great got hot feet, and the first guy I hit will have burns on his back and shoulders. Those could be fatal with their level of medicine."

"Tough, but they made their choice."

"They did, and it'll make them think before coming back, but Jack's sure they will. They need the Queen under their control. I'm hoping your people can offer some support for when they do."

She pulled a face. "I'll put the report in with my comments and my boss will send it upstairs. After what happened, it will get taken seriously, but there's no guarantees what will happen then. We don't have the resources to guard you round the clock."

"It shouldn't be a police job anyway, not the way they're armed."

"Who then? Army?"

"Yeah. After all they'd be facing Lord Faniel's warriors."

"I don't even know who would take that decision. The Chief Constable would have to ask the Home Office, I guess. It might go all the way to the Home Secretary."

"They did it only a few weeks back."

"That was one-off extraction. People were in immediate danger. You're looking at a different kind of operation, one that is potentially open-ended. That's much harder to agree to."

"Yeah, I can see that." I could also see us ending up with no support until Lord Faniel's crew came back again and burned the cottage out.

I didn't know whether Nigel kept office hours. I suspected not, but still left it until Monday morning to phone him on the number he had last called me from. He picked up after a couple of rings, just saying "hello" and not giving his name.

"This is Charlie Somes. Something has come up I think you should know about."

"Go on."

"There's been a coup over there. Lord Faniel has taken over."

"By over there, you mean the place beyond the portal where those raiders came from?"

"Yes. The raiders Lord Faniel sent. We just had another attempted raid at my mother's house."

"Tell me more."

I explained how Lord Faniel had seized his father, but his mother had evaded him and been brought through to this side. How we had repelled their attempt to take her back and finished with: "We're expecting further attempts to take her."

"And more raids like before?"

"If Lord Faniel consolidates his hold on power, then yes. He strikes me as someone big on revenge."

"I see. Thank you. I will pass this on to the people who need to know."

There was a pause then he ended the call. He had said nothing about any action being taken; not a great surprise, we were still on our own.

As Sharon had predicted, DI Brown sent the report upwards immediately with a note that he believed the video to be genuine.

"All we can do now is wait," said Sharon. "This will have to go to the Home Office, and they won't be quick."

I told Michelle this when she phoned on Tuesday evening.

"I'm not surprised, but don't think Jack is going to wait," she said. "He says his people over here aren't doing well. They need to find somewhere safe so they can go back over."

"Well, we've both seen how they've changed. Look at the Queen."

"I think he's going over soon. He said to bring some more of those firebombs."

"Any idea what he's planning?"

"No. He hasn't said." That probably meant it was something mother would not approve of.

"I can make some more. I don't fancy bringing them on the bus, though." Too many ways that could go badly wrong.

"I'll come in and pick you up then."

"Yeah great. See if you can find out what he's planning."

By the end of the week Michelle had still not found out what Jack was plotting, and he had disappeared for a couple of days midweek. I was fairly convinced it was something risky so along with ten new firebombs, I brought two of the non-magnetic swords when she came to collect me.

"You think we're going to need those?" Michelle said when she saw them.

"Maybe. Better to have them and not use them, than need them and not have them."

"I suppose so. He's definitely planning something and won't tell us. He went over on Wednesday and only just got back."

"I guess I'll find out pretty soon."

I put the box of well-wrapped firebombs and the swords in the back of the Polo, and we headed for Langley.

"Did you bring the fireglobes?" was the first thing Jack said when we arrived. His appearance had not changed in contrast to the others.

"Yes, ten." I showed him the back of the Polo. "What are you planning?"

He reached out and took my hand.

"We cannot discuss this in front of your mother," he said in my mind. "I have learned that Lord Faniel's men are holding my brother and his family and some of our friends. I intend to free them and bring them over here. I will need you for this."

I had not expected that, and I could certainly understand why he didn't want mother to find out. "That sounds risky."

"That is why I want you and the fireglobes. Toby will come with us, but the time he has spent over here has weakened him. He may need to work through you."

"Just as well I brought the swords then."

"I hope we do not have to use them, but yes, a good thought. We will go as soon as Toby gets here."

"Have I got time for lunch?"

"Yes. You should eat. We may be gone some time." He released my hand.

I was not best pleased in all honesty by the prospect of being gone for some time. I hadn't left anything important running in the lab, but my absence would be noticed, and I would have to explain. It would also piss mother off, though she would be more annoyed with Jack than me. I took out my laptop and sent an email to Prof pleading an unspecified crisis that was going to keep me away from the lab.

Lunch was a scoop of the stew that simmered on the hob as mother was getting ready to go to work.

"Did he tell you what he's planning?" asked Michelle.

"Yeah. He's going to try to free his brother's family and other friends held by Lord Faniel's men and he wants me with him. We're going any minute."

"That sounds...dangerous. I thought he was looking for somewhere to take people back to."

"Yes. I guess he hasn't found anywhere safe over there yet. He hasn't said what we're facing, but we're taking the swords and firebombs. He says he needs me along."

She bit her lip and reached out to me. "You take care of yourself. I don't want to have to come and get you out," she said, then she kissed me.

Toby arrived just as mother was leaving for work; I heard no car pull up, so it wasn't clear how he'd got here, but his arrival sparked a flurry of activity. As soon as mother left, Jack produced a bag to carry the firebombs and a couple of old sacks to wrap the swords.

"We go now," he announced.

I handed Michelle my phone. She kissed me again and hugged me tight, then Jack, Toby, and I set off down the lane. Alert for every chink of glass from the bag I carried, I followed them towards the Darkwater and the gateway. We paused in front of the blue glow to rearrange our burdens so that we could link arms, then Jack led us through. The place between roared through my mind as we walked forward. I concentrated on not dropping my bag until it passed, and we were standing in woodland. The sun was low in the sky, but it wasn't clear whether it was early morning or evening. As we came away from the gateway, I made sure to try and note landmarks so

I could find it again on my own unlike my first trip over. The energy of the land filled me, fizzing through my veins and I felt about three inches taller. Toby looked back and smiled at me; looked like he was feeling better already.

It was a long walk through woodland before we reached the farm. It hadn't got dark so it must be morning. Jack halted us at the edge of the cleared land, and we looked out across the little fields speckled with miniature cattle to the farm buildings. Last time I'd been here there had been gwasannath labourers mowing the fields, now there were none to be seen

"What do you see?" Jack asked me.

"There's a long white thatched building and a couple of smaller buildings all behind a big ditch. There are five big gwasannath around the gate."

"It is good you see them," he said. "You are getting stronger, and it means our friends are still here." From which I gathered there was a glamour to conceal them that I could see past.

"So what do we do?" There was no cover between the woods and the farm. I didn't see how we could approach without being seen.

"If you can see through their glamour, then they will not be able to see through ours. We can just walk up to the gate."

"You make that sound simple."

"It is. Combined we are too strong for whoever set the glamour on the house. Toby will work it with our support as he has the skill for this. Pay attention, it will be a good lesson for you."

We rearranged the burdens again so that we could join hands with Toby in the middle, then walked slowly out of the trees and into the field. Through the link with Toby, I was aware of the glamour he was casting; the image of the trees behind us, the rough grass moving in the breeze and even the sheep. It was deeply impressive. It was also effective as the gwasannath at the gate did not react as we walked towards them. As we approached close enough to smell them, I watched and prepared to grab a firebomb at their first movement. They didn't look our way, preferring to lean on the open gate yawning and talking between themselves.

I had wondered how we were going to get past them, and it turned out we just walked quietly past without them noticing, though the smell nearly choked me. We walked into the farmyard and around the end of building out of sight of the gate. The dogs that had greeted us last time were nowhere to be seen. Toby released my hand and the glamour dissolved. Jack and Toby took the wrapping from their swords. Jack took my hand for a moment.

"They are holding the prisoners in the farmhouse. Stay behind us but be ready to act."

Taking out one flask, I shifted the bag to my left hand. This was awkward; I hoped I wasn't going to need to move quickly. I followed Jack and Toby to the door of the farmhouse, hanging back a bit. Jack and Toby rushed the door, and I heard a commotion inside. I stood in the doorway, as much to hold it against anyone trying to enter as anyone within. If I had to use a flask inside, then the whole building could go up from the look of it.

I looked into the room. Toby held his sword over three men on their knees as Jack took hold of one of them, presumably to lay on a compulsion. As I watched he finished and moved to the next man. I turned back to see riders and a column of gwasannath approaching across the fields. A big cold hand gripped my stomach. The riders were big, well-armoured and one glowed slightly golden; a glamour then, but powerful enough I couldn't see past it. I ducked inside the doorway out of sight.

"We've got company," I called to Jack. He had a hand on the third man and didn't respond immediately. He finished what he was doing, spoke a command to the kneeling me then turned to me.

"How many?"

"Three riders all glamoured, about thirty gwasannath."

Toby came and laid a hand on my neck. I felt the connection, but together we could not penetrate the glamour on the riders.

The big cold hand squeezed again. Jack came to stand with us, but still between the three of us we could not penetrate the glamour.

"I know this one," said Toby in my mind. "He is strong."

"He is the one to target, Charlie," said Jack indicating the glowing rider. Easy enough to spot, but there were thirty gwasannath between me and him.

The riders reached the gate and halted. One of the gate-guard gwasannath scampered up to the house. As he came through the doorway Jack grabbed him, and moments later he was curled up asleep on the floor. After a couple of minutes waiting the riders dismounted and walked towards the house. The gate guards blocked their way, then glowing guy reached out to the largest gwasannath, touched his hand for a moment, then the guards stood aside.

"Is there another way out of here?" I asked Jack, though I thought I knew the answer. If there was an alternative, we would already be heading that way.

"No. The only way is past them."

I took out a second flask then laid my bag down carefully behind me and watched from the dark interior as the three riders advanced into the sunlit farmyard, their gwasannath following, each armed with a heavy club. Glowing guy paused and looked around, hand on his sword hilt, calling out a couple of times; presumably to the men who were sitting quietly on the floor behind us. Getting no reply, he spoke briefly to the other two, then approached the doorway. I could see his shadow connected to his feet, so he wasn't using Lord Faniel's trick, or he was better at it.

Glowing guy was about eight yards short of the doorway when I stepped out and threw a flask at his feet. He threw up his hands in surprise as the flask burst and ignited throwing flames up his shins to his knees. He screamed and beat at the flames with his hands and the flames stuck to them. He fell and tried to roll but the flames were undiminished.

I looked for the other riders, but they were already moving back. I shifted the flask to my right hand and took a step towards but decided against throwing it at them; it would be too easy to dodge

"Again, Charlie," said Jack from behind me. "Finish him."

Their gwasannath took a step forward raising their clubs.

Toby darted past me and slammed his blade into the body of the burning screaming man. There was one final shriek and then he lay still and silent, smouldering but no longer glowing. The two remaining riders drew their swords and ordered the gwasannath forward as they retreated across the yard. Toby ran back and Jack came to stand beside me, sword in one hand, flask in the other.

I couldn't quite process what I had just seen, but there was no time to think about it. A growl rose from the gwasannath, and they moved forward step-by-step. Watching them intently, I raised my arm ready to throw when they charged. If the first two bombs didn't stop them then we would be in trouble. One of the riders spat out an order – possibly "get on with it!" or similar.

The gwasannath charged. I waited a couple of seconds then threw my flask. The leading gwasannath tried to bat it away with his club. It shattered on contact covering him and the gwasannath on either side with fire. Jack's flask hit another one and the charge dissolved as their fur caught fire. I scurried back through to the doorway in search of more flasks as Jack and Toby pulled back to the doorstep.

I returned moments later with two more flasks. The gwasannath were milling around their burned casualties who were squealing their heads off. The smell was sickening. The two riders were standing beyond them near the gate shouting orders that were not being obeyed. We advanced from the doorway. The gwasannath paid us no attention, the riders watched us with swords raised, then apparently thought better of the confrontation and ran for their horses.

"Let's get our people and get away from here," said Jack. That seems like an excellent idea to me. I could feel my heart thumping and could do with sitting down.

"What about them?" I pointed to the gwasannath.

"Leave them. They're not going to bother us. They were under his control." Jack pointed to the late glowing guy. "They'll find their way home eventually. You stay here and watch them." He and Toby went back into the house.

So I leaned on the doorway letting my pulse rate return to

normal, and watching as they milled around with no apparent idea of what to do. The gate guards watched them with mild curiosity but did nothing to help. I wondered if there was anything I should do, but they posed no threat, and I was not inclined to help the injured, so I left them alone.

They were still milling about directionless when Jack and Toby emerged with about twenty people: men, women and children. If any wore a glamour I could see past it, but then they had not been strong enough to resist the men we had overcome. Jack's brother smiled at me and spoke to the child he was carrying, perhaps pointing out "he's your cousin."

"Is that all of them?" I asked Jack.

"All that are coming," said Jack. "Someone's got to stay and look after the animals."

They looked happy enough to be leaving, though perhaps relieved was a better description of the women as Jack lead us away towards the woods and the portal we had arrived through.

"Who was the glowing man we killed?" I asked.

"He was one of the Great closest to Lord Faniel. I did not expect him to come here."

"Why kill him?"

"He was very strong in the grym hud. Too strong for us to contain, and we could not fight all his gwasannath. He would have killed us all. Lord Faniel will seek vengeance, though. It would have been better to avoid them."

"I think we were already close to the top of Lord Faniel's shit list."

"If we weren't before, we are now."

"What have you told them about where we're going?"

"That it is different from here but safe. That is enough for them now, I think."

"For a few days, yes." Ice creams all round would help.

We reached the edge of the wood and the column of people reduced to single file with Jack leading. I waited for them all to pass and took up post as tail-end Charlie. I didn't think anyone was going to follow us, but I wanted to make sure.

We reached the portal, and everyone joined hands. I decided to go with the party to the camp at Mrs. Barrett's as Michelle should be there and I wasn't sure of my welcome at mother's. I took the hand of the little girl in front on me and caught a shiver of anxiety as we approached the portal. I responded with reassurance before passed into the place between. I tried to keep my mind blank as the wind roared through it as I didn't want to mess with Jack's direction. We emerged into sunlit woodland, and I felt a thrill of excitement from the girl before I released her hand. I looked downhill to a mossy bank with a gravelled road behind it; we were in the right place.

Jack was already leading the column down the slope with a buzz of excited chatter from the group. The buzz grew as the house and the vehicles parked in front came into view. I was pleased to see Michelle's Polo there and even more pleased to see her when we walked round the side of the house. She ran over and threw her arms around me as soon as she saw me.

"I'm so glad you're back," she said between kisses. "We've been worried. Your mum's really pissed off, mainly with Jack but you, too."

That was not a surprise. "What day is it?"

"Tuesday." She glanced at her watch. "Ten past one. So what happened over there? Did you get all the people Jack wanted?"

"I think so, but we had trouble over there."

"What kind of trouble?"

"One of the Great turned up with a pack of gwasannath while we were at the farm."

"That sounds like very big trouble. What happened? How did you get away?"

"He didn't know we were there. I ambushed him with a firebomb then Toby stabbed him with one of the swords I brought."

"Killed him?"

"Yes."

"I can't imagine him doing that."

"But he did, and with no hesitation at all. He was dangerous so Toby killed him." I remembered the King's immediate execution of one of the rebels. "It's a different world over there, a much harder world. We have to remember Jack and Toby are as much a part of it as Lord Faniel."

"Yeah true. But it puts us in more danger here, doesn't it? Lord Faniel will be looking for revenge, and the only place he knows to come to over here is the cottage. Your mum's going to go spare. This is exactly what she was worried about."

"Couldn't be helped once they'd turned up. There was only one way out and they were holding it."

"What's done is done, but you should tell her you're back." She passed me my phone. "Better text her, she's doing a late today."

"Okay. Can you take me to Hythe? I should go back to the lab." I wasn't looking forward to explaining my absence. "I'll let Jack explain why it had to be done."

"That sounds like cowardice," she said with a grin.

"It is. She should come and stay here, but I don't think she will. There're some firebombs in my bag we didn't use that she should have. I hope she won't need them, but they might make her a bit safer."

I opened my phone and saw texts and missed calls from Sharon. I should have messaged here before I left, but it slipped my mind in the hurry after Toby arrived at the cottage. I sent her a quick message saying I would explain tonight and one to mother saying "I'm back. Jack will explain." Then we went into Beaulieu to get ice creams for the new arrivals.

I had plenty of time on the ferry across to the Town Quay and then on the bus up to the campus to think about what had happened. I went through the sequence of events; the original objective of rescuing Jack's brother and family was important. There was no doubt Lord Faniel would mistreat them and use them to demand Jack's surrender. We had to get them out. Which we had been doing with minimal fuss until glowing guy turned up. Then it all went to shit. He and his gwasannath had us bottled up and we had to get past them to get home. It was just the worst luck that they had arrived when they did.

So we'd made things worse. Lord Faniel would undoubtedly strike back, and the only place he knew to hit was mother's cottage. Having been repelled once he would most likely send a stronger force, so she had to be persuaded to leave, which seemed problematic given her previous intransigence. Perhaps Jack would find a way to move her. If not, then a compulsion; not something I would want to do, but she was in grave danger if she stayed put.

I arrived at the lab to find Prof was away with no one sure if it was holiday or conference. My labmates were incurious about my absence and more concerned about my availability for the inter-group five-a-side football tournament. That was fine by me, and I signed up for the team, hoping I'd actually be there.

I had too much on my mind to undertake anything too delicate, so I set up a preparation of an intermediate. I needed more of it, it was a preparation I had run several times before so I knew it would work, and I just didn't need the hassle of a misbehaving reaction. I weighed out the reactants, set up the reflux, and kept an eye on it for half an hour before heading out to shop for dinner. I did briefly wonder what Sharon had done for dinner last night; takeaway and red wine probably.

It seemed my guess was correct when I got to her flat; there was an empty wine bottle and pizza box on the table in the lounge. I cleared them away, texted Sharon to tell her I was there and cooking dinner, then set to making a lamb curry.

Sharon turned up just after eight; I knew enough to serve her a glass of wine and a plate of curry before any serious conversation.

"So what happened?" she said pushing aside her plate and reaching for the wine bottle. "You went over there, right?"

"Yeah. Jack got word that his brother and family were being held by Lord Faniel's people. We went over to free them and bring them back."

"How did that go?"

"Badly! We got them out eventually, but we've made things worse."

"How?"

"Initially there was only a small team of guards and gwasannath holding them, nothing we couldn't handle. But while we were dealing with them a much larger group turned up with a high-level Great. We had to fight our way out. They were between us and the way back. Toby killed the Great. Turns out the guy was one of Lord Faniel's biggest supporters."

"So now Lord Faniel's going to be even hotter for revenge. And the first place he'll go is your mum's cottage. I'm sorry, but we can't give you more than a patrol car passing by a couple of times a day to protect it."

"I'm expecting he'll turn up with a bigger force. That would just put the coppers in danger if they came along at the wrong time."

"Is she still resistant to moving?"

"Yeah. I've left it to Jack to try and convince her."

"You think he will?"

"Maybe."

"Or he could put a compulsion on her." She paused. "So could you."

"I've thought about it, but I'm worried about her response if she finds out."

"Why would she find out? I thought you could do it so people don't notice. Make her think you persuaded her. Afterwards if you're right, which I think you are, it'll just look like a commonsense precaution. That's what I'd do."

That made me feel better about doing it, though I suspected Jack would do it first.

I phoned Michelle after dinner and asked if Jack had spoken to mother.

"I haven't seen him since I got back, so he might have gone over to see her," she replied. "I'll ask him when I next see him."

"We have a few days, I think, with the time difference, but we need to convince her to move. There's no way Lord Faniel is not going to respond. Will you see her this week?"

"I should do at work, and I'll see which way the wind blows. I think we should leave this to Jack."

"I agree." It made sense to me; he knew her in ways that I didn't and was far more skilled in compulsions if it came to that.

I didn't sleep much, turning over in my mind what could be done and felt like shit when I got to the lab. At least the intermediate prep had worked and the clean-up was routine.

I was much relieved then to get a text mid-afternoon from Michelle saying Jack had told her mother was coming to Mrs. Barrett's after work this evening.

My anxiety ticked up again when I got another text from Michelle just as I was getting ready to leave the lab. She asked, "have you heard from your mother?" I called her immediately feeling cold fingers gripping my guts. She answered straight away.

"Have you heard from your mother?" she asked.

"No. Why?" The cold fingers' grip tightened.

"I'm at the cottage. It's all locked up and her car's here, but there's no sign of her. Her phone just goes to voicemail."

That sounded very wrong. The fingers gripped tighter. "I'm coming straight away."

I closed up the fume hood, took off my safety glasses and lab coat and ran for the bus stop feeling cold, numb, and very scared. All my thoughts were focused on getting out to Langley as quickly as possible with no idea what I would do when I got there.

I was at the Town Quay, in the queue for the Hythe ferry when my phone pinged with an incoming text. My heart jumped when I saw it was from mother. I opened it and a great cold wave hit me. It read "We have your mother. We want the queen." I stood frozen in horror. Time passed before the queue began to move, and the passengers brushing past me brought me back to myself.

I boarded the ferry and sat out of deck in a daze barely together enough to text Michelle that I was on the boat. She replied immediately that she would pick me up in Hythe.

By the time we reached Hythe pier I was thinking again. This had to be down to Peter Murphy; no way would Lord Faniel or any of his people know how to send a text on a mobile phone. Besides, Murphy had form; he'd snatched me of the street in broad daylight in Southampton so grabbing mother would not trouble him. The shock faded, replaced by anger. I considered phoning Sharon, but two things stopped me. Firstly, that Hampshire Constabulary would find nothing if they searched Murphy's house; mother had almost certainly been taken through a portal by now. Secondly, I thought it quite likely Jack might want to move against Murphy and involving them would severely limit what we could do. I could always call her once I'd talked it over with Jack and Michelle.

Michelle was waiting for me when I got off the pier train. I showed her the text immediately.

"Fuck!" she said. Then a moment later. "Murphy?"

"Gotta be. Can't think of any other candidates."

"What are we doing to do? Police?"

"Talk to Jack, see what he wants to do."

We walked back to her car.

"I feel a bit better now I know what's happened," she said once we were in the car.

"I agree. Now we can think about doing something. That feeling of being unable to do anything is just shit."

"So what can we do? Get her back from him?"

"I doubt he has her. Murphy may be an evil bastard, but he isn't stupid. He'll have got her through a portal before he sent the text."

Her face fell. "So what can we do then?"

"I want to go after Murphy himself. I figured out on the map where his place is. This is the third time he's fucked me over and it's got to stop. "

"That didn't go well last time."

⁕ Yes. This is something Faniel would do," said Jack. We'd gone to Mrs. Barrett's, and I'd shown him the text and reminded him about Peter Murphy and his connection to Lord Faniel. We waited as he sat grim-faced as if contemplating unpleasant alternatives.

"You know where Murphy is?" Jack said after a while.

"I've been to his place once," I said. "But I don't think mother will be there. He knows the police are watching him. He'll have taken her through a portal before he sent the message."

"There is a portal near his place?"

"There must be. Lord Faniel was there." I shuddered as I remembered that encounter.

"Yes. I remember that," said Jack. "Another wrong he has

done us. It is good if there is a portal nearby."

"What are you thinking?" I asked. "I think we should go after Murphy."

"That is a conclusion I am coming to." Jack said slowly. "We do not have the strength to take her from Lord Faniel directly. He offers an approach, so I think this is our only way."

"But he has guards and guns, doesn't he?" said Michelle.

I remembered the monosyllabic guy who had opened the door to us when Mike Scott took me to Murphy's place and wondered how many men Murphy kept around him. "They'll be guards and CCTV, movement sensitive lights, maybe dogs, too." I hadn't seen or heard dogs when I was there, but that didn't mean there wouldn't be.

"Dogs we can deal with," said Jack. "What is CCTV?"

I started to explain, but Michelle took out her phone and showed him how the camera took video. "They'll have cameras like this covering the approaches to the house. It'll see past a glamour."

Jack did not immediately reply, his forehead puckered in thought. I was tempted for a moment to use the phone to see what he really looked like but thought better of it. I was used to his appearance now and decided I didn't want to know.

"I think we can do this, but I need to talk to Toby," he said turning to leave. I pulled out my phone and sent a quick text to Sharon to tell her I was going over.

"This sounds really dangerous, Charlie," Michelle said. She reached out and took my hand.

"It is," I replied. "And if I could think of any other way to go, I wouldn't do it."

"Be careful. I couldn't stand to lose you now."

I reached out and held her then. I had every intention of being very, very careful, but the prospect still scared me.

Jack returned a few minutes later with Toby.

"Are you ready?" he said.

I kissed Michelle and whispered, "I love you." Her dark eyes looked very moist.

I turned to Jack. "Ready," I said even though I felt far from it and the idea had been mine. That Jack and Toby had accepted it made it only slightly better. "Do we need the firebombs?"

"No," said Jack. "We will do this quietly."

"Do you need me to drive you there?" said Michelle.

"No, we will use the portal," said Jack. It going to be interesting to see how that worked and I was rather relieved that Michelle would not be anywhere near Murphy's place.

"Do I need to bring anything else?" I asked.

"No. Time to go." Jack looked at Michelle then stepped forward and hugged her. Maybe he also spoke directly into her mind before he stepped away. Then Toby and I followed him down the drive and up the grass bank to where the portal glowed blue. We joined hands and Jack spoke in my mind.

"We will go to the other place first. Then you must guide us back to the portal near Murphy's place." It sounded easy enough, I hoped my memory of Murphy and his house would be enough to take us there.

Jack led us into the portal and through the place between into woodland. I looked around quickly; it did not look familiar. Jack also looked around and sniffed the air.

"Good! No one watching us. Your turn now, Charlie. You must lead."

We rearranged hands and turned back to the glowing blue of the portal with me in front. I tried to fill my mind with the image of Peter Murphy's place as I'd seen it from Mike Scott's car; the redbrick farmhouse, the farmyard with its outbuildings. The chill of the portal tickled my face then the noise of the place between filled me as I towed them forward.

We came out into more woodland, but the feel of the air told me were back on my side. It was darker, too, close to twilight even though we'd spent only moments on the other side. There was light enough to pick out a path leading between the trees.

"Is this the right place?" asked Toby in my mind.

"I don't know," I replied. "I think we should see where this path goes."

"We should start the concealment glamour in case anyone is keeping watch," said Jack. I thought it unlikely but couldn't fault his caution.

I felt Toby begin the glamour and tried to analyse how he

was doing it as we followed the path through the trees. We reached the edge of the wood holding hands and, concealed in the shadows, looked out across a field dotted with sheep to farm buildings. The main house was red-brick and a white Range Rover stood in the yard.

"I think this is the place," I said with relief running through me.

We watched for a few minutes but saw no one moving about but lights came on downstairs.

"Someone's at home," I said.

"Let's go and see who." said Jack.

We helped each other over the fence into the field and, still holding hands, walked towards the house. The sheep ignored us, maybe the glamour worked on them. No one came out of the house.

"The CCTV and movement sensors probably only cover the area immediately around the house and farmyard," I said. Otherwise, the sheep would keep setting them off.

"Are these Murphy's animals?" asked Toby.

"I doubt it," I said. "He probably rents out the grazing."

The floodlight came on when we opened the gate into the farmyard.

"Keep moving," said Jack as I hesitated.

The backdoor of the farmhouse was thrown open and two big guys with baseball bats piled out looking straight towards us. They ran a couple of steps then stopped and looked around the yard in puzzlement. Clearly, they could not see us.

"What the hell?" said one. "Check around the Rover."

The second guy ran over to the Range Rover, looked behind it and underneath while the first guy looked sharply around the yard.

"No sign."

"Stay here. I'll go and see what the TV's got."

The first guy went back inside leaving his colleague standing in the middle of the yard. Jack led us swiftly over to him and grabbed his free hand. The compulsion he used was simple enough, complete obedience. He stopped moving and stood quietly beside us, baseball bat dangling loosely by his knees.

The first guy came storming out of the house.

"What the hell, Karl? I saw you talking to them," he yelled.

"I don't know what you're talking about," said Karl.

The first guy came over and grabbed him by the collar. "I fucking saw you on the CCTV. Where are they?"

Toby grabbed his arm with his free hand and laid the same compulsion of obedience on him. The guy released Karl and stood passively with his arms by his sides.

"Where's Murphy?" asked Jack.

"In the house, in the sauna," said Karl.

"Is there anybody else in there?" I asked. If there were any more guards, I thought we would have seen them.

"He's got a girl with him," said Karl. That would account for why he hadn't come outside.

"Take us there," said Jack.

We followed the two guards into the house still holding hands and maintaining the glamour. Once inside we released it. I directed the second guard to the chair in front of the CCTV display and took his hand. "You will wipe the recording, turn off the system and then go to sleep. When you wake tomorrow you will not remember anything about this."

I sealed the compulsion. The guard did as he was told. I waited until I was sure he was asleep.

"Now take us to Murphy," I said to Karl.

Karl took us along a corridor then down a set of stairs. I could smell the chlorine of a swimming pool as we descended. We passed the open door of a seriously equipped weights room then stopped in front of the next door which was closed. A couple of white fluffy bathrobes hung on hooks beside the door.

"In there," said Karl.

"You can sleep now and forget." Jack reached out to Karl. Moments later he was sat slumped against the wall asleep.

Jack laid hand on the door handle. "We'll take Murphy," he said. "You handle the girl."

He turned the handle and threw the door open. We piled into the pine-panelled hot and steamy room. Peter Murphy was naked and sitting on a wooden bench, eyes closed. The girl, also naked, crouched between his spread legs, blonde head at his groin. Three steps and we were on them.

I caught the girl by her shoulder as Jack and Toby closed in on Murphy. She jumped at my touch. Her mind was filled with fear and confusion as I pushed in. With no difficulty I ordered her to get some clothes on, find somewhere to sleep and forget today's events. I sealed the compulsion and released her. She left the sauna collecting her bathrobe at the door.

Jack and Toby both had hold of Murphy. He struggled and yelled for a few seconds and then went quiet. Jack and Toby pulled him to his feet. Even naked Murphy was intimidating. He had the muscles and build of a light-heavyweight boxer; clearly the weights room was not just for show.

"I know you." He fixed me with his dark eyes, the threat clear. I held his gaze until Jack told him to "stop talking and get your clothes on."

We followed him out of the sauna, past the sleeping Karl, up two flights of stairs to the bedrooms. The master bedroom seemed larger than the whole of Sharon's flat and it needed to be to accommodate the huge bed where the blonde girl was now sleeping. You could easily get four people in it; maybe he did. A flat-screen TV covered the wall opposite. I didn't know they made them that big.

While Murphy was dressing, I asked Jack if he knew where mother was.

"It is as you thought," Jack said. "He called Lord Faniel to take her through the portal. The same one we used."

I felt a certain amount of satisfaction that I had guessed right about what he would do and now we were heading the right way. "What are we going to do now?"

"Take him with us. We must think carefully about what we do next."

Murphy reappeared dressed in sweatshirt and tracksuit bottoms.

"Get a jacket," ordered Jack.

We made our way out of the house, closing the doors behind us, and across the fields towards the portal. It was now pretty dark, but Jack and Toby seemed to have no trouble with the path. I kept behind Murphy; he might be under a compulsion of obedience, but he watched me all the time he could. I found his baleful glare unsettling and I certainly didn't want to hold his hand through the portal even though I was sure I was stronger than him.

Jack brought us unerringly straight to the portal. I caught Toby's hand as we passed through into the place between and emerged into woodland. I couldn't tell whether this was the same portal we had passed through previously. We were there for moments before Jack took us back to the place between. I wondered if it was necessary to do it this way.

"We know this way works," said Toby in my mind over the noise of the place between.

We emerged into more woodland in pale daylight to the patter of light rain. It had been dry and dusk when we left Murphy's house, but who knows how much time had elapsed? We made our way to the camp behind the house to find people up and breakfast being served.

Jack caught Murphy's arm then turned to me. "I must speak to the Queen. Find him a place here. He will obey you."

He and Toby walked away leaving me with Murphy who was watching me intently.

"You'll let me go if you know what's good for you," he said. "My father will break you and I have a lot of friends."

So he was Lord Faniel's son. I did not reply.

"I can give you a lot of money to let me go," he continued. "What do you want? A hundred and fifty? Two hundred grand?"

"This isn't about money," I said. "You forgotten you tried to have me killed? Now stop talking."

He stopped talking and grabbed my wrist, his eyes burning. I felt his presence push into my mind. I pushed back, slowly winding up the power, and watching his face as he realised I was stronger. It was like a kids' tug-of-war team against a bulldozer. I wrapped my will around his and squeezed just enough to let him know I was in control, then I reinforced the obedience compulsion and added acceptance of his captivity.

With Murphy thus subdued, I took him to find breakfast which is where Michelle found us.

"You made it. How did it go? Have you found her? Who's

that?" she asked once we'd left him at a table.

"It's like we thought. She was taken through the portal," I said. "And that is Peter Murphy."

Her faced hardened. "What is he doing here?"

"Exactly what I tell him. He's going to be useful."

"What are you going to do with him?"

"Don't know yet. Jack's gone to see the Queen. We'll know more when he gets back."

We sat down to wait for Jack. Michelle got breakfast, I got coffee for myself and tea for Murphy. I hadn't asked he what he wanted; he'd have tea and be happy with it.

It was a long wait for Jack. We wondered if the Queen was still in bed as people drifted in for breakfast. I was on my third cup of coffee when he appeared. I directed Murphy to a table out of earshot and told him to stay there. Jack got himself a cup of tea and sat down.

"The Queen has agreed that we should try to capture Lord Faniel," he said.

"What does she think we should do with him?" Michelle asked.

"She wants to talk to him once he's captured. It will depend on what he says to her then."

"What's the plan for capturing him?" I asked.

"Have his son there summon him to the portal here," Jack nodded in the direction of Murphy. "Take him when he first comes through."

"How are you thinking we do that?" I remembered with discomfort how strong he was. "We're going to have to make sure he can't touch anyone. Gloves for everyone, maybe face masks."

"Why not drop a net on him like we did with the gwasannath?" said Michelle.

"That could work," I said.

Jack nodded in agreement. "Indeed. Can you get a net?"

"We need to check if there are trees close enough to the portal," I said. "Then we can try to find a net."

Jack finished his tea. "Let's go and see."

I ordered Murphy to stay where he was and not talk to

anyone then we walked down to the portal. I hadn't previously paid much attention to the trees surrounding it and was pleased to see a large beech whose branches loomed above it. There appeared to be a number of points where a net could be suspended, though I didn't fancy the job of fixing them for myself.

"It looks possible," said Jack. "We'll need to ask Cal about it, he knows these things."

"Who is Cal?" I presumed he was one of the refugees.

"He's a hunter," said Jack. "He uses traps like this for boar."

"Good. I was wondering how we would rig it." I was happy we had someone who knew what they were doing with it.

"We need a net," said Jack.

There was only one place to start looking for a net; ask Mrs. Barrett. We walked back to the house and, true to form, she knew someone to call. An hour later a pick-up truck drove up and the driver unloaded a football goal net.

"Thank you," I said to the driver. "We'll try to look after it."

"Don't worry about it," said the driver. "It's an old one. We got new ones, so it doesn't matter if it gets damaged."

Jack inspected the net with a wiry little man whose dark hair was showing grey ribs; Cal, I presumed. There was a conversation in their own language. Cal tugged at the net strings, felt its weight and seemed satisfied. There was further discussion then Jack turned to me.

"He needs rope."

"How much and what size?"

More discussions. "The same size as the net would do, and as much as you can find."

No doubt Mrs. Barrett would know someone. If not, Lymington was full of yachts and there would be chandlers that stocked ropes of all descriptions. On my way to find her my eyes fell on the garden shed; there might be something useful there. It was unlocked and a picture of order with everything on labelled shelves. There were a couple of rolls of garden twine, so I took the thicker one. Not quite rope but maybe it would do. I closed the shed door and noticed behind it, between the shed and the hedge, an old-fashioned cast iron two-man garden roller. That might come in useful.

I took the roll of twine back to Jack and Cal. Cal held it up, pulled hard on a length of it, smiled then spoke a few words to Jack.

"This will do the job," said Jack.

We picked up the net and carried to the portal. I went back to the shed for an aluminium step ladder that I had seen there. Cal was already up in the beech tree when I got back.

"How can you carry that if it is metal?" asked Jack.

"It's really light," I stood it in the accumulated mast beneath the beech tree. "Try it."

He came and lifted it easily with one hand. I could see the surprise on his face.

"This is a metal we call aluminium. It's quite strong and not magnetic so I think it would go through the portal."

A call from above reminded us of what we were supposed to be doing. I set up the step ladder beneath Cal, took an armful of net, and began to climb.

Under Cal's direction we had the net rigged above the portal in about half an hour with me up the ladder most of the time. I closed up the step ladder and was about to take it back to the shed when Jack stopped me.

"We need to test it," he said. This was not something I wanted to hear, even though I could entirely see the point; it would be damned awkward if we failed to trap Lord Faniel when he appeared. I carried the ladder a few yards back from the portal and watched as Cal pulled on the dangling end of twine. The net flopped out of the trees a little unevenly, but it looked good to me. It would certainly have engulfed someone standing by the portal. Jack and Cal had an extended conversation with much pointing into the trees then we put it back up. It took less time, and I could not tell if it had been done differently, but Jack and Cal were happy with it.

"Is that ready then?" I asked.

"I think so," said Jack. "We need to find gloves and the other things you said."

"For how many people?"

"Perhaps six."

That sounded like a trip to Tesco at Applemore then. I went to find Michelle so I could borrow her car.

Peter Murphy sat cross-legged on the ground exactly where I told him to sit, a few yards from the portal singing his summoning song. He was no kind of singer, but I guess that didn't matter. Jack, Toby and Cal stood the other side of the portal beside the trunk of the big beech. Jack and Toby had the turbine-blade swords. Cal held the net release twine. Michelle and I each held a firebomb with another pair in a padded basket at our feet. We all wore rubber kitchen gloves.

Peter Murphy reached the end of his song and looked up at me.

"Again," I ordered.

He began the song off-key again and sang it through as the tension mounted in the group. He reached the end.

"Keep going," I said.

After his seventh repetition the tension had dissolved into frustration and Jack called a halt.

"Where is he? I don't understand. He should be expecting a call about the Queen," he said. "We'll try again later."

"Now he knows what it's like for us sometimes," said Michelle.

I called Peter Murphy over to us.

"How often does that usually work?" I asked him, thinking that he shouldn't be able to defy my instructions and sing the song so badly that it didn't work, or the wrong song.

"Sometimes," he said. I took off my glove and held his hand to check. He was telling the truth. I caught a picture of Lord Faniel appearing from a portal.

"Maybe it's night over there," I said and released his hand.

We left the net rigged and made our way back to the house. We parked Peter Murphy and went to get coffee.

"So what are we going to do with Lord Faniel if he does show up?" asked Michelle once we had sat down. "Assuming we capture him."

"I like Charlie's idea of keeping him close to something iron to weaken him," said Jack. I immediately thought of the garden roller.

"How long do you think it will take to weaken him enough?" I asked.

"I don't know," said Jack. "I notice it after a day over here, but I stay away from iron."

"The King couldn't maintain his glamour after a day, but then he had a lot more happening to him."

"It could be three or four days," said Jack.

"It would be better to chain him to something iron," said Michelle. "Use steel chains. That would speed it up."

"Good point," I said. "We need to get some." That meant a trip to Lymington to find a yacht chandler.

"We should go and get some now," said Michelle. "We've got a few hours and we need to be ready next time we try to call him."

She finished her coffee with a gulp, pulled her car keys out and gave me a "come with me" smile. I got up and followed her out to the drive where the Polo was parked.

We headed downhill into Beaulieu and immediately hit traffic with tourists stopping to stare at the donkeys on the grass by the church gateway.

"Fucksake. Have they never seen a donkey before?" said Michelle as we crawled behind a family taking pictures out of their car window.

"It's like this all summer," I said. "I had a job at the Motor Museum for a couple of summers. You wouldn't believe the crowds."

The congestion persisted until we got to Hatchet Pond where most of the tourist traffic kept on for Lyndhurst and we turned off for Lymington. Lymington was as busy as Beaulieu, and it took a while to park. We were nowhere near any chandlers, so we had a long walk, but it was worth it. I bought five metres of anchor chain, shackles, and padlocks then regretted it when I had to carry it all back to the car.

I was hot, tired, and had an odd buzzing in my head that was starting a headache by the time we reached the car. I put the purchases in the boot, then Michelle took us into the traffic again. We made our way slowly back towards Beaulieu pulling into the carpark at Hatchet Pond to queue for ice creams from the van there. Rather than head into Beaulieu I suggested Michelle take the lane to Furzey Lodge. We drove past the nice houses and pulled up in the car park then took our ice creams and walked down the gravel track to the gate and bridge over the stream. A couple of mountain bikers came past us, other than them there was no one around. We finished the ice creams and walked downstream for a couple of hundred yards.

Michelle looked around and smiled at me. "Looks like we've found a quiet spot. It doesn't feel right doing it at Mrs. Barrett's and I've really missed being with you."

She kissed me then started unbuttoning my shirt.

"What are we going to do with Murphy after we catch Lord Faniel?" asked Michelle as we headed down to Beaulieu from Hatchet Gate.

"I was going to put him under a compulsion to confess all to the police," I said. "But I need to shut him off from his abilities first, otherwise he'll just take over whichever prison he ends up in."

"Can you do that?"

"Lord Faniel did it to me, so it can be done. But I don't know how to do it. I'll need Toby or someone to show me."

"That should make Sharon happy."

"And Mike Scott."

"You might need to argue it out with Jack. I think he has rather more direct justice planned."

"Yeah. I imagine he would. I'll talk to him, try and convince him we can do a lot more good by making him confess."

"I agree. I'll tell him that, too. You can always make himself top himself when he's confessed."

Could I do that? I wasn't sure, but I was sure Jack would help with that.

We got back to Mrs. Barrett's much later than we had intended, and it was clear no further attempt to call Lord Faniel would be made today. With help we hauled the old roller out from beside the shed and I rigged the chains around the handles. When I was done, I noticed the buzzing in my head was back. It occurred to me that both times it had happened I had been handling the chains; maybe I was getting sensitive to iron. That would be really inconvenient if it got stronger. And why now? Maybe it was because Toby had been operating through me. He was one of the Great, had he improved me? I'd certainly felt strong dealing with Peter Murphy. Definitely something to ask him about.

I passed the night on the floor of Michelle's room at the top of the house. The room, originally for a servant was tiny, and Michelle alone filled the camp bed. I slept poorly; not only was floor uncomfortable but my time-sense was messed up from the brief trip through the portal. I lay awake thinking about our plan to trap Lord Faniel. There seemed so much that could go wrong, and the stakes were horrifyingly high, but I still couldn't think of what else we could do.

I must have fallen asleep at some point because I woke up in daylight to Michelle trying to step over me.

"Sorry! Did I wake you?"

"I was awake anyway," I lied. "I was thinking about the plan to catch Lord Faniel. I'm really worried about it."

"It seemed a reasonable plan to me. Do you have an alternative?"

"No!"

"Do you want to change anything?"

I sat up and thought about that for a few moments. "Lord Faniel might use a glamour to make himself invisible. You should watch the portal through your phone camera."

"Can he do that?"

"Toby did it for us last time we were over there and at Murphy's place."

"Right. I'll do that then. Anything else?"

"Can't think of anything at the moment."

"Then it's the best plan we've got, and we have to do something."

I looked at my watch; twenty past six. "Is it too early for breakfast?"

"Not too early to start making it for everyone."

We went down to the marquee on the lawn, me feeling scruffy wearing yesterday's clothes which I'd slept in. Some of the refugees were already up, and our appearance triggered a move to the canteen area. We got a brew on and hot porridge for breakfast. I've never been a big fan of porridge but was hungry enough to eat it.

Jack and Toby appeared about half an hour later, collected tea and porridge then came to sit with us.

"We will try again this morning," Jack said before digging into his porridge. This I had expected but my stomach still tightened with nerves and didn't loosen as I watched him eat.

He finished his porridge then drained his mug of tea and stood up. "I'll get Cal. You get Murphy and bring him to the portal. Don't forget your fireglobes."

Peter Murphy was where I'd left him. I gave him a bottle of water but ignored his pleas for a shower and breakfast and brought him straight to the portal; he might get breakfast if he succeeded. Jack and Cal were already there fiddling with the net, Toby watching them holding the swords. Michelle had fetched the firebombs from her car where we'd stashed them. I took Murphy to the spot before the portal and told him to stay there, then retreated a few yards to where Michelle stood.

"Phone?" I said quietly.

She pulled it out and opened up the camera. Jack, Toby, and Cal finished fiddling with the net and stepped away. Cal took hold of the release string. Toby handed a sword to Jack. Jack pulled on his gloves and looked over to us.

"Ready?"

"Ready," I replied. "Start the song, Peter, and keep going."

He began his song off-key. I picked up a firebomb and waited, conscious of my heartbeat.

Murphy reached the end of his song and began again.

"He has to come," I said to Michelle.

Minutes passed and my tension eased slightly as Murphy continued his song like the most annoying loop tape ever.

"He's here!" said Michelle, still viewing through her phone camera. I was looking straight at the portal and could see nothing. Murphy hadn't reacted.

"Net!" I yelled.

Cal must have understood because he yanked on the cord and dropped the net. It came down cleanly, the centre held up as if it had fallen across a pillar. The net surged and tossed as the captive tried to free himself. Jack and Toby ran forward with swords raised. I moved more slowly, firebomb in hand, to stand beside Murphy.

"Stay where you are, don't speak, don't interfere," I told Murphy.

Jack spoke a few words in the Otherkin tongue. The struggles in the net ceased and, a moment later, a tall dark-haired man appeared in the middle of it; Lord Faniel, looking like he had when I met him at Murphy's place. Jack held the point of his sword under Lord Faniel's chin. Toby and Cal set about disentangling him from the net. I kept my eyes on Lord Faniel. He turned his head to look at me, and I raised my hand to show him the firebomb. His eyes widened and his arrogant sneer disappeared.

"Yes," I said to him. "You remember these."

Once Lord Faniel was freed from the net, Jack and Toby hobbled him with twine and walked him back to the camp, their swords at his back. Michelle and I followed with Murphy. When we reached the camp, the refugees came out to watch, there were a few catcalls, but the majority stood in silence. We took him to the shed. I chained him by his legs to the garden roller, padlocking the chains around his ankles. We left his arms and hands free, but Jack set someone to watch him all the time.

"The queen will want to see him," said Jack. "I will bring her."

"What do we do with him?" Michelle indicated Murphy as Jack walked towards the house.

"Right now? Feed him."

"After that."

"Depends on what we're going to do. Obviously, we keep him around if he could be useful."

"And when he stops being useful?"

I looked over at him. He'd tried to have me killed once

and, from the way he was glaring at me, would do so again. "Something permanent."

We took Murphy to the marquee and got him tea, porridge, toast, and jam. We parked him on a table away from us with instructions to talk to no one. We got coffee and speculated on what the Queen would do.

We did not have long to wait. Jack and the Queen strode purposefully past the marquee. We followed them to the garden shed bringing our coffees with us. The Queen was entirely without a glamour. She looked like what she was, a middle-aged woman with a lined face and greying hair, an angry middle-aged woman. She marched up to Lord Faniel and harangued him We could not understand the words, but her attitude was clear. Lord Faniel yelled back at her defiantly, pulling at the chains that held him. Jack watched on stone-faced.

This went on for about ten minutes before the Queen abruptly turned and walked away. Lord Faniel continued shouting at her back and pulling at the chains. He noticed us watching and turned his curses on us. Bit of a waste of time as we had no idea of what he was saying, but he was certainly unhappy and equally unrepentant.

Jack walked over to us.

"That did not sound like he was begging forgiveness," I said.

"No," said Jack. "He claims the people support him and demands we release him."

"So now what?"

"The Queen is finished with him. We wait until he is weak enough for us to take control, then we find out what we need to know to take him back and order the King released. "

"Could be a long wait," I said.

Jack shrugged. "Maybe. He is already complaining that the chains hurt him."

He carried on complaining about the chains and everything else throughout the day. We checked on him several times and a couple of the refugees went to argue or abuse him, but most stayed clear. We brought him food and water, though he threw the food back at us. There was no change in his glamour; I reckoned I would need to be able to see through it before we could work on him and that could take a week.

I was wrong; by midday next day I could see a short guy with long scruffy brown hair chained to the roller. He was done with shouting and was whining instead.

"He looks ready," said Jack.

Toby and Jack held swords over him as I took the chains off his ankles, keeping my gloves on just in case. He glared at me with pure hatred but did not move. Toby put down his sword and reached out a hand to me. I removed the gloves and took his hand. He laid his free hand on Lord Faniel's neck, and I followed him as he pushed in with minimal resistance. Jack came and took my free hand and joined us in exploring Lord Faniel's mind.

I did not understand the significance of much of what we found as Toby searched. I briefly saw the King and mother, both apparently healthy but with compulsions restricting them. There were memories of meetings with many people, plans made and executed. I didn't know what we were looking for, but clearly Toby did. There was a vast amount to take in, and we seemed to be in there a long time. I did understand the compulsion of complete obedience that Toby laid on him before we pulled out. It was similar to the one he had used on Peter Murphy.

"Put the chains back on him," said Toby before he released my hand.

I put my gloves back on and reattached the chains while Jack and Toby talked in their own language. Lord Faniel whined in protest until a word from Toby silenced him. I finished the job and stood up.

"We will need all the fireglobes and airbombs that you have," said Jack.

"They're back at mother's cottage." I glanced at Michelle. "We'll go and get them."

"What about Murphy?" asked Michelle. "What do we do with him?"

Jack shrugged. "We don't need him anymore. End him."

"No," I said. "He can still do something useful, but I'll need some help."

"What do you need?" asked Jack.

"I need to shut him off from his powers like Lord Faniel did to me. Then I'm going to send him to the police under a compulsion to tell them everything about his organisation."

"That's a great idea," said Michelle.

Jack had a brief conversation with Toby, then Toby held out his hand to me. I removed a glove and took his hand.

"Tell me what you want to do," Toby said in my mind.

I remembered how it had felt when Lord Faniel had shut off my powers. "I want this for Murphy."

"I can do that. Take me to him."

We walked over to the marquee; Murphy was sat at the table where we had left him. He looked up at me with fear in his eyes. Good, I thought. Let him fear me. He tried to have me killed.

I put my hand on his neck and reached out for Toby's hand. We slipped into his mind with no resistance. I followed Toby and he brought us to where a large pale stone stood faintly glowing among shadows like some prehistoric standing stone at twilight. I would not have found it without him.

"We must build a barrier around this" he said. He pulled at the shadows which tore as if they were cloth and started to wrap them around the stone. At his touch they grew thicker and heavier, smothering the stone like bandages. I joined in, the shadows feeling as insubstantial as spiderwebs.

"Put your will into them, make them solid," he said. "We have to cover it so that he cannot find it. This will be more effective than what Faniel did to you."

His wrappings were far more effective than mine and in a short time I could not see it in the shadows.

"Is there anything else you want to do?"

"I need to put a compulsion on him to confess."

"Good. I would like to see how you do that."

Toby guided us back to a point I recognised and began to fashion a compulsion to force Murphy to go to the police and tell them every detail of his operation. As a second thought I added visions of the fiery angel for extra motivation, sealed it all then pulled back.

"That was well done," said Toby. "And the vision is a very

good touch. You have considerable promise at this."

I released Toby's hand and we walked away leaving Peter Murphy at the table.

"Success?" asked Michelle.

"Yes. I just need to call Sharon now to come and pick him up."

I had no idea whether she was working and was prepared for her voicemail when I dialled, but she picked up at the second ring.

"Charlie! Where are you? Are you OK? What's going on?"

"Far too much to explain now. I'm at Mrs. Barrett's house in Beaulieu. Can you bring Mike? We've got Peter Murphy here and he wants to talk."

"What? How?"

"I promise I'll tell you it all later, but we've got other stuff to do, and we need Murphy off our hands."

"What does he want to talk about?"

"He's going to tell you everything."

"Wow! Really? Mike's here with me. We'll be there."

"We may still be here, but Jack is taking us over soon. I'll make sure people know you're coming."

"We're on our way."

Based on her previous form, I reckoned she would take about half an hour. Michelle and I went round to the front of the house to wait for them.

I was five minutes out. She and Mike Scott pulled into the drive in Sharon's blue Mini.

"What's going on Charlie. Where's Murphy?" Sharon asked almost fizzing with excitement.

"Round the back," I said. "Follow me."

"Who are all these people?" asked Mike as we came around the side of the house.

"Refugees from over there."

"Where's Murphy?" asked Sharon.

"In the marquee," I said, confident that he would be.

He was, sitting alone with his back to us at the table where I'd left him.

"Don't let him run," said Mike. "I don't fancy chasing him."

"He won't," I said. "He's under a compulsion of complete obedience."

He must have heard me because he looked round. His head came up and he started to rise.

"Don't move," I said sharply, and he froze where he was.

We walked up to him. I put my hand on his and pushed into his mind. I added obedience to Mike and Sharon to the compulsion then sealed it.

"Peter, you will go with these people and answer their questions completely. You will tell them everything and conceal nothing from them." I turned to Mike. "He's all yours now. He will obey you and Sharon."

"That's amazing, Charlie," said Sharon with a warm smile. "This is worth much more than just a dinner."

"Thank me later," I said. "We've got bigger problems to deal with. Lord Faniel's people have got mother."

Her smile froze. "Oh shit, Charlie. What are you going to do?"

"We're going over to get her shortly."

"Is there anything I can do?"

"Can't think of anything unless you've got the Royal Marines on speed dial."

"I haven't." She reached out and hugged me. "Just come back safe."

She released me then turned to Murphy. "Right, Murphy, let's go."

She and Mike walked away with Murphy between them. I hoped it would be the last time I saw him.

"That'll do a lot of good, Charlie," said Michelle. "Really a lot."

Toby and I went to fetch Lord Faniel while Jack assembled his little army. Lord Faniel looked pale and unwell as I removed the chains and said nothing but obeyed Toby's commands. The Queen turned her back on him as we joined the group of about twenty. To my surprise Michelle was there with the fireworks and firebombs.

"We will need to draw on your strength over there," said

Jack. "So we will need someone else who understands how to use these things."

Michelle smiled and held up a lighter.

"Are you expecting much opposition?" I asked.

"It's hard to know," said Jack. "There are many who went with him, and I cannot guess how they will react. Some are very strong. It is better that we have these things and not use them than need them and not have them."

That seems eminently sensible to me. I was pretty sure we would need them at some point.

We all walked down to the portal then joined hands. Michelle took one hand and Toby the other with Lord Faniel at the end of the chain. As we approached the glowing blue oval Michelle squeezed my hand and I reminded myself that this was the only option we had come up with.

We passed through the place between and emerged into woodland lit by the low sun of late afternoon. I filled my lungs with the sweet air and caught a whiff of burnt tyre.

"There are gwasannath near," I said.

Everyone stopped. Michelle released my hand and took a firebomb out of her bag.

I looked around expecting a pack of them to charge out of the trees any second. We waited. The stench faded and the air grew sweet again. Michelle put the firebomb back in her bag.

"Scout," said Toby in my mind. "He'll be halfway to the palace with the news by now. We'd better give them what they expect to see."

A moment later I felt the pull as Toby restored Lord Faniel's glamour then ordered him to take us to the palace. I looked back at Jack and the Queen; she was unchanged. If she had resumed her glamour, I could see through it.

With Toby still controlling Lord Faniel using my power, we marched through the woodland until the palace came into view across the lawns. No longer a chandelier glowing silver, instead it was a grim fortress of high wooden walls and towers. But I knew that, too, was an illusion someone was putting a lot of effort into. I didn't miss the sickly flute music either.

We were halfway across the lawns when a squad of

spear-toting gwasannath appeared from the around the side of the palace lead by a couple of palace guards in bronze armour. The cold hand gripped my stomach once more. Everyone stopped again, and Michelle reached for the firebombs before Toby sent Lord Faniel forward. As soon as the palace guards saw him, they called the gwasannath to a halt and saluted. Lord Faniel dismissed the gwasannath, and we resumed our march with the guards as escort.

Doors were opened for us, and sentries saluted as we passed on into the palace and were hurried to the King's chambers. Before we entered, Toby took my hand again and then caught Lord Faniel's hand.

The King sat head down as if sleeping. On our entry he raised his head, scowled for a moment then broke into a smile at the sight of us. He stood and the glow of his glamour brightened.

"Have you brought the usurper to beg forgiveness?" he said.

"Submit to your father," ordered Toby releasing his hand.

Lord Faniel moved forward and knelt before his father.

"There can be no forgiveness for this crime," said the Queen from behind us. "Remove the compulsion."

"Do it!" said Toby.

Lord Faniel reached up a hand to his father who took it. There was silence for a minute or so as they held hands.

"I cannot," said Lord Faniel. "I haven't the strength."

"Help him," ordered the Queen.

Toby towed me over to them and took Lord Faniel's free hand. Jack joined us taking my free hand. I felt the draw from Toby as he gathered in power to tear at the compulsion. I would have struggled to get any grip on it, but as Lord Faniel had created it, we were able to work through him and gradually pull it apart.

It was hard work. I was sweating by the time the King was free of it. Lord Faniel lay sprawled on the floor and breathing like an unfit marathon runner.

"My friends," said the King. "Once again, I owe you a great debt. How can I ever repay you?"

I was going to say something about putting Lord Faniel permanently out of business, but then there was a commotion behind us and the strong smell of gwasannath. We turned to see two men, armoured in glowing bronze in the doorway, a squad of gwasannath visible in the corridor behind them. Toby immediately identified them as two of the Great who supported Lord Faniel.

"Nobody move!" ordered one. "You are all prisoners of King Faniel."

"Treason!" roared the King.

Jack and Toby released my hands and pulled out their turbine blade swords as the glowing men advanced into the room, bronze swords in hand. Glass broke, one of the glowing men was engulfed in flames. More glass broke and the second man also caught fire. The gwasannath shrieked and a firebomb landed among them setting fur ablaze. Toby dashed forward and with a yell stabbed the nearest burning man in the throat, silencing his screams and nearly taking his head off. He turned to the second man and dealt with him similarly. Michelle stood, mouth open, staring wide-eyed at the mayhem she had initiated.

The King strode forward and picked up the sword dropped by the nearest burning man. He turned towards the prone figure of Lord Faniel. Fearing what here was about to do, I caught his hand.

"Wait! Don't kill him yet," I said in my mind. He turned to me with a flash of anger. "We need him to lift my mother's compulsion."

The anger subsided. "You are right. He must do that," he said after a moment. The Queen came then and took his free hand, so I stepped back.

We needed to get mother as quickly as we could before the King changed his mind and someone killed Lord Faniel. I looked around for Jack; he was at the door, sword in hand.

"Jack, we need to get mother now," I said. "While we still have Lord Faniel to work with."

"Yes. You're right." He took a quick look down the corridor then passed the sword to another man who had come over with us. "Come with me."

I followed him as moved quickly down the corridor past a few doors until we reached a cross corridor. He stopped and looked cautiously around the corner then pulled back rapidly.

"Two gwasannath on guard," he said.

"We should have brought the sword."

"It would not have been useful. They have spears and are ten paces down the way."

He touched my hand and I saw what he had seen. Too far to rush them; that would account for why I hadn't smelled them.

"What's the plan?" I asked in his mind.

He did not reply for a minute or so.

"I think it most likely that the gwasannath were ordered to guard the room by Lord Faniel. I don't believe he would have anyone else do it within the palace. With your help I can try to make a glamour that will convince them I am Lord Faniel, and they will open the door. This is beyond what I have done before, but gwasannath are simple creatures and that favours us. Keep hold of me and the glamour will hide you from them."

I took a firmer grip of his hand and felt him draw from me as he built the glamour. He projected his memories of Lord Faniel's appearance, his voice and mannerisms so that the gwasannath would see nothing else then we walked around the corner. We were dead men if it failed. I scarcely dared breathe, but Jack walked with confidence and the gwasannath instantly stood up straight with their spears held vertical when they saw us.

"Open the door," ordered Jack. "I will see the prisoner."

One of them opened the door and the pair stood back as we went in; just as well as their stench was choking me. Mother was lying on the bed in the sparsely furnished room. I recognised the look of fury on her face when she sat up, steaming angry but physically unharmed. The glamour was working on her, but to reveal ourselves risked doing so for the gwasannath, too. Jack reached out to her and though she shrank back he caught her arm.

"It's me, Jack, and Charlie," he said in her mind. "We've come to get you out. Don't say anything and come with us."

I felt the relief flood out of her. She climbed off the bed and, keeping hold of Jack's hand, walked with us out of the room and past the gwasannath.

"Stay here. I will return with her," said Jack to the gwasannath.

We held the glamour until we turned the corner and were out of sight of the gwasannath.

"I knew you'd come," said mother when Jack dissolved the glamour and she'd finished kissing him. "But what can you do about the compulsion? I can't leave the palace."

"Was it Lord Faniel who laid it?" asked Jack.

"Yes."

"Then he will remove it. We control him now."

"How?"

"We captured him over our side," I said. "Chained him to Mrs. Barrett's big iron garden roller until he was weak enough for us to put a compulsion on him. Then brought him over."

"Sounds like there's quite a story in that," she said.

"There is, and I'll tell you it," I said. "But we need to get the compulsion removed while he's still weak."

"Let's get on with it then."

We made our way back to the King's chamber in a hurry. Lord Faniel was still laid out on the floor with the King, Queen, and Toby standing over him. Jack went to speak to them; Michelle came over to us and threw her arms around mother.

"We were so worried about you," she said. "Are you alright?"

"I'm okay, but I want to get out of here," said mother. "Is the cottage okay?"

"Fine, all locked up," said Michelle. "Your car's still there."

"We'll go back as soon as the compulsion is lifted," I said.

"Good!" said mother. "Can't happen soon enough."

Jack and Toby called us over then. I took Toby's hand, Toby took Lord Faniel's hand and pulled him to his feet.

"You will remove the compulsion on this one," he ordered indicating mother.

Lord Faniel complied and took her hand, not that he had any choice as he was still weak. It was a pretty simple compulsion, and I felt no pull on me as Toby directed him in removing the compulsion. He finished it quickly and Toby ordered him back to the floor.

"What now?" I asked Toby. "Mother wants to go back."

"Then take her back. This one will be executed before the people tomorrow."

"Is that smart? Wouldn't it be better to dispose of him while he is still weakened?"

"I agree with you. But they have decided to make an example."

"It's asking for trouble from his supporters. I guess we'll find out how strong they are."

"I think so," said Toby and I caught a thread of anxiety from him. "I fear they are stronger than the King believes."

"So if I go back with mother and bring some more fireworks and bombs then that would be a good idea?"

"I think that would be a very good idea."

"What time of day is the execution tomorrow?"

"Midday."

"I will be back by then." That should give me time enough back home to collect stuff. "With all the grief he's caused I certainly want to see him get what's coming."

Michelle and I took mother to the portal in darkness. We had two Otherkin with us who were to fetch the refugee families back, so we went to the portal at Mrs. Barrett's. It was late afternoon there and we found we'd been gone three days. Michelle drove us over to the cottage. Mother's car was still there, locked up as she'd left it; fortunately, she had a spare set of keys in the cottage. We found the cottage untouched after Michelle opened up with her keys.

"Put the kettle on, Charlie," said mother. "A cup of tea, then you can tell me the full story of how you captured Lord Faniel."

I made tea, Michelle found biscuits and we settled down fortified by chocolate digestives and strong English Breakfast. I started the tale with the text I received from mother's phone and described how Jack, Toby, and myself got into Peter Murphy's place, captured him, and forced him to summon Lord Faniel into our trap.

"That's impressive! So Murphy is who had me kidnapped?" said mother. "You sure?"

"Dead certain! I've been in his mind," I said. "He's Faniel's son."

"So what happened to him?"

"We gave him to the police with a strong compulsion on him to tell them everything."

"Something good for this side comes out of it then. That was well done. What happens next, are you staying?"

"Tonight yes. Tomorrow we need to buy some more fireworks and anything else we can find to take over there," I said.

"Do you really need to go?"

"Yes. I need to be there to see Lord Faniel pay for all that he's done. Toby thinks there will be an attempt to stop the execution. We're going to find out how strong Faniel's support really is."

"Do you think you can stop them?"

"I don't know, but we have to try. I could wish for something a bit more lethal than fireworks."

"Well, you're going to do it whether I like it or not, so you take care." She finished her tea. "I need a bath, then I'm going to bed to sleep for a week."

Mother went upstairs and neither of us felt like cooking, so we drove up to the village centre to get fish and chips.

Mother was still in bed when we left the next morning to drive into Southampton. We went to the fireworks shop first. We didn't know what numbers we would be facing; we had enough firebombs for small groups and, I presumed, the King's followers could take care of the rest. What I needed was for facing an army, so I bought rockets, air-bombs and, at Michelle's suggestion, smoke bombs. Nothing lethal but all things to upset, confuse, and disorientate soldiers who would not have seen them before. There was no point in buying more than we could carry through the portal, so we filled two medium-sized boxes, I bought three boxes of matches, too, and paid a bill of four hundred pounds. If we didn't use them then we could have a great party.

We debated going to the lab so I could make more firebombs but decided against it. It was more important that we get back through the portal as soon as possible, and I thought we probably had enough anyway. They are for close range anyway, and I really didn't want to get that close to Lord Faniel's followers.

We drove back Mrs. Barrett's and left the car there as the

portal was only a short distance away. Even the medium-size boxes were heavy enough that we didn't want to carry them far. It was not possible to carry them and hold hands going through the portal, so Michelle followed me and gave me an anxious couple of minutes before she appeared on the other side.

It was dark under the trees, but the silvery glow of the palace was back, and we were able to find our way through the wood by its light. It seemed a good sign that it had been restored and, mercifully, without the music.

Just before the edge of the wood Michelle put down her box and caught my arm.

"Can you smell what I'm smelling?"

I stood beside her and sniffed the air. She was right, faint but unmistakable.

"Gwasannath."

"That's what I thought. Lord Faniel's followers?"

"Very likely." While gwasannath were widely used as servants, I'd only seen our enemies use them as soldiers.

We put down the boxes and moved cautiously to the edge of the wood. The sky was lightening and a mist rising over the lawns of the palace tinted silver by the glow. Dawn could not be far away. I put out a glamour to merge us with the shadows under the trees.

Away to our right a horse neighed and, moments later, a group of riders emerged from the mist at a trot following the edge of the woods a couple of hundred yards away on the far side of the broad lawns. They slowed and a second group, a handful of riders and a troop of spear-carrying gwasannath, came out of the trees to meet them.

"We have to get to the palace to warn them," said Michelle. "Should we run for it?"

"They certainly need warning, but I don't see how we can get there ahead of them. Even if we abandon the boxes, we can't outrun them." It was all open ground between us and the palace. While I could produce a glamour to conceal us from the gwasannath, the Great, who were undoubtedly with the enemy, would most likely be able to penetrate it.

"What do we do then?"

I could only think of one thing. "Use the fireworks now. It'll alert the palace and should slow up the enemy at the very least."

"That seems reasonable."

We stepped back under the trees and opened the boxes. There were half a dozen launch tubes for the rockets which I stuck in the ground at the edge of the trees angled towards the enemy. We had bought rockets that burst with a really loud explosion, and I loaded up three to start with. We planted a row of airbombs in front of them also angled the same way.

"We'll keep the smoke bombs back for cover us if they come after us," I said.

The enemy were still milling around on the edge of the trees on the far side of the lawns.

"Maybe they're waiting for more people," said Michelle.

"Don't see why we should wait." I struck a match and applied the flame to the touchpapers of the rockets. We stepped back and a couple of seconds later the rockets soared off towards the enemy leaving a fine trail of sparks. While they were in flight, we loaded up another three and lit them. The first three burst with an eye-searing flash and apocalyptic bang.

"That should wake everyone in the palace," said Michelle.

Among the enemy the effect was gratifyingly dramatic; horses shied unseating some riders, gwasannath screamed loud enough for us to hear and some ran into the trees. The second set of rockets exploded. More horses shied and the loose horses bolted scattering gwasannath. We launched a third flight of rockets. Five riders detached from the group and galloped towards us.

"Smoke bombs!" I called to Michelle then lit the airbombs.

The rockets exploded, further scattering the enemy, but the riders, armed with sword and spear, raced on towards us at full gallop. I stepped back under the trees and reinforced the glamour. I could feel their approach through the ground. The airbombs fired, and Michelle threw the first smoke bomb quickly followed by another. White smoke spewed out hiding the riders from our view, then the airbombs exploded. The vibrations through the ground ceased. We grabbed the remaining smoke bombs and airbombs then retreated into the wood away from the path to the portal. We found a clump of trees where the shadows seemed deeper than most and buried ourselves in it. Michelle took my hand, and I pushed the glamour out for all I was worth.

All was quiet for a minute or two. I hoped they had decided against coming into the dark woods, then we heard men's voices calling to each other, sounding angry, though, of course, I could not understand them. Michelle's grip on my hand tightened. The voices drew nearer along with the sounds of breaking branches.

"They can't see us unless they're Great," I told her in her mind. "And they would not send anyone Great to do this."

"Doesn't matter if what they're doing is sticking their spears into shadows," she replied.

"You have a good point." That was going to be a problem if they came this way.

The voices and noise came closer. They were coming this way.

"What do we do?" asked Michelle. "We can't fight them. Can you scare them off?"

I could feel her fear and she was right, we couldn't fight them. But maybe we could scare them. It was too dark for something visual but there were other options. I drew in her fear, added to my own and pushed it out focusing on the voices, accompanied by as low a growl as I could manage. I amplified and deepened it as if some huge predatory beast was menacing them.

The sounds of breaking branches ceased, and the voices took on tones of alarm. I hoped they were saying "did you hear that? What the fuck is that? I'm not going in there." They were certainly moving, getting closer to each other so far as I could tell. I pushed out another deep growl to persuade them to rejoin their comrades. Their voices got a bit fainter as if they had moved away, but I could still hear them. We were safer and had bought time, but they were still between us and the palace.

"Where are they?" said Michelle in my mind.

"I guess they've gone back to the edge of the woods."

"Where are their horses? They must have dismounted to come into the woods."

"Don't know. Maybe they tied them to trees at the edge."

"So could you scare them into a stampede? It would give them something to think about instead of searching for us."

"Maybe. If it was going to work, they should've already been affected. I think I might need to be able to see or hear them to focus on them."

"Then we have to move."

We moved as quietly as we could, pausing for me to push the glamour out again. I felt more powerful when I was in contact with Michelle, so I kept hold of her hand. The voices stayed where they were and sounded argumentative.

We worked our way slowly around the voices and back to the edge of the woods. The sky had grown noticeably lighter, and we could see a group of horses tethered about a hundred yards away. The voices came from somewhere beyond them, but they were hidden behind their mounts. Across the lawns the palace still glowed tantalisingly, but I could see nothing happening. Looking the other way up the woods' edge, the main enemy force still appeared to be in disorder with gwasannath and men milling around. I wondered if my glamour had reached as far as them.

We hid ourselves in the scrubby bushes at the margin of the wood. I took Michelle's hand and projected fear at the horses. The horses were unaffected. I pushed harder. Still nothing doing with the horses, but shouts of alarm from the voices behind them.

"Doesn't work on horses," I said.

"I know what does," said Michelle. She released my hand, took an airbomb and stuck in the ground angled towards the horses.

"Hold on," I said. "I want to try something first."

I took her hand again and pushed the fear glamour out towards the main enemy force. The effect was immediate. The gwasannath screamed and ran away from the woods and scattered across the lawns. A few of the men ran, too; others clutched their weapons and huddled into defensive circles with blades outward. A few riders seemed unaffected; the Great I presumed.

"Mm, interesting," I said. "That works over a greater distance than I thought it would."

"Why are you surprised?" said Michelle. "The glamour on the palace works over a long distance. Will I light the airbomb?"

"Yes. Do it."

She lit the fuse and I pushed out a glamour to conceal us as we watched from the bushes. The first cartridge launched with a pop and soared over the horses then exploded with an apocalyptic bang. The horses, without riders to control them, panicked, rearing and surging. They broke the tethers holding them and galloped away across the grass. Their riders shouted in vain and gave chase as a second airbomb exploded frightening the horses further.

"Let's see if the rockets are where we left them," I said as we watched the riders pursue their mounts across the lawns.

We made our way along the edge of the wood to where we had left the rockets. The box looked like it had been kicked over spilling the rockets into the undergrowth, but they were still usable. We loaded up the launch tubes and kept watch. The main group of the enemy were still in disarray, but I expected the rockets would still be needed when they got organised.

"When are they going to do something?" said Michelle looking at the palace. "They must know something is happening."

"I think they must. I expect something is being done behind that glamour, but all we can do is wait." Which was true but did nothing to soothe our anxieties.

"Do you think there's going to be a battle?"

"Quite likely, I think. And we should keep well out of it."

We waited and watched the riders fruitlessly pursue their horses and the main group slowly restore order to their ranks. Another small group came up out of the woods to join them, and they looked like they were ready to move.

"Look!" Michelle pulled on my arm. "Something's happening at the palace."

I looked. She was right. Things were moving in front of the palace. As we watched, cavalry and infantry emerged from the ground mist. A whole army marched with banners waving and breastplates shining across the grass towards us; three maybe four times the strength of the enemy.

The enemy responded with frantic activity, moving men and gwasannath around into a defensive formation as the army approached like the incoming tide across Lepe beach.

"There's going to be a battle," said Michelle.

"There is, but how much of that army is real? It looks real enough, but it could just be a really good glamour."

"Does it matter if the enemy can't tell either?"

"Some of them are Great, maybe they can see through it." But then maybe they can't. The King would have assembled the strongest Great available to him plus his own strength. "We're going to find out pretty soon."

I moved to the launch tubes; we had a couple of flights of rockets left. "Let's try to make the best use of these."

We watched the two forces draw closer to each other and I chose the moment with care. We lit the fuses and watched the rockets soar towards the enemy formation. As I had intended, the King's army was about a hundred yards away and beginning their charge when the rockets exploded. The gwasannath panicked and ran as did some of the infantry. The King's cavalry crashed into those that remained, driving deep into the enemy formation through the gaps that had opened up. The illusion dissolved and we could see their real numbers. Far fewer than they had seemed, perhaps slightly more than the enemy, but they had the momentum with them.

There seemed to be no point in launching the final rockets, nor could I project my glamour of fear as the combatants were too close together. We stood at the edge of the wood and watched the battle develop, preparing to run for the portal if it looked like the enemy would prevail. At this distance and with no one wearing uniforms, it was difficult to tell who was on which side. We hoped Jack and Toby were not part of it.

There were some hard men among the enemy. Despite their inferior numbers and tactical disadvantage, they fought for an hour with the desperation of doomed men - which they most likely were if captured. Eventually the numbers told, the back-to-back fighting groups were whittled down one by one until none remained and the King, clearly visible with his full glamour, stood over the last man to fall.

We walked over to join them carrying the remaining fireworks and the full extent of the battle became clear. The grass was strewn with bodies for hundreds of yards, both men and horses, small groups of people attending to the wounded and great stains of dark blood.

The King saw us approach and smiled. A bloodstained man wearing a shirt of bronze scales appeared beside him and beckoned us over. He removed his helmet; it was Jack.

"The King wishes to thank you," he said.

We walked towards him, and the soldiers parted before us as if forming an honour guard. The King reached out and caught my hands.

"Once again I owe you a great debt." His voice boomed in my mind. "You have saved me and my people. Without your warning and magics they would have overrun us."

"But at such a cost," I said.

His smile faded. "He left me no choice, and now there is only one path for him."

I could feel his sadness at this grim outcome and had to feel sadness at his loss, even though I was glad that Lord Faniel would be reaching the end of his road. "A path built by his own actions."

"He is not fit to lead our people, and he would be a danger to the one who follows me. I cannot let that happen."

That sounds pretty final to me, but I wanted to see it.

"You have earned the right to attend."

"So has Michelle."

"So she has. If she wishes to attend."

I thought she would be happy to watch the man who attempted to sacrifice her meet his end.

"Come to the palace and bring her. By the traditions of our people there should be a feast to celebrate our victory, but this does not feel like a victory. Perhaps one day we will feast, and you will be my honoured guest, but not today." He released my hands and called for his horse. He mounted up and with the remains of his escort rode off towards the palace.

"You made a great difference," said Jack who had sneaked up on me unnoticed. "It would have been a much harder fight without your rockets breaking their formation."

"Good. That was what I was hoping for, I didn't know if it would work."

Around us the people on foot were beginning to make their way towards the palace following the King; the wounded supported by one or carried between two. The most severely wounded were gathered together where they could be watched over until carts came from the palace to carry them. Jack and I assisted one poor fellow whose left leg was blood-soaked from hip to ankle and who grunted in pain at every step. Michelle followed carrying the remaining fireworks.

When we reached the palace, we left the fireworks with the door ward who directed us to a hall where the Queen and her ladies were busy tending the wounded. We handed our casualty over to them and went in search of the King. I wondered how many would survive without the treatment that could be offered back home, but it seemed deeply impractical to bring them over. For a moment I imagined the shit that would fly if I turned up at Southampton General with two dozen guys who had major blade wounds, spoke no English, and had no ID.

We found the King in the Great Hall with a cluster of Great and nobles around him in a subdued atmosphere. He had shed his bloodied armour but still wore his sword and had a goblet in his hand. He said very little and looked generally grim. A servant offered us a cup. It was rather rough red wine, but after the day we'd had I was happy to accept it.

More folk came in behind us, took a cup and stood around waiting like us for something to happen. We were the objects of polite curiosity for most people; though no one spoke to us it was clear they knew who we were.

Eventually the King looked around the room, drained his cup and gave an order to the guards at the door. They disappeared and returned a short time later with Lord Faniel. He wore no glamour; his real self was scrawny and pale, his eyes wide with terror. He knew what was able to happen. At his first sight of his father, he pulled away from his guards and threw himself down at his feet, gabbling away no doubt pleading with for his life. The King silenced him with a word then reached down and pulled him to his knees. He growled another word, presumably something along the lines of "stay there," and drew his sword.

Michelle gripped my hand and the whole room held its breath as the King laid his sword beside his son's neck. He spoke a few more words then thrust downward with all his weight. Lord Faniel cried out once then slumped at his father's feet. The King, stone-faced, left his sword in the body, turned away and walked out without a word. The rest of the room stared silently at the body of Lord Faniel. I reminded myself of the men who had died today because of him, of the harm he had done to me and my family but found I could not rejoice.

A few people began to move towards the door, still saying nothing. The movement grew so we joined it. No one around us spoke until we were out in the open air.

"I didn't think he had the strength to go through with it," Jack said quietly. "I thought he would pardon him at the last moment."

"What will he do with Lord Faniel's followers?" asked Michelle.

"It depends on what they do. I would advise a period where he seeks reconciliation, but if it is refused then bloodshed will follow, and we cannot afford that."

"No," I said. "Enough people have already died."

"I agree," said Michelle. "I think I would like to go home now."

ABOUT THE AUTHOR

Martin Owton was born in Southampton and grew up in the shadow of the Fawley oil refinery, he studied for a PhD in Synthetic Chemistry at the University of Southampton but there the similarity with his characters ends. He now lives in Surrey working as a drug designer for a major pharma company, and is a cancer survivor. He is the author of the non-epic Sword & Sorcery Nandor Tales novels *Exile* (mybook.to/ExileOwton) & *Nandor* (mybook.to/NandorOwton).

His website is at http://martinowton.com

Curious about other Crossroad Press books?
Stop by our site:
http://store.crossroadpress.com
We offer quality writing
in digital, audio, and print formats.

Printed in Great Britain
by Amazon

85970909R00130